Dear Tim

I very much appreciated the engagement with my first book.

This one is a bit old...

Published by Crazy Otter Publishing

Produced and manufactured by Softwood Books

EU Responsible person: Maddy Glenn

Office 2, Wharfside House, Prentice Road, Stowmarket, Suffolk, IP14 1RD

www.softwoodbooks.com, hello@softwoodbooks.com

EU Rep:

Authorised Rep Compliance Ltd., Ground Floor, 71 Lower Baggot Street, Dublin, D02 P593, Ireland

www.arccompliance.com, info@arccompliance.com

A CIP catalogue record for this book is available from the British Library

Paperback ISBN: 978-1-9192631-0-6

Hardback ISBN: 978-1-9192631-1-3

eBook ISBN: 978-1-9192631-2-0

and it was far from finished. Reading my great-grandmother's book was not going to speed things up.

On the other hand, the publisher never got back to me with edits or indeed anything when they said they would. Never ever. Moreover, for a writer, all reading is research and research is work.

I swung round on the floor so I couldn't see my reproachful cursor, and got to work.

I read the story in one sitting, pausing only to fetch food and coffee, and to capture and release a bumblebee about the size of a guinea pig.

I enjoyed my great-grandmother's story as much as anything I've read, and certainly more than everything I've written. Which was quite annoying, but also, when I realised that I owned the story, quite exciting.

And that is how you come to my great-grandmother's tale, set in eighteenth-century America and written in the second half of twentieth century. Not wanting to be a Julian (you'll understand what that means), I edited not a word. Well, hardly a word. Some of the attitudes and language are different to today's, but you'll take that in your stride because you're not stupid.

The book introduces itself, so this preamble is really nothing more than me putting myself into the tale for no reason, apart from perhaps to justify the fact that I'm taking the proceeds. So, with no more ado -

GOLD
MURDER
BY ELEANOR SALMON

DISCOVERED BY
ANGUS WATSON

CONTENTS

INTRODUCTION BY ANGUS WATSON

Finding the Story

Like all great Westerns, my great-grandmother's murderous Wild West adventure story begins in a care home near Henley-on-Thames. Before we go there, I'm going to tell you how I found it.

It's easy to get distracted when you work at home. A while a back on a Thursday morning, instead of typing away like a secretary in a 1950s cartoon and whizzing towards the current novel's completion, I found myself sitting on my study floor, surrounded by the belongings of my late grandmother.

It was three years since the "Granny Cheeseman's dead" phone call.

A week later, mustered descendants crammed into her musty room in the old people's home. Jenny, or possibly Sue - the lady from the old people's home who delighted in guilting us for not visiting enough - produced a dusty old box. She opened it and lifted out a three-legged wooden fox, probably - given its sombrero – from Mexico.

"I think this box is full of lovely *keepsakes*, like this dog. Would anyone like to take it?" I could see she was keen for everyone to say no, so she could hate us even more.

I didn't want it. I have enough junk.

"I would love it, please," I said.

"Just the dog?" Jenny or Sue smirked like a shop assistant who loathes the stupid customers but is on her final warning for not smiling at customers.

"I think it's a fox, but no, the whole box please."

Jenny or Sue managed a tight smile while also looking outraged about having her wooden canine identification skills brought into question.

"It could be a dog," I admitted as she handed me the box. That seemed to annoy her all the more.

Going through that box was the second oldest entry on my to-do list (*sort the garage* remains the oldest). So, of course, I decided to go about it on a morning when I was meant to be writing to a deadline.

As well as the Mexican canine, Granny Cheeseman's box revealed an ancient china doll, dressed in a home-knitted light blue onesie. Its enamelled skin was criss-crossed with cracks which made it look like a prematurely elderly baby. Wrapped in a cardigan that smelled of dead skin and talcum powder were some egg coddlers (I immediately planned to coddle some eggs but haven't quite got round to it yet).

Then there was a large, old, brown book. Printed squarely on the cover in a neat hand were the words:

GOLD MURDER

On the first page it said:

By Eleanor Salmon

I knew that name. I'm afraid I sat there for a moment with my mouth open, trying to remember where I'd heard it before.

Then it came to me - Eleanor Salmon was my great-grandmother. *Gammy Elly*. I had only one memory of her - sitting on her knee, pretending to be a doctor mending her broken wing. I don't know why I wasn't a vet if I was mending a wing. I was about three, she was about a million, so I guess the appropriate medical profession was less important to us than the story.

She must have died not long after that. Not of a broken wing, I'm pretty sure. I couldn't remember anybody mentioning her since. I hope my ancestors take a little more interest in me.

I wondered what she'd written about. With the title *Gold Murder*, two of her themes seemed pretty clear.

I paused as I opened the first page.

I looked back at my computer. The cursor was blinking accusingly, halfway through the word *dependable*. The novel was late to my publisher,

The Rooms of Eleanor Salmon, Home for Dying Crones, England, 19 -

Looking out at the dreary sky and slimy leaves of an English November, it's surprisingly easy to recall the feel and smell of the American western desert in the last century. From my turret, I can see a way westwards through dank English mist to a wooded rise on the far side of the River Thames. The view is grey, soft and unexciting. It is the exact opposite to the blazing-bright, jagged-edge canyons, merciless mountains and crazy towers of teetering red rock on the far side of the American Rocky Mountains, where I spent my younger years.

I've never before considered writing my story, but I have been pressed into joining the home's creative writing group, so I've got to write something.

I don't, in fact, live in a turret. I occupy a bunch of rooms on the top floor of a Victorian school converted into an old people's home. They call my rooms a "suite." They also say "yourself" when they mean "you." Is the temperature alright for yourself? they'll ask. Here's the poached eggs for yourself, they'll say.

Neither the money-grubbing, pompous owners, nor the generally well-meaning but grammatically inept drones who work here, quite know what to do with their residents while they wait for us to die. However, this is the most expensive old folks' home in the county, so they need to look like they're doing something.

To that end, they established a creative writing group. It's led by an earnest, effetely-bearded man called Julian who drives over from Oxford in his rusting automobile and tells us to how to write creatively.

They say activities like this one stave off mental atrophy. 'They' should glance in the mirror every now and then. The staff here are young, as are my insincere and vacuous grandchildren who visit as often as they judge to be enough to ensure their inheritances. I've got a whole lot of atrophying to go before I'm half as dumb as any of them. I'm very well aware that I'm not the first to say this - every generation thinks the same, back as far as the Ancient Greeks and no doubt before - but young people are idiots. Five-cent heads in ten-dollar Stetsons, the lot of them.

However, there's not a whole lot to do here in Hell's waiting room, so six weeks ago I went along the creative writing group. I've been every week since. Before this evening, I hadn't penned so much as a sentence (but I have learnt that Julian approves of using words like "penned" where "written" would do).

Julian has whinged that my lack of production is a bad example to the rest of the codgers. I couldn't give two rats' asses for Julian, nor for the other fogies, but I am bored of listening to everybody else's efforts to show and not tell, vary sentence length, use small details to describe large scenes, and follow the rest of Julian's earnest instructions. Moreover, If I have to endure much more of Mrs Terbangun's smug prose - "mercurial skein of damask'd rain" isn't even the most puke-inducing phrase thus far - then I will have to kill again. I'm joking. I won't kill her. But I'm not joking about having killed before. The American West back in the day was simply beset by "kill or be killed" situations. And just "kill if you want to and definitely get away with it" situations of course, but I didn't go for those.

I digress (does Julian approves of digression? I don't think we've covered that yet). The point is, it's time that they listened to my efforts. I will attempt to be creative. I will try to remember how it felt to be a girl and write as if I were back in the Old West, looking out of those young eyes. The shell may have sagged and wrinkled, but my brain is pretty much the same, so it shouldn't be too hard.

Using what I discovered later, I'll write some of the story from the eyes of the others involved. Nobody knows what goes on in the minds of other folk, and there is a lot I don't know, so those parts will be more on the creative side.

I'll start the story a few days before it went really crazy, because one must start somewhere. I rather enjoy the pretentious device used by Mr Dickens and his ilk of being vague with dates and places, so I'll do that too.

I should also note that my memory is not perfect. Whose is? Yours? I doubt it. So, don't complain if I misremember the odd bit of historical detail. As my old friend Frank Lloyd Wright said, truth is more important that facts.

So here we go. My name is Eleanor Salmon. The following happened an awful long time ago in the West.

ACT ONE

United States of America, 18 -

ACT ONE, CHAPTER ONE

In a Canyon

"You've got blood on your hands." I realised the double meaning as I said it.

Was it Loretta? Impossible. But could it be? Shivers ran along my arms and legs. *Had mild-mannered Loretta done for them all?*

Loretta had dragged the bench out of the big dorm, set the parasol, and was sitting sentry over the canyon. *Was she waiting for the law? Ready for a shoot-out?* I hoped for a shoot-out. I'd only seen one before and it had been dark, so I hadn't seen anything juicy.

Or was it too hot for a shoot-out?

I sat next to Loretta, closed my eyes, and tried to enjoy the shade, but the parasol offered about as much protection from the heat as it would have done from a landslide. They said Death Valley was the hottest place in the world. They had it right, far as I could tell.

I scooched along the butt-broiling wood closer to Loretta. I reckoned it would be cooler next to such a cool woman. She didn't seem so affected by the heat as the rest of us, maybe because she did everything a little more slowly.

I got a big whiff of her scent - she smelled like a pretty, white-tailed deer in a bed of hot flowers - but did not discern any decrease in temperature.

She lifted her hands. There was dried blood on her dark skin. Red drops flecked her white sleeves. "Dern lion," she said. "I ain't no good with a knife and I ain't no good with blood."

"Lot of blood in a cougar!" I bounced on the bench, picturing red geysers fountaining from the big cat's split belly, drenching gawping onlookers with gore, and them coughing when it got in their mouths.

"Cougar?" Loretta asked.

I looked at her in case she was joking, but she really didn't know. "Cougar's the same as a lion. They get called panthers, pumas, and painters, too. All the same thing; huge cat with a bitty head that'll eat you first and ask questions later."

"Whatever they're called, Eleanor, my dear, they sure do have a lot of blood, and a lot of smell, too!" She shook her head, laughing, "I'll try again later. I never skinned an animal before."

I raised an eyebrow. Had Loretta really lived so many years without skinning so much as a cottontail?

Almost half of me wanted to skin the lion myself, to pull it open and delve through the slimy innards to see what I could find. A finger? A head? But the lion hadn't eaten Happy Days Frida, just killed her dead with its claws, so I'd be disappointed.

A little more than half of me - I knew it was more than half because that inclination won - did not want to skin the lovely animal. I was sad it was dead. I didn't care that it had killed Happy Days Frida. Truth be told, I hadn't much liked Frida.

"Crane shot it," I said. "He should skin it."

"Men don't like to do that sort of work. Besides, Crane did a job for us, killing the lion, so I'm doing one for him skinning it. He might get fifty bucks for the skin in town."

I sniffed. A cougar skin fetched ten bucks. Fifteen maybe, if you found a someone as green as Loretta. Boy, she did not know much.

I'd learnt pretty early that adults weren't perfect - time was I'd thought proving that was my ma's sole calling - but Loretta was something else. Even though she was clever. And, in her defence, she was, as the Forty-Niners said, a greenhorn, a tenderfoot or *not from around these parts*. Of course, the Forty-Niners weren't from around those parts neither. Nobody was, save from the Timbisha Shoshone, who dumb people called Indians.

We stopped talking for a while and sat. It was too hot to be outside, but it was hotter in the shacks. It was cool in the tunnels of the Fabulous, but Loretta *never* went underground, not so much as a few yards along an adit.

I wasn't meant to go into the mine tunnels neither. It was too dangerous after the flood, said the men, and also full of drowned miners. The drowned miners didn't bother me, but I was scared of tunnels collapsing and squashing me like a worm with a rock dropped on it.

And I was scared of the killer.

I imagined him finding me there in the dark, me trying to run, but with my left leg being shorter than my right, I wasn't much of a runner. I'd probably trip and land face-first on the soft, dead belly of a drowned miner. It would burst and fill my mouth with maggots, and I'd scream a chokey, maggotty scream. *Then the killer would grab me …*

I shuddered despite the heat. I'd leave the men to avoid the killer while they hunted for The Prize in the mine. Loretta and me ran the camp, the others mined. We'd all share The Prize, that was the deal. Loretta and me wouldn't get as much as the men since we weren't doing the hard work, but Silver had promised that the five percent Lorretta and me were getting each would still be more than we could possibly imagine.

That was, *if* they shared The Prize at all. We only had Silver's word, and he was about as straight as a dog's back leg. Crane would share, I reckoned, but the other three who hadn't been murdered (yet) were the most rat-faced, mean-mouthed varmints west of the Rockies.

I hoped that we would get our share. It was hard living in the heat, and I missed my ma something rotten. I didn't let the others see, but I felt sad and scared a lot of the time. I even cried sometimes when I was on my own. All the fetching and carrying made my leg hurt quite a bit. I really wanted it all to be for something. I really wanted to take all that money to my ma.

So I really really hoped that the killer didn't do for us all before they found The Prize.

The grown-ups said there wasn't a killer. Didn't mean much. Grown-ups were wrong nine times out of ten. *Accidents happen in threes,* Crane said. We'd had three so we were safe. That's what Crane said.

He was wrong. One of them was a killer, I knew it, just waiting to strike again.

But who was it?

Masterton, Monk, and Silver were all despicable enough to kill. But in stories it was always the one you expected least, so that meant it was Crane, Loretta, or me. But I knew it wasn't me. Or Loretta, of course. She moved too slowly, and besides, she was too scared to go in the tunnels where two of them had been killed.

We sat in stillness. Sun blazed off tin roofs, red rock baked in the sun. Nothing moved. It was too hot even for lizards and bugs.

"This dang blasted land!" I said, I'm not sure why. I didn't mean it. It was just something to say.

"Dang blasted?" asked Loretta, eyes still fixed down the canyon. *Waiting?*

"Monk said. No crop'll grow. No grass for cows. Even a goat couldn't live here. Land's no use to anyone. That's what Monk said. He said it was ugly, too, what with no trees nor streams. Only goodness in this godless land is underground, said Monk."

"Is that what you think, Eleanor?"

I looked at Loretta. She turned and smiled at me, blue eyes all the more dazzling in her dark skin. I wished I looked like Loretta. She had a calm beauty that I knew I'd never have, no matter how pretty I got. I'd never be calm. And I'd always have one leg shorter than the other, and that was not high up on the list of what made a girl beautiful.

What are you looking for in a wife, Johnny?

First and foremost, beyond all, I'd like her left leg to be shorter than her right, so she hurts a lot and she walks funny and can't run as fast as the other women.

"Well?" Loretta pressed, tipping her head towards the huge view.

I squinted. The rugged red and brown sides of Fabulous Canyon were dotted with brave cactuses and frail-looking bushes that were far from frail. *You think they look frail? Try pulling one up!* Their roots went right down to Hell, mister.

Over to the left, tramway buckets draped from a heat-limp wire. Below them, the destroyed road followed the jagged, winding gully to the breath-takingly broad Death Valley below. The salt-white valley floor was lower than the ocean, they said. They were wrong this time. If it was lower than the ocean how come the ocean didn't flood in and fill it with water? Hadn't thought about that, had they?

On the far side of the salt flats the land backed up like a great rock wave, up to a mountain so high it had snow on it, even as we cooked. Canyons tore into that far valley side. I reckoned trolls had clawed out them gashes in the mountain back in the time of giants. Each canyon spewed alluvial fans the size of cities onto the Death Valley flats. Big old Death Valley hardly noticed.

"It's not dang blasted. Not at all," I admitted. "It's beautiful nearby, and looking across that valley it's so wonderful that it hurts my heart. My ma told me there is no God, but looking around here I declare that there must be."

"Listen to it." said Loretta.

"What?"

"Just listen."

I did. There wasn't a waft of wind. The smell of baking rock hung in the air, mixed with Loretta's musk. The only sound was my own breathing. I held it and strained my ears. "I can't hear anything!"

"Exactly," Loretta nodded. "That is a precious stillness. Monk's wrong about the goats, too. I saw one yesterday."

"That would have been a sheep. A bighorn."

"Oh."

I was embarrassed again. How could a grown woman not know about bighorn sheep? It's not like there were lots of big mammals around. The only other two were coyotes and lions. Coyotes didn't look a bit like bighorns, and you didn't see the lions. Not until they ripped your throat out.

"Crane likes the land, too." I said, to get off the subject.

"I'm not surprised. He's bright."

"And handsome?" *You shouldn't tease adults!* I knew that, but Loretta was more of a friend than a grown up. Friends tease friends. I'd learnt that from the start. Someone doesn't mock you, it's because they don't respect you.

"I feel sorry for the places I've always known, where soil and plants cover the rock and you can't see the beauty below." Loretta continued, as if she hadn't understood my implication. "I'd heard the West was desolate and it is, but it's also beautiful."

I looked at the woman. I wasn't totally sure what desolate meant, but I was pretty sure that Loretta was desolate and beautiful too. *But why had she come West?* People are like donkeys, or so Ma said. They reach for the carrot or they're driven by the stick. I couldn't see how the West, with its heat and its snakes, could be a carrot for Loretta. So, what was her stick?

"Is that why you're always sitting here, looking?" I asked. "Because you like looking? Or are you waiting for someone?"

Loretta raised an eyebrow, pursed her lips, and turned her face so she was looking out over the wide valley again.

I felt even hotter. A moment before, I'd have denied that was possible. I'd pried.

Rule number one in the West - no prying. Even with a friend. Folk didn't generally make the long, often deadly trek across plains, mountains and desert to shout about what they'd run away from.

I sure didn't want anybody asking why I was there.

"Sorry," I said. "Are you worried about the ghosts?" I tried, hoping my prying might be forgotten or forgiven.

Loretta smiled. "I've been scared of ghosts long as I can remember."

I swung my legs because my short leg was cramping. It did that sometimes. It did worse sometimes. "Don't waste your fear. There are plenty of real things to be scared of out here."

"Such as?"

"Well, there's no point being scared of a lion, my moth- ... people say. Lions come from behind, noisy as a shadow. They leap and bite your neck in two. You're dead before you know you've been bit."

"So Happy Days Frida didn't suffer?"

I pictured the dead rock doctor's face, eyes wider than eyes should go, mouth set in a scream. She sure did look like she'd suffered a whole lot.

"Well, maybe she saw it coming." I admitted. "Or maybe the lion bit her neck and paralysed her!" I continued, warming to my subject,

"Then stood over her and clawed her stomach open with a swish, swish!" I swept my arms though the air. "So she had that look on her face as she watched the lion pull out her guts and chomp on them while she was still alive and-"

"So, lions *are* scary," interrupted Loretta, "but not as scary as spiders."

"*What?*" I peered at Loretta to see if she was joshing. She didn't seem to be. I was hot from standing in the sun and swishing my arms, so I sat back down in the shade. "*Spiders ain't scary!* They're furry little critters, bite no worse than a bee! They're more cute than scary."

"They scare me."

"You want to be scared of something? It's a shame we've got no grizzlies here. They're ten times the size of a big man and you can't kill 'em. They'll take fifty bullets and still catch the shooter and rip off his arms and legs, leaving him looking mighty silly." I stood to show how a grizzly might rip the limbs from its victim but pain shot up my leg and into my butt – it was worst when it got that high – so I sat. "But we do have rattlers," I continued, hoping Loretta didn't notice me bouncing to try to stop the spasm. "They'll kill you easy. So don't go jumping into shadows or rummaging in wood piles. When you're climbing, look where you're putting your hands. Or you'll get bit."

"I should be safe, then. It's been a good while since I jumped, rummaged, or climbed."

I mused for a moment. True enough, Loretta wasn't much for mousing about. But I wasn't going to let her off. She still might get bit. There were people at the Fabulous just asking for a rattlesnake bite, but Loretta wasn't one of them. "You still got to be careful. You could open the outhouse door and it could be coiled there and shock of the sun would make it STRIKE!"

"What happens then?" Loretta chuckled.

I took her dry hand in my own sweaty paws. She wasn't taking this seriously enough. "I saw a boy - name of Scampo Bender - get bit once. If he's anything to go by, you go red, do some swearing, then you cry for a bit and ask for your ma, then your neck swells up like a toad's and you turn purple and die. Don't get bit."

"I'll try not to. Is that dangerous?" Loretta pointed at a gigantic, red-winged black wasp, flitting from rock to rock, waggling its long antennae.

"Tarantula wasp," I kept an eye on the mean critter. "They kill big spiders. You do not want to get stung by one of those, but I reckon they'll leave you alone if you don't trouble them. Masterton tried to kill one not long before you got here. It stung him. He ... do you mind if I say 'crap'?"

"I don't." Loretta laughed. I wasn't sure why. Loretta was highfalutin and highfalutin people were generally disapproving of cuss words.

"When Masterton got stung, he screamed for an age and crapped his pants."

I couldn't help but smile to remember the usually sombre man jumping about and smelling of crap.

"Was it funny, Eleanor?"

"I guess not," I grinned, "but he shouldn't have been messing with the wasp and, well, the thing about Masterton ..." I stopped there. My mother had taught me not to bad-mouth people.

"You don't like Masterton?" Loretta asked.

As always, just thinking about Masterton made me feel like I had centipedes all over me. "He talks to me too much. He looks at me too much."

Loretta's blue eyes fixed on me. "Does he touch you?"

"He puts his hands on my leg and squeezes sometimes. It makes me want to puke."

"You should slap his hand away."

"I do! And I scream. He stops sharpish."

"Good. Make sure you're never alone with him."

"Why not?"

"Just don't be. Now tell me, should I be scared of Indians?"

I blinked. How did she get from Masterton to Indians? Well, never mind, I thought. The people who'd lived in Death Valley for ever, as far as I knew, were the Timbisha Shoshone, so that's who she should have been worrying about, but if she didn't know the difference between a bighorn and a goat I wasn't about to explain how all the tribes were different.

"Indians do kill white folk sometimes," I said, "and sometimes they do nasty things to them, but it ain't nothing compared to what white people have done to the Indians. A white man'll kill five Indians cos he thinks one of them looked at him funny. It's cos all the white men have got guns, and there's not much law. Man with a hot head and a gun at his hip sees red and an argument becomes a murder. So, Indians get killed by an angry man with a revolver and then the Indians retralliate. No. What's the word?"

"Retaliate?"

"Yup, that's it. Five Indians'll get shot and killed. Then Indians'll retaliate and beat up maybe one Forty-Niner. Then the other settlers will retaliate right back and then some. They'll muster a posse – that's a lot of excited men on horses. They'll gallop off with a lot of whooping and cussing and guns and other manliness, then shoot dead all the Indians they can find. Women, children, and all."

"I heard the Indians were awful, that they'd tortured people and killed babies. They hung three hundred of them for raping and killing in Minnesota."

"I don't know about Minnesota. Out here, in the desert, I've seen murdering and I've seen crookedness and a lot of downright evil. Ain't much of it was Indians." Pretty much all that was taken directly from my ma, but I believed it too.

"You know a lot about Indians, don't you, Eleanor?"

"I knew someone who talked a lot about the people who were here first, and how badly they're being treated," I explained.

"Who was that?"

"I'll tell you a story," I said, instead of embarrassing her by telling her it was none of her business. "A man named Rockwell stole a mule from the Timbisha, who live round here. Rockwell butchered the mule and ate it. The Timbisha caught him. If Rockwell had been an Indian and the Indians whities, they would have strung him up. But these Timbisha just stripped Rockwell naked and took all his stuff.

"That night, Rockwell crept into their camp and killed two Timbisha women, one man, and a kid while they were sleeping."

Loretta gasped.

"Yeah. While they slept. Four of them! Including a kid. Next day the Timbisha went to the mine that Rockwell came from, told the other miners what Rockwell had done. The miners wanted to give him up but he'd fled. So, there was a fight, and twelve more men were killed. Eleven of those dead were Timbisha because the Timbisha didn't have guns."

Loretta was listening in respectful silence. I was impressed. Not many adults listened to me. They often started talking over what I was saying, which made me hot, I can tell you.

"First time the person who told me came across the story of Rockwell and the Timbisha, she heard it was a heroic defence of the mine against an Indian horde, attacking because that's what murderous savages do. She only heard the real story later. She told me to be wary of any story which has the Indians as the evil side."

"I'll make sure I do that."

"Of course, you can go too far the other way and ignore the terrible things that Indians do do. Tonkawas are cannibals, for example, but some pilgrims won't let themselves believe that because they want to see all Indians as wonderful and noble."

"Pilgrims?"

"That's what they call folk from the east. Some people say the more states between you and the Indian, the rosier your picture of the Indian. The people who say that though are the people who hate Indians just because they're Indians … even though there's some truth to it. Point is, it's complicated."

"So, I'm a pilgrim?"

"I guess …"

"But I believe you about the Tonkawas! I'll watch out for them."

"I think you'll be alright. They're worried their medicine won't mix if they eat invaders' flesh. And they live further east. The Timbisha Shoshone, who live round here, won't hurt you if you leave them alone. Most Indians are like that."

"Indian Moses seemed pretty dark," said Loretta.

I pictured Indian Moses' pinched face and mean eyes. "He was horrible, but he wasn't an Indian." I don't mind admitting I wasn't too sad when he got killed, but I couldn't tell Loretta that.

"Indian Moses wasn't an Indian?"

"He was half Indian by blood, but he never lived with any tribe, and he didn't like Indians much, either. He was a white man who looked like an Indian."

"You see a lot, don't you? You're a very clever girl."

Her praise pleased me mightily. "I'm interested in things, is all."

"You certainly spent long enough looking at Moses' corpse when Crane pulled it out of the mine."

His head had been smashed so it was just bits of skin and yuk on his neck bone. I reckoned the rest of it got left behind when Crane was dragging him out. It had been pretty interesting.

"Like I said, I'm interested in things." I blushed.

"It's not just bighorns," said Loretta. "I saw a little fox yesterday." I think she saw I was embarrassed and wanted to change the subject.

"Foxes are everywhere," I said.

"Everywhere?"

"Yup!" I confirmed.

Loretta reached up to my ear then plucked her hand away. "Oh yes! Here's a fox that was right in your ear. They are everywhere!"

I giggled, picturing foxes all over the place. "Darn right! The whole of the air is thick with foxes! You've got two in your nose!"

"You're sitting on a whole pile."

"Foxes everywhere! Can't move for foxes!" I swung my arms to push away imaginary, floating foxes.

"Look at their little heads," Loretta pointed, "sticking up out of the tram buckets!"

I pictured fox heads poking from the dangling quartz carriers and laughed till I coughed.

A skinny-legged lizard ran onto a rock and stopped, knees high, staring at us with an expression on its face that looked an awful lot like outrage.

"Zebra-tailed lizard." I said, nodding at the critter.

"You just make up that name?" Loretta asked.

I looked at her. She still wasn't joking. "No, that's what it's called, on account of it having black and white stripes on its tail like the stripes on an African horse."

Loretta nodded. "You know everything. How old are you?"

"Twenty."

Loretta laughed. "I'm not much more than twenty. Try again."

"Sixteen?"

"You might get away with that. If you were talking to a blind, deaf, and dumb dog. But why not say how old you are? You're a kid, be a kid. Don't rush to be a woman. The West is a tough place for women. There aren't many. I've heard of towns where men outnumber women a hundred, even two hundred to one. A woman doesn't need to be beautiful to make a lot of money selling herself. But I won't do that."

I knew what she meant, but I wished I didn't. I sat quiet and Loretta didn't say anything more. I guess she knew she'd touched a nerve.

Down in the valley there was a little black hill that stuck out from the valley floor like a mole from a man's back. Crane called it a volcano. He was wrong. It wasn't a volcano (*how come adults didn't know this stuff?*) but I liked it all the same. Funny, in this land where hills could be green, purple, red, or whatever colour they chose to be, and might soar so high that they had snow on the top even in this heat, I liked that little black lump best.

"Come on," said Loretta, standing up. "It's not going to get any cooler, and we've got laundry and tidying to do. And those men'll be hungry when they come out of the mine."

"I hope they find The Prize today," I said.

"Me too," Loretta nodded, hands on hips. "Me too."

ACT ONE, CHAPTER TWO

The Bounty Hunter

I read the first chapter to the biddies and duffers of the creative writing group yesterday evening. Mrs Terbangun, hitherto the keenest and most popular reader, yawned a few times. That was a good sign. She always tries to belittle when she feels threatened.

"Were you really not scared of the Indians?" asked Mrs Skillet.

"Well, like I said, Indians is a very broad term, and—"

"We should not be calling them Indians," interrupted Mrs Terbangun. "It's a racialist term, made up by white invaders who thought they'd reached India."

I do actually prefer the term Aboriginals," I said, "because that means the people who were there first, but people think I'm talking about Australia if I say Aboriginals. So I just say Indians, so that people know I'm talking about America, which is odd if you think about it, but there you go. I don't have a problem with the word. If we are to use one term to describe all the varied people who lived in the Americas before the white man came, one is as good as another."

"Words matter!" barked Mrs Terbangun.

"Do they, though?" I replied. "I never met an Indian who minded being called an Indian."

"They don't know they're being demeaned and belittled! You should not use that word!"

"I reckon policing others' words comes second to learning about the people you're patronising and doing something to help them. I am surprised how often folk these days seem to think it's the other way round. Minding other people's

language only serves to prove how morally superior you are, and only to yourself. So at best it's pointless. At worst..." I left that hanging. Mrs Terbangun was already gulping like a toad having a stroke and I didn't want to goad her into a tantrum with a direct insult.

"As if Indians need help!" scoffed Mrs Hopkins. "Quite the opposite. I saw plenty of people in headdresses when I was in the States who were only too happy to take the dollars out of your hand. They own huge swathes of land in the West. One of them asked for five dollars when I tried to take his photo!"

"Did you give him five dollars?" asked Mr Hillier-Edwards.

"Did I bunnies!" Mrs Hopkins quivered. "I took the photo and walked away!"

"You shouldn't have done that!" chimed in Mrs Terbangun. "They believe that being photographed takes their soul."

"So how come I bought a book with hundreds of Indians posing for photos?" barked Mrs Hopkins.

"You're the expert, Mrs Salmon," said Mr Hillier-Edwards. "Can one take a photograph of an American Aboriginal?"

"Yes, in the same way you can take a photograph of anyone. It's fine, but you should probably ask before sticking a camera in their face. Although there were some Indians who didn't like it and refused to be photographed," I said. "Crazy Horse for example."

"What a silly name," opined Mrs Hopkins. "But they've all got silly names, haven't they? And they're all the same. Beggars and thieves who'll take anything they can get from the white man."

I looked into Mrs Hopkins' watery blue eyes. I was there and I saw what happened. Perhaps I'll write more about it one day, if I manage not to fall down the stairs, choke on a fishbone or simply die in my chair any time soon. I didn't want a row, but I couldn't let that one lie.

"Have no doubt," I said , "that the treatment of the American Indian was, and continues to be, a travesty and a tragedy."

"Tragedy! That hardly covers it," cried Mrs Terbangun. "It was a holocaust, exactly the same as the Nazis' evil persecution of the Jews."

"Well, no," I said. "It wasn't like the Holocaust."

"Oh no?" Mrs Terbangun was shaking. "Pray tell why not?"

"It's complicated. There were murderous idiots who loved killing Indians, sure, and thousands of tribes were destroyed. But, for the most part, it wasn't done on purpose."

"Not on purpose?" sniffed Mrs Terbangun. "What nonsense!"

"Why did the white people want to destroy the Indians?" I asked.

"Because all white people are murdering racialists!" Mrs Terbangun blurted.

I should probably mention that Mrs Terbangun is a white person, as were all the people in that room. I could have gone along that tack, but I was keen to get my point across to the others. I knew there was no hope for Mrs Terbangun. She'd made her mind up a long time ago and then closed it.

"Well, yes, some were murdering racialists, but they were few and they killed relatively few. The tribes destroyed each other as much as the whites destroyed them. And many more deaths were caused by smallpox and cholera. Yes, the diseases came from Europe. And yes, a lot of the inter-tribal violence was a result of the European invasion and connected factors, including the introduction of horses and guns, but that's the point. The destruction of the tribes was a side effect of European expansion across the Americas in the pursuit of land and riches. It was never a goal."

"A side effect!" spat Mrs Terbangun.

"I'm not saying it was right, but it was not the Holocaust. It was not, a deliberate attempt by one group to erase the other. Yes, it was bad. Maybe as 'bad' as the Holocaust, but it was not the same. Rape is bad and murder is bad, but they are not the same. Just because two things are bad, it does not make them the same, and it's stupid to suggest that they are."

"Are you calling me stupid?"

I paused. I was calling her stupid, but I couldn't quite think of the right way to put it. I was saved by Mr Hillier-Edwards, who piped up, "You said Death Valley wasn't below sea level. But I understood that it was?" Mr Hillier-Edwards has the most wonderful accent. Very posh, but also capable, reassuring, and kind. Many men I've met who fought in the last war have that accent, but I've never heard it from anyone born after 1925. Shame to think that it might die out with the War generation.

I nodded. "Yes, Death Valley goes down to two hundred and fifty-six feet below sea level, but I didn't believe that when I was eleven."

The conversation turned to how somewhere could stay dry when it was *below sea level. I'd worked that out when I was about twelve, and I'd had enough of other people for one evening, so I returned to my room to write a little more.*

So, here we go, a little further east this time. We're going to join another of our main characters on his way to the Fabulous mine, even though he doesn't know that yet.

James Willow's companions in the coach were American brothers Orion and Samuel Clemens. He'd rather have been on his own, but at least having company meant that he couldn't dwell on what had happened, because weeping in front of two other chaps would have been embarrassing.

Orion Clemens, perhaps five years older than Willow, had large but piercing dark eyes, and a fine black beard grown army style; in other words his beard was untopiaried beyond the occasional trim. Samuel was around two years younger than his older brother Orion. His curly hair crested in a waxed wave over a broad forehead and eagle nose. Mutton chops adorned his jowls like spaniels' ears, framing his otherwise clean-shaven face.

Willow was jealous of their facial foliage. He himself had what people called – at least what his brothers and father had called – an effeminate face (they'd often used the pronoun "she" when referring to him, which had rankled). A manly bush jutting from his chin like the prow of a warship would have helped him a great deal in almost every endeavour. So, he'd been looking forward to sprouting bristles. Now in his twenties, that sprouting was yet to manifest. All he could grow was a fluff not dissimilar to the agglomerations of drifting hair and dust that might gather under a bed. Even that feathery fuzz would grow only in irregular patches.

The older brother Orion Clemens was travelling west to take up a government post. Samuel's role, so far as Willow could tell, was to make whimsical and witty observations.

And he, James Willow, was a bounty hunter. Could one call oneself a bounty hunter if one had never collected a bounty? Yes, he reasoned. Here he was, heading West, hunting a bounty. Very hard to argue, therefore, that he was anything but a bounty hunter. Even if he didn't have any facial hair.

If you'd told him a year ago that he'd be a bounty hunter heading West across America, he'd have assumed you were drunk or trying to be funny (without being funny). But here he was. It really was very exciting. Forgetting, for a moment, that he had company, he jiggled up and down in his seat and giggled a little.

The brothers both raised their left eyebrows in such a similar fashion that they might have been trying to prove they were brothers, and regarded Willow as if he'd just pulled a large caterpillar out of his nose.

"Sorry!" he said, ceasing to jiggle.

The Clemenses both treated him to a benign smile and a single nod.

Sorry seemed to be the only word that Willow said as their coach zoomed past extraordinary cactuses and twisted trees - the last two times, because he had made a smell. He was not used to the volume of beans and bacon that people consumed out here.

If he was honest, the brothers intimidated him.

Back in England, it was widely accepted that Americans were too stupid to know they were stupid, which led to brash loudness. Oafish words, loudly spoken, were expected on the Western shores of the Atlantic.

Before this coach trip, Willow had seen little to disprove this notion and much to support it. Yet the Clemens brothers were different. Willow had attended Oxford University. He accepted that he wasn't the brightest person in the world, or even in most rooms if he had company - but he'd certainly mingled with the very cleverest, or so he'd thought, as earnest young Brits had theorised their theories and argued their arguments beneath dreaming spires.

Yet the Clemens brothers, particularly young Samuel, seemed more erudite, educated, and eloquent than any of Oxford's scholars, and by some margin. They contemplated and concluded almost without cease as the coach jiggled along, a barrage of convoluted but clever wisecracks, bon mots, and hypotheses that were so well-observed, and often so funny, that Willow didn't know whether to laugh or ask to shake their hands.

They travelled for a while before Orion cleared his throat and broke the silence. "This road we've had the luck to traverse for the last three days is matchless." His accent was definitely American, yet, to Willow, paradoxically polished and intelligent. "It surpasses the roads of New York City and leaves them choking in its dust."

Samuel raised his eyebrow. Willow had learnt the look. Clemens Junior was about to be clever. "I've walked storm-pelted mountain trails that surpass the rutted routes that New Yorkers claim as roads." His eyebrows danced to emphasise their owner's archness.

"Ha!" said the elder, delighted by the younger man's observation. "You're right. New York City is a bad example. Instead, imagine, if you will, a triangular district of thoroughly fair thoroughfares. Its points are Pittsburgh, Boston, and Richmond."

"New York City lurks within that triangle." Samuel asserted.

"I'd say New York perches a little west of the line from Richmond to Boston, but let's quibble not. Draw a circle about New York City's treacherous trails, my good man, and remove that circle from consideration. Picture the finest city street or country avenue from elsewhere within the sector."

Clemens Minor closed his eyes. "Indulge me a moment. I am strolling the routeways of your triangular, infrastructural nirvana. I'm rounding a perfectly curved and evenly paved corner … and here I am, striding with giddy happiness along the finest avenue that lies within the newly established Pittsburgh-Boston-Richmond catchment of carriageway comparison."

"Good," nodded his big brother. "I posit that this road along which we are whizzing with such satisfactory alacrity is superior to the road you are picturing, as far as a coach's ease of passage is concerned, if not for passing scenery."

"The view from my imagined coach window is spring flowers, live oaks, and smoke curling from the chimney of a productive and reasonably priced bakery. Such a vista does indeed surpass dirty rocks, dust-coated scrub, and boarding houses that charge, with breathtaking brazenness, five dollars for inferior ham and eggs. However, the surface of the road here is, as you suggest, superior. And I shall explain why!" The younger's customary cynicism was cast aside. His eyes shone with intellectual fervour as the carriage sped along, "This passage to the West seldom - if ever - suffers the ravages of frost."

"But surely the ravages of heat are more injurious to long-suffering hardcore?"

"Not nearly! And here's why. When a fall in the mercury nudges water from playful liquidity into sober solidity …"

Willow looked out the window. He was lost, and, if he was honest, not entirely interested in road surfaces. Whilst the brothers argued on, he scanned the dusty rocks and scrub for rangy jackass rabbits, heavily armoured tortoises, guiltily slinking coyotes, and his favourite of all, the pert pronghorn – a wonderfully elegant deer which ran so fast it looked like it was flying and kissing the ground with its hooves as a dainty dance, rather than as a gravitational necessity.

The brothers were right about the road. It was immeasurably better than Willow had expected. The coach made astonishing pace, not least because they changed horses every ten miles. Rather excitingly, the way west was superior to the Oxford to Newbury road. Even the Oxford to London.

What glories lay ahead?

The coach slowed and they passed the skeleton of a long-dead oxen, skin tight over its empty frame like desiccated seaweed stretched between the beams of a shipwreck on a desert shore.

More and more dead oxen lay by the roadside. Soon there were piles of them, shoved off the road to rot in the desert heat. *No, not rot*, thought Willow, *not in this heat. Their carcasses would simply become dryer and dryer until they turned to dust.*

What had happened here?

"Hay prices." said Clemens Minor, as if reading his mind.

"Excuse me?" Willow replied, not sure that he'd heard the man correctly.

"Hay prices." Samuel leant forward, fingers steepled, and looked Willow in the eye as if he was about to reveal the key to everlasting life. "Three winters ago, dozens upon dozens of waggons headed west. Their doughty oxen found little grazing. Several wily hay merchants, knowing that fodder would be scarce, followed the brave pioneers and charged whatever they desired. Hay prices rose to eight hundred dollars a ton. Eight hundred dollars. You can guess the consequences."

"Hay merchants became rich?"

The younger Clemens blinked. "Well, yes, indeed, purveyors of agricultural foodstuffs indubitably bolstered their coffers, but that was little comfort to the beleaguered beasts whose remains we pass. No, the darker consequence of the obscene price hike struck these bovine innocents. If one indulges the difficult situation of their drovers, one might say the oxen were emancipated."

"And if one does not indulge?" asked Orion.

"The oxen were abandoned," replied Samuel, as if reporting a great crime. "The kind animals did not venture here voluntarily. The good beasts were ignorant of fortunes to be found below ground. Yet those pressed servants marched west uncomplainingly. In return for wholehearted duty, they were left alone and incapable in a land free of grace or graze. Conditioned to receiving fodder from their erstwhile masters on the road, to the road they returned. Here they found that humans were no longer generous. Here they waited to be fed. Here they starved."

"The bones glow at night." added Orion.

"I'm sorry?" Willow blinked.

"On murkier nights only, when there's moisture in the air. The phosphorus in bones luminesces."

Was Orion teasing him? The bounty hunter looked from Clemens to Clemens. They smiled back, obviously pleased with themselves.

Willow was flustered. He had been teased a great deal in his life, and he had never come to like it. He returned to his usual pursuit of scanning the scrub for jackass rabbits, which were actually hares, coyotes, which were actually big foxes, and pronghorns, which were simply wonderful.

Presently there was another cough, and James Willow's eyes flicked expectantly towards Orion Clemens.

"Now, my good fellow," said the older brother, "we've been travelling together for some time, so I hope you won't mind me asking: what brings a fine Englishman such as yourself to the West? Do feel free not to answer, it is none of my business. I am interested in others, and I enjoy conversation, yet I take no offence when denied. I do implore you not to indulge me if you would rather not share the inspiration of your odyssey."

Willow's mind flicked for a moment back to England and the reason he had crossed the ocean, and recoiled as if burnt. Instead, he made himself remember that day in the coach office in St Louis, and the more immediate reason for his presence in a carriage hurtling westwards.

Ahead of him in the line had been a tall, dark-skinned woman with a bearing and dress as elegant as any he's seen. She'd reached the window and spoken quietly but confidently, and - Willow had concluded, after thinking about it for quite some time - smokily.

"First class ticket one way to Denver, please."

The cashier, a lofty and scrawny man with a nose that could have opened a tin, smiled at her as if she was a pupil and he was a teacher who hated children. "Those tickets are expensive." He'd oozed smug superiority. We don't accept credit notes from your kind."

"I have cash."

"We do not accept confederate dollars!"

"I don't carry them."

Holding the cashier's gaze, the woman had removed a wad from her neatly sewn leather bag and placed it on the counter.

"Where did you get this?" he asked.

Willow could see only the back of the woman's hat, but he could *feel* her staring at the cashier.

The man's expression morphed from piggish defiance to confusion, then something that wasn't a mile from fear.

"What name s-should I take for the register?" he stammered.

"You don't need a name," she said.

The cashier had opened his mouth as if to say something but then thought better of it. He scribbled on a chit, then handed it to his intimidating customer.

Willow saw her face for only a moment as she headed out. It wasn't her beauty that was striking, although she was beautiful. It was the pride that flowed from her in waves. Never had he seen a head held so well.

So, weeks later, when he'd seen her face looking out from a bounty poster, he'd known immediately that it was her, and he remembered that she'd bought a ticket to Denver. He knew straight away that he'd quit his current employment as a saloon plongeur - or glass-scrub, as they called them here - and chase her.

He wanted to see her again, and he wanted the money for capturing her and turning her into the law. Somehow these two desires could exist side by side in his head without troubling each other.

He pictured her face and smiled. He thought about the money and nodded. *Money will solve most of your problems,* his father had said. *The rest you can live with.* He'd said it of course to Willow's older brothers or possibly his sister and Willow had overheard. His father wouldn't have deigned make such a proclamation to James himself.

Thinking of his family made him scowl.

Yet another small cough brough him back into the present, reminding him that his facial dramatics had an audience. He'd been smiling and frowning like a loon, and the Clemens brothers were looking at him as if he'd quietly vomited into his own top pocket.

"I'm looking for a woman," he said.

"Ah!" they said, nodding as if the male sex was one great conspiracy.

They peered at him expectantly.

He wanted to tell them - he really did, he was a natural chatter - but he'd made a resolution when he crossed the Atlantic to be cannier, and this seemed like a good opportunity to prove his canniness. These brothers might decide to chase the easy bounty themselves.

Willow nodded and smiled politely, then carried right on looking for wildlife.

Hours later, the carriage crested a rise and the lowering sun lit all aglow. In the broad valley ahead, pioneers had cleared cactus and scrub and hammered into being the network of sheds which passed for a town in these sun-blasted badlands. Larger sheds flanked a wide, central road. Flat shopfronts were daubed in once-gay paint, sun-scorched into a peeling pox, browns of varying shade all tending to the overwhelming brown of the desert.

The flat shopfronts were two stories high, but the buildings behind were only one story. Willow had seen the like all over America. It was a bizarre, obvious affectation that fooled nobody, like combing hair over a bald pate, or wearing black in an attempt to disguise fatness. Willow wondered why they did it.

Leaving his coach companions crafting cleverly hilarious quips about the relative importance of drivers and division agents, James headed along the street, mouth agape. He'd been in America for several months now, but everywhere was so strikingly different from home that he constantly felt like he'd just stepped off the ship in New York.

This town was all men, for a start. Young men at that. There were no children, no women and no old duffers. This did not greatly suit Willow, who much preferred the company of woman and children to his own sex and age. The old he could tolerate. At least they weren't threatening - not most of them, anyway.

Secondly, it was all very, very brown. The buildings, the clothes, the carts, and the road were brown, and even the men's faces were tanned to a level of brown that, back in England, one found only on aging furniture and some horses.

Despite the drab colouring, there was a bustle here that he'd never experienced at home. People had pep - a word that he'd never heard in England, nor that was needed there. Everybody strode as if there was something going on, or, more accurately, many things going on, and they were on their way from one of them to another. Even the dogs marched about as if they had somewhere to go, and that somewhere was important.

This was the Gold Rush. He might not be in a gold mining region yet, in fact they were still a good way from the gold as he understood, but everyone was going to or from the gold. Overwhelmingly, people were going towards it.

He pushed his way along the street - the words "excuse me" had little currency here - through the crowd of stinking humanity and barking conversation, all about mother lodes, placer deposits and other terms alien to Willow.

Back East, in the relative sophistication of New York, the Englishman had heard tales of the West. Across the Rockies, they said, were thriving towns packed with sassy women and charming gentleman-prospectors spending money like generous royalty, all set to a background of jaunty piano music. Funds exhausted, these debonair fellows strolled into the hills, picked up some of the gold that was lying about like acorns under an oak in autumn, and strutted right back into town to resume the high life. The very different reality of the west made the Willow nostalgic for that bright and shiny time that he'd never known. A time that hadn't, in fact, ever existed.

He climbed the wooden steps to a saloon. Or "SALON," if you went by the foot-high letters above its door, daubed jarringly by a painter who'd presumably been suffering from at least one broken arm.

The saloon was heaving like an overstocked livestock shed at the beginning of feeding time. It stank of fetid booze, cigar smoke, and unwashed men. The shouted chat and general yeehawing was near deafening. With some effort, pushing past three bearded men on their way in, Willow struggled back out again.

He stood on the veranda. To the west, clouds were huge, tending downward from pale yellow on high, to orange, to pink and then a bloody carmine soaking the horizon. The metamorphosis of the sky was staggeringly beautiful, and a sign, Willow reckoned, that he too could change.

He had come here to change. Memories from England shamed him. Remembering what had happened immediately unleased the familiar, all-pervading nausea and despair. In those moments he could be objective about it, he reasoned that his grief and shame felt like terror. When those emotions weighed on him, he struggled to breath, let alone think, eat or sleep.

He shook his head. He raised his eyes to the wonderful sunset.

He would be that man no longer. He would be brave. If not quite a hero, perhaps he could at least be an adventurer. Yes, the saloon had been terrifying at first exposure. However, it was populated presumably by people who not terrified of being in there. Was Willow less than all those people?

Perhaps he had been in the past.

No longer.

He took a deep breath, then another, then one more for luck, and re-entered the saloon. He pushed through the crowd. "The only way to cross a dancefloor is to dance across it" was an expression that he'd made up at university (it had never caught on, despite his efforts). Here, the crowd was jostling and shoving, so, reasoned James Willow, since *excuse me* didn't work, the only way through this crowd was to jostle and shove.

One particularly muscular shoulder wouldn't budge, so he thrust a palm into it.

A mistake.

The owner of the Brobdingnagian shoulder turned. His face was huge and extraordinary, as if a sea monster had mated with an overly-muscled bull, squeezed its offspring into human clothes, and despatched it into America to frighten nervous Englishmen.

The monster-man looked down. He was over a head taller than Willow.

"I don't like being pushed." His voice was like railway sleepers dragged over rock.

"Do any of us?" asked Willow.

The man's brow furrowed into a ridge like a fat dog's neck-roll.

"I really am sorry. I didn't mean to." Willow tried.

"You did. Else you wouldn't have done it."

The logic was undeniable.

"I am sorry," Willow stammered on, "I was hoping to get a drink and–"

"Round here," said the large man, leaning in, "you want a man to move, you say "*excuse me.*" Round here," he leant further in, "people got manners."

His breath smelled of tobacco, raw meat and manliness. The bounty hunter felt like he was shrinking. He felt the crowd clear all around them. Presumably they were making space so they could watch this man mountain pound Willow into a greasy spot.

So much for bravery! thought Willow.

"I really am sorry," he said again, "but I've found that '*excuse me*' doesn't always work in America."

"You're English?"

"Ahhh," Willow wondered if being English was a good thing. He seriously doubted it. "Well, I'm half Scottish by blood but … but some Scots are far from pleased when you claim Scottishness with an accent like mine … yes, I am English."

"Well, in that case it's my turn to apologise." The monster stepped back. "I was English once and I know it can be difficult. Have you been here long?"

"In America? Not long at all. I got the boat across-"

"EXCUSE ME!" the large man shouted.

The bar fell silent.

The large man continued, voice loud as a town crier, "Our English friend here would like to make his way to the bar. Everyone step aside, please."

The throng parted, creating a passage. They were all looking at Willow, smiling as if they were in on a joke he didn't understand. One toothless old chap with a nasty-looking facial fungus was wringing his hat in his hands and grinning like a greedy child at Christmas.

Willow's eyes were wide. What was this? A joke? Was he about to run a gauntlet; to receive painful, public punishment?

"Well, go on then, chum! They won't wait forever," said the huge man.

He took a step, then another, feeling like he was in a dream and hoping that he was because he was fairly sure he was about to soil himself.

The crowd closed behind him. The monster turned away to resume his conversation. Willow let out the breath he didn't know he'd been holding, and carried on towards the bar. It was busy with leaning men.

"Move aside! Customer coming through!" called the barman. He was a squat, silver-haired fellow with wide-spaced eyes that looked in different directions like a flounder.

Willow reached the bar, alive and unmaimed. He looked back across the saloon. The giant nodded at him with something that looked a lot like manly respect, then turned away.

"Howdy, stranger. What can I get you?" The barkeep smiled.

Willow leant in, aware that the people either side had stopped talking so they might hear him. He saw no option but the truth, however. You never know, one of the eavesdroppers might have seen his quarry. He'd keep his wanted poster to himself though. He didn't want competition.

"Actually, I'm after some information. I'm looking for a woman."

"Aren't we all!" chimed an onlooker. The superb quip near brought the house down. The bounty hunter waited for the thigh slapping to subside.

"She's dark-skinned and-"

"Drink first." announced the barman. "What'll it be?"

"What do you have?"

"Whiskey or slumgullion."

"Slum …?"

"Gullion."

Around them, the customers returned to their previous spaces and conversations.

"Slumgullion, please." Willow the Adventurer was determined to try new things.

The barman turned to do whatever one needed to do to produce slumgullion. A small man sidled up, Mexican and handsome.

"I saw your dark-skinned woman, and I know where she is gone. I will tell you."

"What colour were her eyes?"

"Blue. Like Ice." The man looked puzzled for a moment. "Maybe not like ice. Like a bird's wings. Well, like a blue bird's wings. Have you seen the bird that sings like an angel at dawn, but by the time the sun has-"

"I understand. Her eyes were blue."

The Mexican nodded. "I told you, I know her. Give me some money and I'll tell you where she went."

The bounty hunter reached for his wallet, plucked out a dollar bill and slapped it on the bar.

"You will need more of those," said the Mexican. "Quite a few more."

ACT ONE, CHAPTER THREE

Moses Meets God

The second chapter was warmly received. Mr Hillier-Edwards and Mrs Hopkins joined my table at breakfast, which I'm secretly pleased about as my usual table mates are the drooling, odorous, chat-free versions of the biddy that I will become if I live long enough. Mrs Hopkins was full of questions and Mr Hillier-Edwards full of wartime stories of his own dealings with the "yanks," as he called them. I caught Mrs Hopkins glancing at me when he said "yanks," perhaps wondering if I was offended, me being a yank and all. I smiled back to show that I wasn't.

It's just like Indians I suppose. Intention is important. Words are not. To Mr Hillier-Edwards the word "yank" was synonymous with "American" and he spoke of his yanks with affection and admiration.

I have heard the term yanks used pejoratively, but that doesn't upset me either. It tells me nothing about me and everything about the speaker. When someone uses the term yank as an insult, all I hear is "I am a moron." Same goes for any derogatory term about any nation or group of people. A hurled insult only an insult if you catch it.

Anyway, let's return to the mine.

Indian Moses jumped. Someone - or something - was coming along the tunnel towards him. He held the candle aloft and peered into the murk. His hand shook, throwing jagged shadows onto the tunnel walls and floor. There was the noise again. And again. The tunnels sloped gently upwards into the mountain to make it easier for ore-laden carts to roll out, but it looked to Moses like this tunnel spiralled down to the darkest pits of hell. Candlelight didn't pierce much into the gloom. The darkness underground was different to nighttime outside. The dark here was a solid, closing in all around.

He held his breath. Deafening, roaring, crushing silence.

Then the noise again. It was a drip of water, he realised. Indian Moses exhaled, near faint with relief. His sweating back was wet as a pupfish.

The blackness seemed to pulse, shrinking his pathetic sphere of candlelight with each beat. Shadows all around could have hidden a buffalo. Or any of the others. They'd kill him if they knew he was down here searching for The Prize on his own. Gold warped minds. There were stories of men - women too - killing friends and kin for a whole lot less than The Prize. Monk, Silver, Masterton and Crane were neither friends nor kin. Nor were the woman or the girl, for that matter.

Oh yes, they'd kill him and not lose sleep. He was an Indian. He'd seen the way they looked at him.

But they were all scared of the ghosts. None would have followed him into the adit at night. He was safe down here. In the darkness.

Wasn't he?

Only kin Indian Moses had known was his pa. He knew his ma had been Indian because his pa wasn't, and everyone said Moses looked Indian. That was all he knew about his ma. He didn't have much memory of his pa. Him stung, cussing and crying after raiding a bee nest, wolfing down the little bit of honey he'd managed to pilfer, snot running into his mouth along with handfuls of amber-dripping cone. Not sharing. His pa hacking apart a tree with a stone axe, Moses terrified that he might hit his own hand and hurt himself so bad he wouldn't be able to get food for them. Other cloudy memories, like the smell of the woods after rain. Waking cold and uncomfortable at night, unable to get back to sleep. Being left alone for days, stretching out supplies so he wouldn't starve, climbing a tree when a grizzly roared nearby, staying quiet and peeing himself when the enormous animal padded below his tree.

He remembered walking out of the hills. He'd followed his pa along an increasingly good trail, then finally along an actual road to an actual town.

His pa hadn't looked back the whole journey.

He'd followed his Pa along the street. Flat-faced buildings had towered on both sides. Hairy, smelly, enormous men were mostly busy with their business, but some stared. Moses stared back and the starers stared back at him.

His father led him into a saloon, dark and dusty, just a few men lurking in the shadows. Some nodded greetings but none spoke.

"Moses, this is Crazy Hips Sid," his pa said, not looking at his son, pointing at the man behind the wooden counter. "You're going stay here. Crazy Hips Sid is your pa now."

Then his pa walked out without looking at him again. Moses wanted to follow, but he knew to do what he was told.

He never saw his pa again.

"Shall I call you Pa?" he asked Crazy Hips Sid.

"Crazy Hips'll do." The man stepped around the bar and Moses saw how he'd got his name. God had seen fit to cram a horse's pelvis into an otherwise slight man. Not content with that, the good Lord had set that pelvis at an angle, so Crazy Hips lurched like a shot mule.

For maybe five years - maybe three, maybe seven, if anybody was counting, Moses didn't know - Moses ran errands for Crazy Hips and got older.

Then, in a town grown to three hundred men with no women and no other children, Crazy Hips realised he had a golden goose. It wasn't eggs that he wanted Moses to lay.

The new work was disgusting, painful, and strangely lonely given that there was always at least one other person with him.

Crazy Hips made Moses do the horrid work, but he also looked after him. He shot two men who hurt Moses, killing one of them. The sheriff, a regular visitor to the boy's crib, declared that both incidents were self-defence.

Moses became good at his new job and, like any job well done, it began to satisfy him. It pleased him to please his customers. Some of them still tried to hurt him, but Crazy Hips usually sniffed out the bad eggs before anything happened. If something unwanted did go on, Crazy Hips was always nearby with his Navy revolver and a stout club.

Then Christians came in the night and rescued Moses. Father Antonio and his followers took him south, to a walled house that they called a hacienda.

Here the boy learned from Father Antonio that he, Moses, was a beautiful devil, sent to tempt men. Father Antonio, explaining that he was but flesh, gave into temptation regularly. Sometimes twice a day. Every now and then, three times.

When the good Father was done, he would weep or beat Moses. Often both.

After a summer and a winter, God showed Moses a way to free the father from temptation. The boy crept into Antonio's cell when he was asleep, picked up the good man's horn-handled Bowie knife and plunged it into his skull. Moses took the knife and fled over the wall.

He walked and walked. Snatches of memory from that trek still haunted him. Animals growling and flashing away in the darkness, the relentless sun, the circling vultures. Cutting his arms with the Bowie knife and sucking his own blood to try to slake the agonising thirst. Giving up. Falling down onto the dirt to die.

A sudden noise snapped Moses' mind from his memories.

He held his breath.

Someone, or something, was following him along the dark corridor.

He turned slowly and stared back along the rough-sided tunnel, widening his eyes in an effort to penetrate the cloying blackness.

Was that a glint back there - Silver's glass eye?

Or, much more likely, a chunk of quartz angled just right to shine at him ...

Moses stared, making monsters out of shadows. The noise had been another drip, he told himself. Maybe the same one. He turned and crept on, deeper into the mountain.

God sent a one-mule prospector to save him.

After his rescue, Moses stayed with the one-mule prospector until the winter, walking a winding passage steadily north, stopping every now for some pocket mining. They found a little gold, maybe a hundred dollars' worth in all. The prospector shared everything, and did most of the setting camp, cooking and clearing up. He never even mentioned that Moses was an Indian, and never tried to touch him.

Moses resolved to kill the prospector and take all the gold pretty early on, but the very day he planned it, the old man had given him half of their findings with a knowing smile and headed off alone.

With nowhere else to go, Moses went back to Crazy Hips Sid. Sid was dead, it turned out, shot to death in a row over a bottle of vinegar.

The new owner of the saloon had Chinese women to do Moses' old work. So, Moses set up on his own in a crib on the edge of town. Technically, his line of work should have taken place in the tenderloin district, but the sheriff renewed his custom and granted him dispensation, on the condition that Moses claimed he was an Indian masseuse with marvellous healing hands.

Moses grew all the more skilled and raised his price, but he gambled his earnings, drank it, and spent it on opium which he smoked with the Chinese women. The women were child-like and spoke not a word of English, but Moses enjoyed his time with them despite this, or perhaps because of it. They laughed a lot, and he hadn't heard much laughter – not the good kind, anyhow. He liked the opium. He felt clean after a pipe. He missed it now. He could taste the burnt sweetness and remember the calming, smoky waves of peace. He'd have all the opium he wanted when he'd got The Prize. He'd pay Chinese girls to prepare his pipes and laugh while he sat on a big cushion.

The years in town went by, who knew how many, before a huge man came to his crib, old and fat but strong. Silver.

Bring a man to the edge and hold him there, Moses had discovered, and he'd give you pretty much anything to bring him over it. Silver had asked him to do something he didn't usually do. Moses could see how much Silver wanted it. He held back. Even when Silver offered him ten, twenty, thirty bucks. Something made Moses hold out for more. God, he reckoned.

Silver had purpled with rage. He'd raised a fist.

"Hit me and I'll never do it," Moses said, calm and brave for once, the good Lord with him. "Find the right price, and I will."

It looked nasty for a long moment. Then the big man said, "All right. How would you like to be the richest Indian in the world?"

So here Moses was, in the broken canyon, miles from town. As part of the deal, he had to service the big man every few days. It wasn't difficult, in fact Moses quite enjoyed putting to use the only skill he had. But Moses was a good reader of men. Silver had started to look him in the same way that Father Antonio had done. He was ashamed, but he couldn't stop himself. He didn't expect Silver to hit him like Antonio had. Silver would kill him.

So, it wasn't just greed that had brought Moses down here in the dark. He had to get out before Silver snapped. Might as well, he reckoned, take The Prize with him.

There was a noise ahead. Drips again? No! Something was coming towards him. He brandished the candle. A weapon against the darkness, useful as a stick against a raging buffalo.

He saw his attacker! A darker patch in the darkness, knee high, coming fast.

It wasn't a person. It was a skittering demon that had clawed its way up from Hell. Moses had been told he was going to Hell more often than he chose to remember. Here came the creature to pull him down.

He fumbled for his Allen. The six-barrelled pop gun caught in the holster. They joked that an Allen pistol hit everything but what you were aiming at, and they weren't far wrong. When it hit anything at all. Most of the time it didn't fire.

He yanked the gun free. He blinked away stinging terror-sweat.

The creature was coming still, the tick-tick-tick of small feet counting down the time Moses had left on this world.

He fired.

In the flash he saw his enemy. Frozen for the moment in the light on the far side of a shaft that it might have fallen down had he not fired - unharmed by the Allen's wayward shot, of course - was a small fox.

A fox.

What was a fox doing down here?

Moses blinked, eyes blazing from the Allen's flamboyant but useless flare. The fox must have come down to eat the food they put out to encourage rats. Rats foresaw earthquakes and floods and warned miners by fleeing the tunnels, or at least they were meant to. Obviously, the rats in the Fabulous hadn't been very good at their job.

He blinked again, wondering if foxes knew when earthquakes and floods were coming.

Something shoved him from behind. He staggered forwards, fighting to stay on his feet. He dropped his candle. The unprotected shaft was maybe a pace ahead. It could be twenty feet deep, it could be two hundred. Either way, it was too deep to fall down.

So, one of them had followed him. He spun, shifted weight foot to foot, hands ready. They'd learn. You didn't do what he'd done for years without learning how to-

A fist slammed into his cheek. He knew that feeling all too well. He was far from beaten. He dropped, ready to strike low, then use his attacker's weight t -

A punch crashed into his jaw, cracking his head backwards, knocking him upright and sending him staggering backwards again. Two palms were on his chest. For the blink of an eye, he thought his attacker might be grabbing him, saving him from the shaft, keen to teach him a lesson but not to kill him.

But no.

The hands pushed.

Arms flailing, hands grasping at nothing, Moses fell.

Wind whistled. He wondered why he wasn't screaming. His leg hit a crossbeam and a bone broke. Now he was screaming.

He tumbled head over ass over head over-

His head whacked into rock. Everything was very bright and then very dark.

He woke. It took him a moment to know where he was. The realisation

did not please him.

He had fallen down a shaft. Been pushed! He was lying on his back in the dark, head reeling. But he'd survived! The good Lord loved him. He was blessed. Blessed and tired. So very tired. He'd have to move soon, see if that broken leg could be walked on.

But it was peaceful here. He couldn't remember feeling so very relaxed ever before. All his troubles were flowing out of him. He felt good. He felt right! He smiled. In a moment, he'd get up and start really living - a whole better life than before. But for now, he'd rest a while, maybe have a sleep in the comfortable darkness.

Rumbling from above roused him. Thunder, down here? No. It was a tailings wagon, rolling above. But the track was broken above. A wagon full of ore, weighing more than ten men, would never make it across the collapsed …

The rumbling stopped. There was a moment of silence, then a terrible clattering. He reckoned he could see the wagon plummeting towards him. He needed to move, and fast, he realised as the sturdy metal wagon full of stone landed on him and he thought no more.

Left in the Dark

Some of the biddies were shocked. Possibly all of them.

Mrs Hopkins shook her jowls like a plum-coloured chicken. "I've seen dozens of Westerns and read several Zane Greys. That ... depravity did not happen in the Wild West! It simply didn't. The were no ... " she looked down her nose as she struggled for the right word. I sympathised. It's annoying when you can't remember things.

"Homosexuals?" I suggested.

"That's it!" she called triumphantly as if she'd not only come up with the word but also proved her point. "There were no homosexuals in the Wild West!"

"James Buchanan, president of the USA 1857 to 1861, in the heart of the Wild West years, was a homosexual man." I told her. "He was far from the only one. People teased him a bit, but most weren't too bothered about it."

"A nancy boy president! Ha!" laughed Mrs Hopkins. "Whatever next!"

I shrugged and let it go.

You might as well shout at a tree as argue with some people. I'm not sure why I gave Indian Moses the role of a boy prostitute - or catamite, if you want to be more Classical about it - but chances are he was one. There was an awful lot of brotherly love out west in the pioneering days. What do you expect when there were almost no women west of the Rockies? Well, there were the natives of course, and there were more settler and native relationships than we see in movies and books, but that was more the beaver trappers of earlier days. Miners came later, in greater numbers, and didn't mix so much with native women. Or natives at all for that matter. The beaver trappers traded with the natives and often lived among them. Miners tended to keep the natives at arms length at best, and shoot them at worst.

Men last maybe a week without women before they look for alternatives. In the West, they found each other. And animals too, of course. Steel-jawed heroes of the type you find in Western books and movies were outnumbered a hundred to one by, if you'll pardon the expression, goat fuckers.

Julian, also a little pink in the cheeks, suggested that we should have a break from my story and perhaps listen to someone else's?

To my surprise, the codgers, including Mrs Hopkins, shouted him down. They were unanimous that I should finish my tale to the exclusion of anyone else reading theirs, unless, of course, it became boring.

I was not miles from becoming misty eyed.

Julian asked me to reduce the violence and what he called "unnatural sex." I'll see what I can do. However, I've never been very good at doing what I'm told.

Also - there's nothing much more natural than sexual urges, no matter how counter to the current culture they might be (as I reckon Julian knows only too well). Plus, while we're here, I should say that natural does not mean right. It's natural to want to kill someone, doesn't mean you should. I guess what you have to consider is whether it hurts anybody else. But don't listen to me. I'm trying to be a novelist, not a moral guide, and it's not healthy to try to be both. If I do ever sound preachy, please feel free to ignore me.

So, let's rejoin me, about eighty years ago, in a canyon that runs into Death Valley, and still will do long after we're all gone.

I froze, tin clamped between my knees, tin opener aloft. There was a commotion on the far side of the mine camp.

Silver's, Monk's, and Masterton's voices were echoing up from Gila Canyon, the narrower gulch which joins Fabulous Canyon below the main mine. They were laughing and barking, pretty excited about something.

"Why don't you see what's going on?" said Loretta. "I'll carry on here."

I did not need asking twice. Cooking made me hot and angry. So much effort for something that would be destroyed. *Turned to turd!* But cooking was better than cleaning pretty much anything, especially the outhouse.

I dried my hands on my apron and headed off. Sun glinted off the teeth of huge circular saw that stood menacingly at the end of the dorm shed, unused since I'd been at the Fabulous.

There was all sorts of yahooing and noise coming over the ridge. Had they found The Prize? I quickened to a swift but ungainly march. I considered running but it was too hot, even for The Prize.

Cresting the ridge, I saw my three least favourite people in the world heading up the pale trail towards me, looking mighty pleased with themselves. Monk was near shouting with laughter, teeth gleaming. Silver was beaming like a sweaty, fat cat. Even Masterton had a mean little smile on his wrinkled face.

"What's got you lot tickled?" I asked.

Monk grinned, showing those even teeth and twinkling brown eyes. Loretta said Monk was good looking as a healthy stallion and attractive as a scalped rat. I didn't think he was good looking.

Silver's dark, fat face was split by teeth the colour of peed-on snow in the crevice of a burnt stump.

Masterton's eyes lapped me up and down like a paintbrush dunked in fish slime, his wrinkle-edged mouth twisted into a smile that would have turned the stomach of the toughest bighorn.

"You going to answer me or stand there grinning like dumb wolves?" I asked.

Monk squeaked, trying to hold in a guffaw.

"Nothing to concern a child." rumbled Silver. "Run along, Eleanor."

I shook my head. I did not like these men. What could it … I realised what was wrong.

"Where's Crane?"

Monk's guffaw was like a whipped mule's bray.

Silver chuckled, "Let's get back to camp. There'll be all the more dinner for the rest of us tonight."

They all laughed at this. They did not have what might be called senses of humour.

"Where *is* he?" I demanded.

The three dolts walked on up the path. Monk would have walked right into me if I hadn't jumped out the way.

Masterton, coming last, stopped. He dropped his head, then lifted it slowly, looking at me from top to toe. His lizard tongue flicked between his lips, and I wanted to tear him apart and feed the bits to a hog.

"Crane's lost," Masterton hissed. "But aren't we all?"

"I'm not," I said.

He walked away, following the others up the ridge.

"Where *is* he?" I called after them.

Monk turned. "You don't make it back for dinner, Eleanor, we'll eat your share." Then they were over the rise.

I wrung my hands and looked up and down the sun-cracked canyon. Fat cactuses, spindly bushes, and the smashed detritus of the once busy mine looked back. The land smelled of cooked brick. Way above, a turkey vulture circled.

What could they have done to Crane? Even they wouldn't be laughing if they'd killed him. Surely they wouldn't?

I galumphed down the gully, straining my bad leg, wishing I was faster. I stopped to listen, pulling my sweat-glued dress from my back. Hot silence pressed down from the blue and squeezed in from the canyon sides.

Movement caught my eye. A six-incher scorpion was watching from a flat rock on the gully side, pincers aloft. It was the biggest scorpion I'd seen and for a moment I was fascinated. But I didn't have time to investigate. I hurried on.

Ahead, the sandy gulch-bed went over dry falls, between bluffs, and through a couple of slot canyons before opening into Fabulous Canyon. This side canyon was called Gila Canyon because, I guess, someone had seen a Gila monster there once. I never had, which was a shame because I loved those big black and orange lizards.

Cut into Gila Canyon's sides were half a dozen adits. These passages, man high, wide as my outstretched arms, were dug horizontally into the living rock. They linked with other stone corridors and shafts that plummeted right into the middle of the Earth as far as you could imagine. There was a network of the Lord knew how many miles of tunnels and shafts criss-crossing inside the mountain.

All there so men could run about like ants, looking for gold.

Somewhere in those dark passages were the bodies of fifty drowned miners. I told myself that ghosts couldn't hurt Crane, but I didn't believe it. And there were plenty of other ways to die in a flood-damaged mine made by men in a hurry to find a fortune.

Focus, I told myself. They'd left Crane down there alone. They must have done. Had they hurt him? Was he dead? I hoped not, so much. Not Crane. I hadn't minded too much when the other three were killed. People died. But I liked Crane.

Had they killed him to get a bigger share of The Prize? A man not far to the east had murdered his family for a couple of thousand dollars' worth of gold.

I had to find him.

There was no point fetching Loretta. She might be cool as an icicle in the bright day, but she wouldn't even go near the entrance of an adit, more terrified of the dark than any grown woman had a right to be.

"Crane!" I shouted up and down Gila Canyon. "Crane!"

My voice echoed back, quieter and quieter until it disappeared into the ancient silence of the mountains. I wanted to shout Crane's first name, feeling that might be more effective, but I didn't know it. Crane could be his first name, for all I knew.

I rounded a marbled curve in the canyon and climbed a fan of smashed rock to the entrance of the first adit, hardly watching for rattlers in my hurry. I peered in and couldn't of course see a thing - even when my eyes recovered from the sun's violent glare, I wouldn't be able to see more than half a dozen yards into the cloying gloom - but I felt like I was looking into the depths of the world. Where the monsters lived. I half grinned at the idea.

"Crane!" I shouted down the tunnel.

"Crane! Crane! Crane! Crane!" came back, the last one like the whisper of a mocking demon hunched just out of sight in the darkness, maybe taking time to whisper back in between bites of drowned miner.

Every adit had locofoco friction matches and candles in an alcove by the entrance, so I could have lit a candle and headed in. But there were five other adits in the canyon, and he could be down any of them.

I'd shout down each of them before lighting a candle and entering the darkness, I resolved. It was the sensible thing to do. It wasn't because I was afraid of the dark. The dark was exciting. Definitely not scary.

There was no reply at the second adit either, then I remembered that one was caved in not far from the entrance.

I shouted down the third, then the fourth, then the fifth. Nothing.

I'd have to go in and look for him.

But which adit? Judging by when I'd first heard Monk, Silver, and Masterton, when I'd been up at the camp, and when I'd seen them ... the third one. I'd try the third adit first.

I stamped back up Gila Canyon, fists clenched.

"Eleanor!' called a voice.

I jumped.

Crane emerged from the tunnel behind me, smiled, and nodded. "Good day," he said, tapping his forehead as if it was the brim of his missing hat.

"Where have you been, mister?" I demanded. "I thought the others had ... well, I don't know what I thought they'd done. What did they do?"

"They played a trick."

He smiled but it wasn't his real, warm smile. He freckled skin was pale. His ginger hair hung in sweat-soaked strands and his shirt was sodden. He looked a bit like a frightened horse, eyes wide and nostrils flared.

"What kind of trick?" I asked.

"They left me quite a long way into the mine without a light."

My own eyes widened and my mouth fell open. "They. Did. What? No. How did you ..."

"It wasn't so difficult." His hands were shaking. "The tunnels all slope down towards the exit."

"But not much! Not so much that you could tell in the dark!"

"I admit it was some relief when I saw the light."

"Oh, Crane!"

He shrugged. "Come on, let's get back before they've eaten everything."

"I can't believe it!" I announced, as we crunched across a shoulder of grit between brave shrubs, treading slowly in the stunning sunlight. "We've got to get them back! I know where I can get a whole bunch of tarantulas. A whole big bunch of them. We can put them in their shoes one night … Now what can we use to glue them?"

Crane laughed, sounding a lot more like himself. "There's no need for revenge, Eleanor."

"They wronged you!

"Life'll crap on you every now and then."

"It wasn't *life*. It was Silver, Masterton, and Monk. *They* wronged you. You owe-"

"What would Jesus do?"

"He'd *smite* them. He'd fill them with frogs and shoot them with lightning bolts so they'd burst and he'd stamp on the frogs and-"

"No. Jesus forgives all sins. We should too."

"All sins?"

"All but the Ten Commandments."

I struggled to remember the Commandments. Surely there was one about being the lowest varmints there ever were and leaving a good man alone in the dark?

"Take an eye for an eye, Eleanor," Crane continued, "and you make the whole world blind."

I pictured people walking around a town's streets, arms outstretched and feeling their way. That's how Crane must have been in the mine. Testing each step, knowing he could fall any moment, not knowing whether he was heading to the light or deeper into the rock, where the drowned miners and who knew what else lurked …

I shook my head. "That sounds pretty, but it's wrong. Bible says wrongdoers get what's coming to 'em. Everyone knows that."

"Old Testament, Eleanor. Before Jesus came along and made everything right."

"Old Testament is still the bible!"

"And it's justified a lot of horror in these parts, and all over the world. Men rape and kill and call it God's work. It's not. And nor is revenge."

I looked at him. His colour had come back and his smile seemed genuine again, but I didn't like people badmouthing the bible, even Crane. But I let him off. He'd had a difficult afternoon. And he was a nice man. Too nice to get them back for what they'd done.

But I wasn't.

The three varmints sat at the table watching me and Crane walk up the hill, fat smiles on their toad faces, Masterton turned round on his bench like we a spectacle worth gawping at. I didn't like people watching when I walked. I tried not to limp, but you try and walk regular with one short leg. The harder you try, the weirder it looks.

Back at the camp, I joined Loretta at the greasy pine plank that passed as a serving table and slipped a dead beetle from my pocket into Silver's beans. It was a start.

I usually had a dead critter or two in my pocket, in case you're wondering. Always in my left. Right one was for food. I used my legs to remember. Bad one was on the left.

We sat at the long table in the shade and sweated and ate in silence, other than the slurping and chomping. The sun was near done with the day, but it was still hot as the Devil's drawers. Despite the heat, Silver, Monk, and Masterton looked pleased with themselves. Crane tried to be cheery, but you could tell he'd been shaken.

Silver finished his bowl first. No surprise. "More," he said, sliding his bowl across to Loretta without looking at her. She did his bidding without question.

Wouldn't be so smug if you knew you'd eaten a beetle! I gave Silver my sweetest smile.

Loretta came back with the bowl. Silver didn't thank her.

"By the face on you sometimes, Loretta," said Monk, all teeth and aren't-I-handsome, "I reckon you did for the others."

The dark-skinned woman raised one of her lovely eyebrows. Was she going to talk back and rile him? I bounced on the bench.

"Sounds about right." said Crane before Loretta could speak. "Loretta persuaded the lion to kill Happy Days Frida. And she went down into the mine, where she's terrified to go, and pushed Indian Moses down the shaft, and someone with no knowledge of explosives, who's afraid to go underground, went deep into the mine and set the dynamite to drive the chisel through Denny's head."

"She could have done it." Monk's smile had no warmth, just a devil's wickedness.

"Those were accidents," drawled Masterton, looking at me as usual, even though he wasn't talking to me, scratching at his beardless face with a fork.

"Accidents happen in mines," Masterton continued. "You can engineer them, sure, by leaving someone down in the dark, for example," his gaze shifted to Crane, "but some people are stubborn bastards who don't want to die. Now, get me more supper Eleanor." He shoved his bowl to me.

I could feel his eyes on my back as I limped to the serving table. I knew the tip of his tongue would be sticking out between his lips. I was all out of beetles so I considered taking the bowl behind the shed and peeing into it just a little, but Masterton would have noticed me going, so I had to make do with drooling a mouthful of spit into his food.

They talked nonsense for the rest of supper, then they turned in. When I'd arrived at the Fabulous all the men had slept in the mine because it was so much cooler. They slept in the huts now, even though the valley had got hotter. Whatever they said, they didn't think Denny or Moses had been killed by accident. Maybe Frida had, I had to admit. Hard to think that anyone could have persuaded a lion to slash her to death.

Who's next? I thought, picturing elaborate and exciting ways in which the three men I hated most could be killed. I didn't for a moment consider that the murderer might come for me.

ACT ONE, CHAPTER FIVE

Frida and the Lion

Julian thinks my story could be published. He has offered to edit it, and charmingly pointed out that, given the speed at which publishers move, I am unlikely to live to see the publication date. However, it may provide a nice income for my grandchildren, he reckons. I intend to prove him wrong. I'm not planning on dying any time soon. And I will kill him before I let him edit one word of my story. And I decided a long time ago how much money I'm going to give to my grandchildren. It's not a lot. I've encountered quite a few people who've been given a heap of money at a young age. It never turns out well.

I'm not sure why, I'm usually pretty unflappable, but queer little Julian talking so glibly about my death got me a little riled. So maybe I've been meaner to Happy Days Frida in this next chapter than I might have been.

Happy Days Frida looked over her shoulder. She was alone. She let out a breath she didn't know she'd been holding.

It was good to be away from the others.

They were too stupid to realise how special she was – how lucky they were to have her there - and were not treating her accordingly.

Sure, Monk paid her plenty of attention, for all that meant. She'd encountered his type before. For men like Monk the conquest was all. If she slept with him, it would be one time only. Afterwards, she'd have to carry her own tools into the mine.

However, she maintained the suggestion that he had a chance, which made her life a little easier and somewhat made up for the others' indifference. It was all about the twinkle. You looked at them a little longer than necessary, with that light in your eye that said, "you really could, you know. Keep trying. You could get me." A touch here and there that lingered just long enough helped matters long.

Frida had practiced in the mirror until her twinkle was like dawn light on a diamond.

Men would do anything for that twinkle.

Most men.

She couldn't play Silver and Crane so well. Some men weren't attracted to women and there was nothing to do about that. Crane, at least, was kind and civil. And her magic still worked a little on men of their kind. Nobody, she believed, was wholly one thing or the other.

Except maybe Masterton. But he was different. His proclivities made her flesh crawl, and she had no interest in twinkling for him, and much less in touching him. The way he looked at the girl sickened her. It was so disturbing that she'd almost had a word with him. However, she couldn't see any benefit to herself in calling him out, in fact Masterton may have reacted angrily, so she'd kept her counsel.

She reached the top of the valley and looked back. Nobody following. Good. Mountains towered above. Below, the main valley faded to haze then rose up to even higher western peaks. It wasn't technically a valley, of course. It was two horsts and a graben, formed by the movements of the earth's plates rather than the fluvial or glacial action that created a valley. Try explaining that to the idiots at the camp! Actually, she had. Crane had listened, but he hadn't understood.

Geologically, the area was fascinating. That's what she tried to tell herself. Fact was, she was a little tired of geology. If she was honest, she regretted the path that had led her here. The Prize would put her back on track. And, if her calculations about the layout of the Fabulous were right, she'd be able to keep all The Prize for herself and she'd became head over heels, buy-a-country-in-South-America rich.

She headed into the next valley northwards, along a bighorn trail that traced a gentler downward gradient across the precipitous incline.

She tried to guess at the others' reasons for needing The Prize. Why were they desperate enough to put up with the heat and the horror? How could the girl Eleanor possibly need The Prize? Crane's motives, too, were impossible to grasp. He seemed more relaxed than anyone who needed The Prize had any right to be.

And Loretta? How had she ended up here? Dumb luck probably. Her sort didn't have the capacity to plan more than a day ahead, so how could they deal with riches? Giving Loretta that sort of wealth would only confuse her and make her the target of thieves. Yes, Frida consoled herself. If Loretta got a share of The Prize, she'd be killed the first evening in town. She was doing the woman a favour by taking the whole lot for herself.

She was pretty sure Zack Monk's and Halicore Silver's motives were simple greed.

Masterton's reason she knew. And by all the saints, it was a dark one.

She'd found out Masterton's secret by a stroke of luck. She'd been in Pandora's Saloon in town, drinking and thinking, failing and failing to come up with a way out of her predicament. A hoary, horny old Forty-Niner had taken the seat next to her - as if he'd had a hope. Men were so stupid.

She ignored his initial leerings

"Too good to talk to me?" he burped.

"Of course not, sir," she replied. "I have a lot on my mind, that's all." It never hurt to be polite. Some of these filthy old miners were stinking rich and keen to prove it to women like her.

"I bet I could tell you something you'd be interested in." His breath was a mix of Valley Tan whiskey and diseased gum. "It's about that man over there."

He gestured to two men in a corner – Silver and Masterton. Back then in the saloon, she'd never seen them before. Now she knew them as well as her own brothers. Funny things, she mused, time and knowledge.

"Which one?" she asked, intrigued despite herself.

"The paleface. His name's Masterton." The Forty-Niner leaned in, far too close. "Masterton's got a debt to pay, or his own brother-in-law'll kill him."

"What's the debt?"

"Buy me a whiskey and I'll tell you."

She wanted to hear the tale, but she wasn't in the habit of buying drinks for men. She wasn't in the habit of buying drinks for herself, for that matter. She unleashed the twinkle. Half a minute later, the Forty-Niner bought whiskey for himself and champagne for her, then began Masterton's story.

"I was in the Tenderloin, a-squeezing and a-pushin and-"

"Spare me the details," she interrupted.

He smiled lasciviously and continued. "All right. I was wiping up when I heard shouting outside. I peeked through a crack in the wall and saw it all."

He downed his whiskey.

"Saw what?" She asked.

"Give me a kiss and I'll tell you." He lurched forward and grasped her thigh.

She seized him by the balls with one hand and grabbed his pistol wrist with the other. He struggled but she was a good bit younger, and she was a geologist. Years of hammering rock had given her hands strong as a prize fighter's. She wasn't proud of her mighty grip. Her mother would have been horrified. But it was useful.

"You'll tell me and then we'll see what happens." She twinkled again and relaxed her grip so that her fingers were squeezing his balls rather than crushing them.

She pulled her hand away as he began to harden, but kept that smile playing through her horror. She'd learnt to decouple her facial expressions from her true emotions around the same time she'd learnt to walk.

The old miner blinked, smiled, then continued. "I saw Masterton there lying on the dirt. The other feller was none too happy. Turns out our friend Masterton had been far too friendly with his sister's daughter. His own niece! His attacker, it soon transpired, was his brother-in-law, father of the kid. "She's eight, you sick bastard!" he kept shouting, "I'll kill you!" I thought he would kill him for sure. People don't like it when you mess with their kids."

"Indeed."

"So, the brother-in-law took out his gun and aimed it at the sick bastard's face. But Masterton shouted, "I can make you rich! Let me live and you'll never need to work again!" The brother-in-law roughed him quite a bit more, but eventually, after much worming and toadying, Masterton persuaded him to listen."

The old Forty-Niner paused, suddenly reluctant to continue.

"Listen to what?" Frida asked, hand on his knee, turning her head so the candlelight would enhance the twinkle, and he'd get a waft of her shampooed hair.

"Told him about a mine destroyed by a flash flood. Fifty miners dead."

"I heard about that." He was talking about the Fabulous, but he didn't know the mine's name. She knew the story better than he did. She prepared to be annoyed that he had wasted her time.

The miner leant in, breath reeking. "But did you hear what they found?"

"No," she had to admit.

"Just before the flood struck, they uncovered the mother-lode to end all mother-lodes. A seam of pure gold, thicker than your lovely waist, and who knew how long. That's why all the miners were down there, despite the storm. The boss knew that a flash flood was coming. He was worried the lode would be lost in the flood. He reckoned by sending them all down, they could get it out before it hit. He was wrong."

"So, the gold's still there?" Frida was interested, despite herself. There were countless stories in the West of huge finds that fate had prevented finders from exploiting. All of them were lies; fables fabricated by campfires and embellished in saloons. But there was something about this story. She'd heard about the disaster and wondered why so many men had still been down the mine.

"That's right!" the Forty-Niner nodded, ordering another drink for each of them. "And that there Masterton's going to go to find it and pay off his brother-in-law. Man he's talking to goes by the name of Silver. He knows where the mine is. Talk is he was there when it flooded."

Frida stood.

"You going to talk to them?" the Forty-Niner asked.

"I am."

"I want to come, too!"

She looked at him. He'd clearly been in the West a long while, so, despite his appearance, he must know how to handle himself. He might be useful, especially if she was dealing with a fortune, a man mixed up in the death of fifty miners, and a pervert.

"Alright. I'll get you involved as well, but stay here while I do it. What's your name?"

"I'm Denny."

She walked over to their table, twinkle at the ready.

And so here she was, weeks later, picking her way down a tricky slope in the insufferable heat like a common working man. She deserved better! She was beautiful, goddarnit! She should have been rich, instead of working shoulder to shoulder with the likes of Denny and Masterton.

Most sickening of all, the only other woman in camp was Loretta. How low had Frida sunk when someone like that was her company? Well, not company as such. Loretta was just the help, but the men let her eat the same food at the same table. It simply wasn't on. The sooner Frida was back east the better. She never wanted to share a table with one of those people again as long as she lived.

A rattlesnake rattled on the trail ahead of her. She'd almost stepped on it, deep in her musings. It raised its rattling tail and waved its head from side to side.

She backed away across the slope, off the path. The snake stayed put.

She walked on.

The worst of it all was that her mother had been right. Frida was beautiful and she was a geologist. She should have stayed just beautiful. She shouldn't have gone to university. If she'd used her twinkle, and not her brilliant brain, she'd be sunning herself on a rich man's yacht like Patricia Pittsburgh or Chloe-Goddarn-Vandelay.

She reached the valley floor and turned almost back on herself to walk west, upstream, into the mass of the mountain.

She followed the dry bed until she found what she was looking for

- a gap in the valley's southern flank. She squeezed through the crack, climbed a couple of boulders, and, as she'd suspected it would, found that the crack widened into a slot canyon. The slot opened into a clearing with high rock walls all around. Cut into the west wall was an adit. She smiled. She was right! This passage led from the neighbouring valley into the same body of rock as the Fabulous. By her reckoning, this passage would not have been blocked by the flood. There was a good chance it led directly to The Prize.

She swung the bag off her back and sat. She pulled out five candles and laid them on the sandy ground. Now where were those locofoco matches? She was sure she'd put them -

WHACK!

She fell face first to sprawl on the sand. Her head felt like it was expanding and contracting and, all the while, whirling. She turned over, blinking and rubbing sand off her lips.

"You!"

Her attacker was holding a stick with claws on the end.

"What are you going to-"

The claw lashed out. Pain lanced through her head and there was blood in her eyes. She flailed an arm. She felt the claw bury in her neck and rip free, pulling a good deal of her neck with it.

She tried to scream but only gurgled.

Her arm flopped. She couldn't lift it again. She felt the claw strike her chest and tear flesh. It was strangely painless.

She was going to die, she realised. She was being murdered!

She managed to blink the blood out of one eye. Her attacker was squatting, watching her.

Her final thought was that she really, really should never have become a geologist.

ACT ONE, CHAPTER SIX

A Mormon Caravan

Mrs Skillet took me aside for a word about the gore in last night's instalment. I told her to go suck an egg. Not really.

"It's not me," she said, wearing her concerned-for-others face. "I don't mind blood and guts myself, and I do love your story, but I wonder if the gore is necessary? It might upset some of the others. There is no gore in Agatha Christie's novels and yet those are very popular."

Mrs Skillet is concerned for other people around a hundred percent of the time. She loves nothing more than finding out people's troubles or ailments and being concerned about them. I enjoy telling her how marvellous my life is, then watching her frustration. "Are you sure there's nothing wrong?" she will ask, eyes wide. "You were limping earlier." "No, I'm all tickety boo," I'll always say, and she'll sign and sail off like a modern-day Florence Nightingale to delight in someone else's problems.

So, I reassured her that I would take heed of her wise words and cut the gore. I will of course do precisely the opposite. I'm trying to paint a picture. People got killed, injured and sick the whole time in the West, and it was rarely pretty.

The slumgullion had been an error. Every lurch of the coach churned the rancid contents of James Willow's stomach around and around, then upwards in another bid for freedom. Swallows and gulps and tightening the throat had kept it down thus far. The Englishman couldn't see himself winning that battle for much longer.

Thank heavens, the Clemens brothers were almost as subdued as he was. He hadn't seen them in the town but perhaps, he mused, they'd found a different saloon. He wasn't going to ask them. He didn't want to listen, and he was fairly sure that, if he tried to talk, he would regurgitate whatever it was he'd eaten the night before.

Had he eaten?

From what he remembered, he'd enjoyed the evening. He'd been heading out after listening to the Mexican's information, intending on an early night, when a group of four men at a corner table had beckoned him over.

"You look interesting, partner," one of them had said, "let's hear your story." And so, he'd sat and chatted to the affable and intelligent chaps. Round after round of slumgullion had come to the table. Try as he might, he could not remember how the evening had ended.

He'd woken in the coach, with no idea how he'd got there. Going by the evidence, he'd been dragged there by badgers who'd stolen most of his money, beaten him about the head, and defecated in his mouth.

They hadn't been going long when the coach slowed. At crawling speed, with hollers and "yahs!" from their driver, they passed a desperate group. Dozens of men, women, and children tramped along, dusty and hatless, not so much driving as accompanying a clutch of dusty cattle and a solitary horse. A good dozen or so of them were pushing rickety handcarts with obvious effort.

Never had the Englishman seen such a sorry gang. They looked like they'd given up a good way back but somehow carried on.

"Mormons," said Orion Clemens.

"Headed for the paradise of Brigham Young's Salt Lake," added Samuel Clemens.

"Where a man can enjoy as many wives as he desires," the older declared.

"Surely as many wives as any man would desire would be one." replied the younger brother.

"Six mothers-in-law!" Orion chuckled.

James Willow closed his eyes. Thousands of miles away, almost a year since he had last seen her, the thought of his own wife made him feel even sicker. The face he loved and hated flooded his mind and he had to open his eyes again.

"Can Mormon men really marry as many women as they like?" he asked, keen to wrench his mind from his wife.

Outside the carriage, a Mormon child plodded from the track, off between dusty desert bushes, in pursuit of a recalcitrant cow. Neither child nor cow seemed to be in any kind of hurry.

"There is no limit, so far as I understand," asserted Clemens Minor, looking to his brother for assent.

"There are limiting *factors*," explained Orion. "You have to be able to support a new wife, and her father has to agree to the union. So, essentially, you can have as many wives as you can afford – or, perhaps more accurately, as many as it *seems* you can afford."

The bounty hunter imagined dozens of Elizabeths looking down their noses at him and shuddered. "Seems like a lot of hard work."

"I should imagine it is," agreed the older Clemens, "but the more wives you have, the higher your place in Heaven."

The Englishman's jaw fell open. "Really?"

"That's the Mormon way," nodded the younger.

Willow's mouth opened. "But they can't think that God wants that. Can they? How did they get everyone else to agree? Why do the women stand for it?"

"I had the same reaction as you, my friend." said Samuel. "It's clear to any rational thinker, surely, that a man who takes many wives will be all the warmer in the afterlife."

"The whole scheme was concocted by the horny old goat Brigham Young." Orion was gazing out at the struggling Mormons and shaking his head. "He inherited the religion from its founder - fellow called John Smith, after that good and well-loved man was beaten to death by an outraged mob. Young developed the ingenious practice of sleeping with as many young women as he wanted and calling it God's work. His harem numbered twenty-five when we were in Salt Lake City not long ago, each new wife younger than the last."

Willow gibbered. "But … What did the girls' fathers say?" Now that he knew what to look for, the Englishman could see that women outnumbered the men in the ragtag group of refugees by some degree. There were many children, too. None of them looked happy.

"I guess the fathers were consoled by the taking of their own friends' daughters to the wedding bed. I don't think that humans have ever found it hard to persuade themselves that their god or gods approve of their behaviour. No man is happier than he who can construct a morality to suit his immorality."

"A morality to suit your immorality!" Samuel smiled "That could be the slogan of our young nation."

"Indeed," smiled the older. "We have certainly applied the same concept to our treatment of America's noble Aboriginals. The very men who slaughtered the Cheyenne and Arapaho children at Sand Creek sing to the Lord every Sunday with clean consciences."

By the way some of the Mormons were walking, the Englishman wondered whether they would make it through the day. "Do you think they will reach Salt Lake?" he asked.

"I suspect they will. Large groups of people with a determined mind and a singular purpose usually achieve their goals," said Orion.

The carriage passed the Mormons and sped up through the wide desert.

Would James Willow achieve his goal, he wondered? He'd learnt from the man in the 'salon' where his quarry had headed next, but not where she'd gone from there.

Was God on his side as he crossed a continent to bring a fugitive to justice and win the bounty?

His motive was financial, which was never the best moral standpoint, but, surely, he was also on a crusade? The system would collapse if everyone like her ran free.

Or had he constructed a morality to suit his immorality?"

ACT ONE, CHAPTER SEVEN

Chisel Breach

After I read last night's bit, Mr Hillier-Edwards asked me about the slaughter of Cheyenne and Arapaho at Sand Creek.

"Settlers had been settling for a while," I said, "and the Indians had been less and less happy about it. Gold was discovered in Colorado, late 1850s I think. Miners felt compelled to dig, so people flooded in. Colorado was made a territory and given a governor. His first order of business was to raise a militia to protect the miners and other settlers.

"Unfortualtely for the Indians, the militia were not a great bunch of people, led by one of the worst, an ex-minister called Chivington. If he'd had his way, they would have slaughtered all the Indians. When he was asked if it was okay to kill Indian children he pointed out that "nits make lice." The bastard should never have been given a command. However, the Civil War was beginning in the east. If the governor, whose name escapes me, was going to keep his militia, it had to be seen to be busy. It suited him to have it led by a man like Chivington, who was definitely going to use it.

"It was getting towards winter, November I think, and there was a village led by a guy called Black Kettle. He, like many Indians, was pro-settler. He thought there was enough land to share. However, the Indians are an individualist lot, who tend to only listen to leaders when they agree with them. Against Black Kettle's wishes, there had been raids on settlers, a few murders and some thefts. Chivington set out with maybe 700 rowdy men to teach the Indians a lesson.

"They found Black Kettle's village of Southern Cheyenne and Arapaho. The men of fighting age – the warriors – were almost all off hunting. The militia attacked and killed about 150 women and children. The women tried to surrender. At one point a few dozen of them in a hollow send out a six-year-old girl with a white flag. She was shot and all the squaws were killed.

"The details are horrible. Babies and pregnant women were hacked to bits. Corpses were mutilated. With the warriors away, there was no resistance. The cowards attacked without mercy, on and on. The only militia killed were shot by mistake by their own side, because a lot of them were drunk. There seems to have been a focus on cutting out women's private parts and stretching them over hats and saddles. Afterwards, the militia paraded through Denver with their gory trophies and the people cheered."

I looked round the biddies and Mr Hillier-Edwards. They looked about as comfortable as if I'd taken my top off, waggled my boobs and started swearing at them in German. Maybe I'd gone too far, but Mr Hillier-Edwards did ask, and I guess I was a little riled that people – well, Mrs Hopkins – could have opinions about Indians without knowing about events like Sand Creek.

"What happened next?" asked Mr Hiller-Edwards. "The Indians can't have been too happy."

"They had their revenge. The chap who's name Mrs Hopkins thought was silly – Crazy Horse – was a brilliant warrior, and an all-round great man. Some called him the Sioux Jesus. Years before I met him, he- "

"You met him?" scoffed Mrs Terbangun, as if it couldn't possibly be true.

I pictured Crazy Horse - that beautiful, enigmatic, tragic young man. I knew him years after both Sand Creek and the happenings in the Fabulous Mine.

"It's getting late," Julian interrupted my silent reminiscing. "Please can we get back to the creative writing?"

"Would you like me to read my next bit, or tell you how Crazy Horse avenged Sand Creek?" I asked the oldsters, enjoying Julian's impotent bristling at being ignored.

"Perhaps we could have Crazy Horse another time?" asked Mr Hillier-Edwards. "I'm very keen to hear what happens next in the mine."

The others murmured agreement.

"Sure thing!" I said, and began to read.

They called Denny a Forty-Niner. He called himself a Forty-Niner. Being a Forty-Niner was an honour. It was a club like the New York clubs he'd been a member of, during what he thought of as his previous life, but even more exclusive because if you'd got there later than 1849, you couldn't join. People pretended, but you could always tell. You might get away with it if you'd come in 1850, but that was about it.

Like his fellow New York clubbers, Forty-Niners looked down on outsiders. If someone didn't know a placer digging from a pocket digging, a stamp mill from a ball mill, or a doré bar from a soap bar, they were mocked and they were shunned.

But what did it really mean to be a Forty-Niner? He had nothing in common with the rest of them. They had nothing in common with each other, apart from that they were all gullible idiots.

He'd believed. They'd all believed. Go west, cross the Rockies, and you will trip over gold lying about in piles like dragon's treasure.

So, he'd left his work that had promised so much. He'd thought he'd be back within the year, he really did.

He'd paid for the coach. How he and his fellow coach jockeys had laughed as they'd sped past the poorer men tramping west. How they'd scowled when they'd crossed the Mississippi and found no coach service, no road even, only the deep-worn trail of thousands of idiots tramping west to dig up a fortune.

A few found their fortunes. There were stories, and more stories, spreading like diseases back along the column of westward hopefuls.

Denny had found his fortune a couple of times, then lost it again. For a while he made a fair bit buying and selling claims. Few people made money actually digging stuff out of the ground. The real fortunes were made by exploiting other fortune hunters. But, because everyone was trying to make a fortune from everybody else, and because there were genuine supply issues, everything was so very expensive. If a man drank well, ate well, and whored well, his fortune soon went down the well.

So, it had been a boon overhearing Masterton's fight, then meeting Happy Days Frida who could use his knowledge and her feminine wiles to bring them aboard this mixed-up crew of miners.

They were searching some of the lower shafts today, cleaning the flood's mud from the walls, hoping at any moment to find that glint of gold. The passage was a strange one here, taking advantage of a natural fissure. Its base was packed mud and stone like a normal mine tunnel, but it had no ceiling, just tapering walls that disappeared up into the black.

He was furthest along the shaft. A little way back was Crane, hard at work clearing mud, like Denny. Then it was Happy Days Frida, pretending to work. She thought this labour beneath her. She thought Denny beneath her. Not literally. It would be a very cold day in Hell before Happy Days Frida was jumping about on top of him, no matter the looks she flashed at him, and those fingers that trailed across his forearm when she reached for the salt.

For a while he'd been fooled. He'd believed her "you are going to have me" eyes. He'd wanted to be fooled. But then he'd remembered what he was and realised her game.

So far as the casual observer could tell, he was a grizzled loser who'd tried and failed and had his boyish good looks destroyed by sun and toil along the way. They knew nothing of the money he'd made in Virginia City and lost in San Francisco, nor the monster strike he'd found with a partner, nor the partner who had run off with the lot.

Happy Days Frida wanted drinks and information she could use. That was all. She couldn't care less that he was a Forty-Niner. He could try to look down on her for not being a Forty-Niner, but he'd fail because she was young, she was beautiful, and she knew it.

So, she was a user. But that was fine. So was he. And there was little greater pleasure than using a user, so he'd been tickled when she'd been true to her word and persuaded Silver and Masterton to take him along too to find the fortune in the Fabulous.

Leaning in to get more pressure on his trowel, he looked down the passage, into the dark, and noticed something sticking out of the wall.

He looked back to Crane. The good, diligent man was focussed on his work.

Denny picked up his candle and walked slowly towards the mystery shape.

There was a chisel protruding from the rock at shoulder height. It was left over from the days when they'd been extracting quartz ore from the mine. You'd make a hole with a chisel, ram in blasting powder and a fuse, light the fuse, and run. You were meant to walk, in case you tripped and got caught in the explosion, but everybody ran.

He rubbed the wall next to the chisel, carefully. A classic mining mistake - or possibly just a good campfire story - was the unfortunate who'd used an iron chisel instead of a wooden rod to tamp the blasting powder. They'd been talking about it just a few nights before. Whack iron into blasting powder and they'd be scraping bits of you off the shaft wall for weeks.

It was unlikely that some fool had stuck this chisel into a hole full of explosives, but it didn't hurt to be careful.

More likely, or at least just as likely, someone has stuck the chisel in the wall here as a marker for the mother lode.

The mud came away easily. He held up a candle. The small patch he'd cleared shone gold.

He'd found it.

He wouldn't mess it up this time. He'd take his share in dollars and book every seat in an eastward coach, so he could stretch out and sleep all the way to New York City. Sure, he was a broken old man now, not the beautiful boy who'd set out from Manhattan all those years before, but that didn't matter. Money was all in that great city, and he'd have more than just about anybody. He'd buy a big house, get a pretty, young wife and re-join all the clubs. They wouldn't mind that he was bald and wrinkled as a Mojave tortoise. As long as he splashed around a vulgar amount of dollars they'd listen to his stories and slap his back.

Hands shaking, he scraped away the mud.

He hadn't found it.

He'd found a lump of gold the size of a small man's thumb stuck into the rock. He griped it with his fingertips and pulled, but it held firm.

It was an odd one. Owners of mine claims sometimes peppered ore by firing a shotgun cartridge full of gold into a lump of quartz. You could sell a claim for an awful lot if you could fool someone with that trick, as

Denny knew because he'd done it more than once. With mixed levels of success, it had to be said. He still had a sore shoulder from the whupping he'd been handed the last time he'd tried the ruse. Fools were getting wiser out West.

This lump was like a peppering - it didn't sit naturally in the rock - but it was just one lump of refined gold, and underground, where it wouldn't help anyone sell anything. Most odd. By the position of the chisel, somebody had been interrupted in the process of prizing it out.

He grabbed the chisel and pulled it. No good, it was stuck firm and deep. He looked back along the shaft. Frida was sitting against the shaft wall. It looked like she was asleep. Crane was still busy cleaning. He'd have a hammer - he was the prepared type - but Denny didn't want to share his find. He looked down. There was a hammer at his feet! Had the flood struck right when someone was trying to dig out the nugget, removing the man but leaving the hammer and chisel? Maybe not, but he needed a hammer and here was a hammer, so it looked like fate was on his side for once!

And maybe he was wrong. Maybe this wasn't a nugget. Maybe it was a protrusion of the mother lode! They did say it was pure gold …

He picked up the hammer, gripped the chisel in one hand and whacked it.

There was a blinding light and great slam as if he'd been punched by a giant. He felt himself sliding down the rock wall, slumping into a sitting position. There was something very wrong with his head. He tried to lift a hand, but he couldn't.

Crane was first to him. Denny was sitting on the tunnel floor. One eye was wide and blinking with surprise, the other had a chisel through it, handle first. By the amount of point showing, the chisel had gone through his head and out the other side.

Denny was not going to get up and dust himself down.

Crane spotted the gold nugget on the ground next to the dying man. He looked back up the corridor. Happy Days Frida was standing there, mouth open and face ashen even in the warm light of her candle.

"Is he okay?" she managed.

"He's a good long way from okay."

Denny's remaining eye stopped blinking. Crane flicked his cheek. He felt very dead already. "Can you go and get a couple of the others? I'll need some help with his body."

"His body?"

"Hurry along now. I don't want to spend too long here with a dead man."

She turned and was gone. Seemed she wasn't too keen to spend too much time down there with a dead man either.

Crane leant forward, picked up the nugget, looked up the shaft again to check she was gone, then slid the lump of gold into his pocket.

When the Bough Breaks

Mrs Skillet was very thin-lipped at the end. She's not annoyed about the gore. She's annoyed that I ignored her diktat to remove it. In my experience, moral guardians always know for certain that they are right, so, boy does it irk them to be ignored. But, boy do I enjoy ignoring them.

Mrs Terbangun caught me on the way to bed and said that she'd loved the bloody bits. "Makes the whole thing more thrilling!" she said. Shows what Mrs Skillet knows.

Julian has asked me for the manuscript so far so he can start "sprucing it up." Making it more boring and taking out all the bits about Indians, I shouldn't wonder. He'll never get his soft hands on it.

My Hillier-Edwards wanted to hear about Crazy Horse's revenge for Sand Creek, but he was shouted down by the others, who wanted me to get on with the story. So that's what we did.

Breakfast was bread with bacon in sauce. Masterton, Silver, and Monk were lucky enough to get the special added ingredient of a few velvet ants. So I hoped. I got the tin plates a bit mixed, so it was possible that Crane got one of the special dishes. Never mind, I thought, velvet ants couldn't be poisonous. Or could they?

We sat around the big table, pulled out from under the veranda of the big dorm. It would be a while before the sun made it over the mountain top to the east, so we could be out in the morning breeze blowing up canyon.

The men ate in silence. I watched them. I was a bit worried. Velvet ants weren't really ants; they were misnamed wasps with nasty stings. I'd decided the stings wouldn't work if they were cooked, but now I was questioning myself.

"Ahh!" Silver cried, and I felt myself reddening. He hooked a finger into his mouth and pulled out a shard of bacon bone.

"You're meant to take the bones out," he growled at Loretta.

"Sowbelly's got bones. A few are going to get through. They won't kill you."

Everyone looked at each other, forks still, food sitting unchewed in every mouth. Sweat shone dully from every face even though the real heat was a way away.

Nobody was saying it, but we were all thinking it.

Bacon bones might not kill you, but was one of them going to?

Denny, Indian Moses, Happy Days Frida. All accidents, all in the last couple of weeks. Were they really accidents? That was the question on everyone's mind at the Fabulous yet again that hot day.

"Get me another bowl, no bones." Silver pushed his plate across the table to Loretta.

She looked back at him, somehow managing to chill the warm air.

"What you waiting for, Loretta?" said Monk, smiling like a crazed wolf. "Your kind like to fetch and carry, don't they?"

"I'll get it!" I said, reaching over to grab the plate.

Masterton squeezed my hip as I rose. "There's a good girl." If a snake could talk it would have sounded just like him. Or maybe that's mean to snakes.

I pulled free and glared at him. He smiled back. I wanted to get a gun and shoot him, but I had no grounds. He'd given me a friendly pat, that was all.

"We going to try Gila Canyon again today?" Crane was saying when I returned to the table with Silver's refilled bowl.

Since they'd got back the evening before, Crane hadn't mentioned being left alone in the dark by those varmints. How could he just take it like that? I'd have found the others one by one, tripped them over, stuck a six-shooter up their nose and told them to never try no goddarn low trick like that ever again if they knew what was good for them. How he could just sit there and smile and eat bread and bacon - and possibly velvet ant - like a goddarn saint …

"What's got you?" Loretta's smoky voice always cheered me.

"Oh, nothing, just listening to the silly men."

Loretta and I cleared breakfast as the men headed off to their various cabins. There was plenty of space in a mine built for fifty and manned by six, so everyone had their own building to sleep in.

I filled a tin basin and sat on an upturned candle box to scrub at the plates and pans with yellow soap. Now I was feeling bad about killing the velvet ants. What harm had they done? I resolved to put only dead animals in the men's food from now on. Or - I knew where there was a gathering of jackass rabbit crap. That might have to do. I'd be more careful not to give any to Crane.

As I cleaned up breakfast, Loretta went around the cabins collecting clothes for washing, moving slowly in the heat. So, it must be Saturday, I thought. I finished up washing, emptied the bowl, then rinsed it because we'd need it for the clothes.

I spat. I did not like laundry.

A hundred or so paces up the mountain, next to the wooden scaffold that housed the top of the aerial tramway, was a tall, metal tank, bigger than a house, cylindrical like a giant tin of beans. Wire-wrapped wooden pipes led away from it, some down shafts, several through the camp to shafts and adits lower down the mountain, and one right to where we washed the clothes.

I did not like that tank. Sure, we were never going to run out of water and that was good, I supposed, but having enough water to do laundry meant we had to do laundry.

I stood for a moment - there was no rush, you couldn't rush in that heat - and looked out over the Fabulous Canyon, across Death Valley, to the clouds fringing the snow-topped western mountains. They were silky and delicate, still tinged pink with morning light. Those beautiful clouds would be blasted away pretty soon by the cold-hearted, super-hot sun that didn't care nothing for nobody, just blasted and blasted and blasted with its rays, burning it all up.

The aerial tramway's hefty wooden pylons were spaced down the canyon, wire and carriages dangling between. The road down to the valley was smashed. There'd be no more waggons coming up to the mine, but you would still walk it. There was a path around the steepest dry fall, and a baby could have scaled the other falls.

Would my ma come walking up that path today, I wondered? Loretta was nice and Crane looked out for me, but I missed my ma something rotten. I understood why I'd been sent to the mine with Silver. Ma could make more money dancing without me around and save money not having to feed and lodge me. When I got my share of The Prize, we wouldn't worry about paying for things ever again. Ma could stop dancing. I could study and become a veterinarian and get paid lots of money and look after Ma as well as people's dogs and horses. I'd look after wild animals that got hurt too.

As I put the final dish on the rack, an almighty crash rang out not far up canyon.

A cloud of dust rose near the top of the tramway, then cleared quickly in the morning breeze. I rushed on up, quick as I could.

Loretta was already there, hands on hips, looking at an elevator housing with a broken crossbeam and no wire, no lifting wheel, and no elevator. The elevator and all its workings must have fallen down the shaft into the mountain.

I looked at Loretta and Loretta looked back, blue eyes wide. She was thinking the same thing as me. *Who had been in the elevator?* The men were headed for Gila Canyon. The elevator was one way to get there - one lazy man's way. You could go down into the mountain, then walk along underground. It took longer but would save you a hot hike down the canyon.

Only one man was lazy enough to do that. Silver. He'd done it before. *Please let it be Sliver!* I asked God, trying to stifle a smile. I corrected the prayer: *I didn't mean to ask you to kill anyone, God, I know you wouldn't do that, and I wouldn't ever ask you to. What I meant was, if someone's dead and there's nothing that can be done about it, because in your wisdom you've done it, and it's not ours to question why, please let it be Silver. Not Crane. It could also be Masterton or Monk. Maybe Masterton instead of Silver. But not Crane.*

I thought about Masterton's greasy gaze never sliding over me again, and never being grabbed by him again, and I smiled.

"Eleanor!" I opened my eyes. Loretta was looking at me from the other side of the shaft. Her expression was the same as when she saw lizards, snakes, spiders, and all the other critters she wasn't used to.

I tried to rearrange my smile into more of an "oh no, someone's just died" look.

Loretta shook her head at me, and I felt hot. How long was it, I mused, before you were allowed to smile after someone died? It depended on the person, I supposed. If it was Silver or Masterton or Monk ... well, then it probably wouldn't be that long. Not for me, anyway, and I doubted if Loretta would mind too much. But if it was Crane ...

It couldn't be Crane, could it? Maybe it was all four of them? Maybe lazy Silver had persuaded them to all go the easy way and the elevator had fallen because the load was too much?

Scuffing footsteps sounded out from the camp. Crane came jogging around the corner of the big dorm house. I near shouted with joy.

"What happened?" he yelled when he spied us. "Are you alright?"

"It's the elevator!" I hollered back, "It fell! I think maybe Silver is dead?"

Crane ran up and stood, breathing hard.

"What do you mean, Silver's dead?"

"The elevator fell - look, the crossbeam's broke - and I guessed that maybe ..."

Crane raised an eyebrow at me. I was sounding a bit too excited about Silver being dead.

"I mean I hope there wasn't anybody in it," I continued in a lower voice, "but I guessed if there was someone it would be Silver, him being so, well, like him I guess, but maybe-"

"It wasn't Silver. He's in Gila Canyon."

"So it's Masterton!" I gasped, then remembered and continued in my sombre voice, "I mean, oh no, it must be Masterton or Monk all crushed and broken down there, dead or breathing their last as we speak with nothing we can do for them except mourn and make plans for their-"

"It's nobody," Crane shook his head. "The other three are all over in Gila Canyon. We were almost there when we heard the crash. We thought something had happened to you two."

"Yet only you came?" said Loretta.

Crane walked over to the shaft, peered over the edge, then looked at the beam and nodded.

"It's dangerous out here," he said. "You ladies should watch yourselves. Try to stay together."

"There *is* a killer!" I just knew there was.

"No, Eleanor, there isn't," said Crane, "apart from the land itself and what we done to it by digging all these holes. Watch yourself, is all. And do not go into the mine."

"You don't have to tell me that!" said Loretta.

ACT ONE, CHAPTER NINE

A whupping

"What was the point of that chapter?" asked Mrs Hopkins afterwards. "Nothing happened and we didn't learn anything new about anybody."

"What's the point of you? You're a mean-faced waste of space and air who could only help the world by being killed and made into soap," I nearly answered. Funny how tetchy I've become about my writing. I can't remember being tetchy before. I guess maybe writing makes you vulnerable. Never thought of myself as vulnerable neither.

"Well, I liked it!" said Mr Hillier-Edwards. "I loved it, in fact! The part about when you're allowed to smile after someone's died really stuck a chord. It was like that in the war. We joked the whole time of course - one must when the alternative would be to break down weeping - but there were those awkward times after a chap was killed when one didn't know if a joke was appropriate. And it's the same here in this house we all share. Now remind me, who died last Thursday?"

"It was Lady Beveridge," Mrs Skillet shook her head. "She'd had a terrible time of it."

"Yes, yes, poor woman. But I thought of something very funny to say about our breakfast eggs, and I didn't because we'd just heard she'd died."

"Perhaps you can crack the egg joke at breakfast tomorrow?"

"Oh, I can't remember it! I can't remember my own name most mornings. Now you say that though, I think it was probably something to do with cracking."

I do like him. I think he likes me too. If we were both a few decades younger, I might have encouraged him to get sweet on me.

"Can we get back to how pointless that last chapter was?" asked the delightful Mrs Hopkins.

"It wasn't pointless," said Julian, a surprise white knight. "It told us more about some of the characters, Eleanor in particular, and it's helped us see where the mine is in relation to that dramatic valley, as well as how dangerous the environment is. It highlighted the dichotomy that every character is at risk, and every character is a suspect. Excellent writing."

Julian gave a little clap of congratulations. I think he wanted me to thank him, but I just nodded as if that was what I'd planned all along. It wasn't. I just sit and write. Do people plan these things? Secretly, I think Mrs Hopkins may have had a point, and that Julian is trying to suck up to me so I'll let him edit.

However, as I said, I'm tetchy about criticism, so I'm tempted to make nothing happen in this next chapter too. However, that would be tricky given what's coming next, and I'll be deader than a can of corned beef before I let Mrs Hopkins influence what I write.

Not long after they'd left the Mormons, the coach carrying James Willow, Samuel Clemens and Orion Clemens swept smoothly down a long hill, slowed, then trundled along the main street of another town. The three young men peered from the windows.

On the face of it, the town was the same as the last. Paint peeled off flat-faced clap-board stores, smiths, and saloons. The air was heavy with the stench of unwashed humans and horses, and both species' faeces. Men stood in conspiratorial clusters, clad in the uniform brown that matched their tanned faces.

"It's different," said Samuel, for once seemingly awed into not trying to be clever or funny.

Willow knew what he meant. There was something heavy in the atmosphere. Mean-faced men eyed the carriage like wolves sizing up an injured bison calf. There was an air of menace so thick that it hampered his breathing; although that could, he admitted to himself, have been the stink.

"I wager every man on this street has a price on his head," said Orion, leaning back from the window as if to hide.

"Indeed," replied Samuel, "and I'm fairly sure I've seen a good number of these horses looking out from wanted posters, too."

Willow chuckled, relieved that Samuel had recovered his wit. The joke made it all a lot less frightening.

"You're right," smiled Orion. "There's the desperado Snorty McHoof. They say she's killed a dozen stallions with her bare hooves."

"That horse," said Willow, pointing to a black and white beast attached to a hitching rail, "is, ironically, a cat burglar."

The brothers laughed. Willow was fairly sure they were faking, but it was convincing fakery, and he was grateful that they had encouraged his foray into wittiness.

After that though, they were quiet for a little too long and Willow began to wonder if he'd used the word 'ironically' correctly. Was it ironic that a horse was a cat burglar? He honestly didn't know. What was irony, really? He was damned if he knew. He'd been pretty sure that nobody else did – irony was surely like gravity, nobody actually knew how it worked - but these brothers were jolly clever. In the silence you could almost feel them telepathically communicating the shared knowledge that the Englishman had proved his ignorance again.

A fresh flush of sweat prickled Willow's brow.

"Thank the lord we're not stopping here," said Samuel after what seemed like an age, but was really only moments.

But they did stop there. The coach pulled over outside the town. The driver explained that the thoroughbrace had broken, or was about to break, or had some other problem. Willow was no expert on coach construction and found the driver's extraordinary accent difficult to penetrate.

"The thoroughbrace is the contraption of belts and springs on which the coach balances in order to smooth the ride. I think," opined Orion Clemens, when the driver had left them.

"With the utmost respect," argued Samuel, "I believe it's a more specific part of the workings. I believe the thoroughbrace to be the metal spine which *holds* those belts and springs, much as a beast's spine is the supporting beam, as it were, for the superstructure of ribs."

"I'm going into town," announced Willow.

The brothers turned to him, eyebrows raised in concern and alarm.

"This town is no place for the likes of us." Orion shook his head. "Come, English friend, you're not in the Cotswolds now. Let's leave this world to Snorty McHoof and the other desperados. We can stay in the coach. We'll turn a few hands of cards whilst there's light. Who knows, they may have the mainbrace mended before long."

"Thoroughbrace," said Samuel.

"What did I say?"

"Mainbrace."

"Oh. What's that?"

"Part of a ship, I believe."

"I see. Thoroughbrace, then. The point remains. This town is a den of wolves. It's fine and peaceful while it's all wolves, with perhaps the odd yap or snap here and there. However, should a rabbit walk into that wolf den, there would be a brief but bloody explosion and the rabbit would cease to be. You, Mr Willow, are, I'm afraid to say, a rabbit."

Willow opened his mouth to reply. He'd been called names in England many a time. His shame and misery, never far from the surface, threatened to overwhelm him again. No. He fought against it. He wasn't going to put up with insults in his new life. He's been called a rabbit, and he was damned if he was going to stand for it. However, he couldn't muster up an effective response. Should he attack the man or insult him back? Call him a squirrel, perhaps? No, squirrels were better than rabbits. Or were they?

His slumgullion hangover still had his brain wrapped in wet wool, which did not help.

"Orion means no slight," Samuel rescued Willow from his internal struggles. "We two, too, are rabbits, and glad for it. In this animal metaphor, the wolves are gun-slinging murderers and the rabbits are decent folk. So, Orion was saying that you are a decent chap, and we decent chaps would be fodder for the very un-decent denizens of this borough. You may avoid appearing on their menu by remaining here with us."

Willow shook his head. He had three reasons to brave the town. First, he was keen to find information on his quarry. Second, he was a tourist,

He enjoyed seeing new things. Thirdly, he had to admit to himself, he didn't mind too much the notion of being killed. Nobody would mourn him, and he would be free from his endlessly gnawing memories.

"I'll see you shortly." He declared.

The Clemenses looked at him sadly.

"Try not to talk to anybody," advised Orion as he walked away.

"Or look at them!" called Samuel.

Horses were bucking and snorting, and men whooping and yeehawing like animals, or - let's be straight here, thought Willow - like Americans. A gunshot rang out not very far along the street. Willow started and ducked. Nobody else seemed to notice, not even the horses.

It was impossible to believe, mused Willow, that a town like this and peaceful, genteel English towns could be made by the same god and populated by the same species.

What was the whooping all about? You would not catch Englishmen whooping. Were Americans particularly childish? Were they faking, trying to prove how happy they were to the world and to themselves? Or was it a genuine, free and fresh expression of excitement, severed from the stiff social structures of the Old World? Willow had resolved on each of those explanations in turn and was now fairly certain that the shouting and yeehawing and general gleeful loudness was unaffected. Perhaps it was childlike, but it wasn't childish. These men hadn't had their exuberance stifled by an education obsessed with forcing children not to behave like children. Willow rather liked it, and wished that he could join, but it simply wasn't in him. He could have faked it, but he was sure that everybody would be able to tell.

He strode up to the first saloon, "The One-Legged Crab," according to its sign, then jumped back as a chap flew out of a mercifully glass-free window. The man landed with a whump, rolled across the veranda, fell between two hitched and uninterested horses, and lay in the street. After a heartbeat's rest, he stood, dusted himself down, and, to the Englishman's slack-jawed amazement, headed back into The One-Legged Crab, tipping his hat as he passed.

Willow gibbered.

There was don't-care-if-I-die bravery and there was stupidity.

Perhaps he should try the next saloon.

The fear that he'd felt as they'd arrived in the town returned. He reasoned that these people wouldn't even notice an impecunious traveller, and that he had no qualms about dying, but fear had no interest at all in what reason had to say. Fear was a sodden mass in his stomach, a weakening poison in his limbs and a debilitating despair in his mind.

Men stared at him. Two young Chinese ladies came sashaying along, twirling gay parasols. They stopped their giggling when they saw him, batted their eyelids, then smiled and sashayed away smoothly, as if they ran on rails.

The fear dissipated a little.

Willow knew the women were Chinese by the epicanthic folds covering the inner corners of their eyes. He'd seen pictures, but never a real Chinese person. He'd heard that Chinese men had crossed the Pacific to find work on the Californian railroad, where they renowned for being more skilled, harder working and cheaper than their western counterparts. Chinese women were shipped from the Orient, slaves from another direction, to serve the men of the West. They were known as sporting women.

Sporting women in England were ladies who partook keenly in outdoor leisure pursuits. They were typically ruddy-faced, horse-haunched, massive-bosomed ladies, who'd take a whip to a lazy stable lad and laugh while they did it. These Chinese sporting women were different. Their skin was pale and flawless, with a slight chalkiness, like the petals of a white rose. They looked hale and carefree, hardly Willow's idea of indentured labour. Their silk dresses swished on the first womanly figures he'd seen for a long time. He wondered what it would be like to talk to one. He wondered what it would be like to- No. No, he was better than that.

He tipped his hat and walked on, resisting the urge to turn and see what the women looked like from the rear.

He passed smiths, goods stores and a stinking tannery. Horrific, heart-stopping screams rang out from one building. Willow shuddered and stood with a severe case of the willies. He was about to run back to the carriage, when he spotted the sign saying "Doctor" that hung across the top of the store front.

The town's second saloon was freshly painted, standing out from the other buildings like a princess amongst paupers. No, not a princess, more like a queen past the first flush of youth but served by the finest dressmakers and make-up ladies in the land.

"*Ossian Slade's Public House*" was written in elegant gold letters above heavy, closed doors. It was the first bar in the West that Willow had seen with proper doors, rather than a couple of planks on hinges. And what doors! They could have graced a stately home. Either side the windows were closed, the shutters painted with scenes of Italian countryside that wouldn't have looked out of place on that stately home's walls.

What, wondered the Englishman, *lay inside this opulent exterior?*

He walked up onto the veranda and reached for the door handle.

"Ahem."

He turned.

A man was sitting halfway along the veranda, his posture so relaxed that it looked like he'd been poured into the rocking chair. His face was stubbled, a cheroot hung from his lips, and his large, brown hands cradled a polished rifle. His short-brimmed hat was tipped back to reveal a wide, intelligent brow above eye slits so narrow that Willow wasn't sure if he actually had eyes.

"Can I go in?" Willow asked, not feeling much like a bounty hunter.

"You're English?" the man's voice sounded like it was being filtered through the coarser type of desert sand.

"Uh, yes. I am English." He hoped that was a good thing. "I grew up near Banbury," he added before he could stop himself. "In a village called Fenny Compton."

"Thanks for the life story. Head on in, partner."

Willow wasn't sure if the frightening man was a guard or just sitting there. He opened his mouth to ask, but another glance at the well-weathered gunman convinced him otherwise. Whether he was an official guard or not, he certainly had authority over Willow, and heading on in made a lot more sense than challenging the chap.

The latch opened with a solid click and the doors swung on well-oiled hinges.

It was much brighter inside than he'd expected in a saloon with closed shutters, due to high windows and cleverly oriented mirrors. A wide balcony ran across the far side of the room with stairs sweeping down from each side. Large paintings of religious fantasies in gold frames loomed from the walls. A spectacularly well-polished bar between the stairways was backdropped by shelves of gleaming bottles. Willow would have wagered a tidy sum that not one of those bottles contained slumgullion.

The main floor was filled with round tables and light, expensive-looking chairs. There was no barman to be seen, but four Chinese women occupied one of the tables. They were even more lovely than the ladies he'd seen outside. They smiled at him.

He heard a chair scrape. There were two men at another table whom he hadn't noticed, so busy had he been studying the room and the ladies. One stood and walked over, hand outstretched, a good head taller than the bounty hunter and clean-shaven apart from a huge moustache which sat on his upper lip like a well-trained Scottish terrier. He wore velvet pantaloons and a flamboyant waistcoat, and he wore them well. He had the broad shoulders and narrow waist of a prize fighter. Despite his size and dense moustache, he looked to be in his early twenties, around the same age as Willow.

"Good day, partner. My name's Slade. Will you take a drink? We have malts from Ireland and Scotland." His voice was confident and rugged, but also beguiling. This was an attractive man, Willow couldn't help but realise.

He looked at the shining golden bottles behind the bar, then to the Chinese ladies, then back to Slade. The Mexican's information had cost him almost all his remaining dollars. He could probably have afforded a drink with the dollars in his pocket, but he could probably have eaten for a week with those same dollars.

"Actually, I'm looking for someone. A woman."

Slade took a step back and smiled.

"Aren't we all?" He glanced over at the Chinese ladies, who giggled.

James felt himself reddening. "Not like that. I'm a bounty hunter." He regretted it as soon as he said it, but he was keen to claw towards some semblance of equal footing in this town of manly men.

Slade smiled handsomely. "Don't tell me. You're after a dark-skinned woman with the most striking blue eyes you ever did see."

"Why yes, how did you ..."

"She came in here a while back and we got talking. She told me all about herself. She said folk might come after her."

"Did she tell you her plans?"

"That she did."

The Englishman could not believe his luck. "Well, that's marvellous. Please will you tell me where she's gone?"

"Nope."

"Oh." Willow looked up at Slade, trying to decipher meaning from those shining eyes. "Should I give you some money?"

"No, you should give up your chase."

"Oh, should I? Why?"

"She deserves her freedom."

"Did she tell you what she did?"

"Sure."

"I see. And you don't think she should return and face justice?"

"Nope."

Willow was confused. He understood that the West was wild, but surely murder was still the most heinous of crimes?

"You would let her and all like her run free?"

Slade took a step back. His face darkened and he glowered down. His hand went to the white ivory grip of a very large pistol, nestled in a black leather holster supple from regular use.

"You don't think they should be free?" the big man asked.

Willow didn't know quite what to say. "But of course not. It would be carnage. Nobody would be-"

Something hard and fast whipped into the Englishman's chin. He was falling before he knew he'd been hit. The back of his head hit the wooden floor. A bulbous, moustachioed face appeared, became five faces which swirled round a couple of times in a darkening miasma, then disappeared.

Willow woke, confused and terribly uncomfortable. His thoughts swung wildly as he tried to make sense of his situation. Finally, he worked it out. He was trussed, hands behind his back, bent face first over the back of a walking horse.

Strange.

He remembered Ossian Slade's Public House. And Ossian Slade himself, and - he'd been hit!

He lifted his head and opened his eyes. The light was so bright he almost cried out. He closed his eyes and lowered his face again. The back of his skull was very sore. As was his jaw, now he came to notice it.

There was shifting pressure to his left, presumably a person riding the horse in the more traditional legs either side, arms free position. Slade? Probably. He certainly smelled manly.

Willow braved another lift of his head. He bore the initial explosion of light blinkingly, then the scenery resolved itself into ... surprise, surprise – scrub and rocks, predominantly brown. In the distance, red-brown mountains.

"Slade!" he tried. No response.

"Sir?" he ventured. Nothing. "Can we stop please?"

"Shut up," said Slade.

Well, at least he'd replied.

The Englishman relaxed. What else was there to do? He closed his eyes.

It was as if Elizabeth had been waiting behind his eyelids, an unbidden but clear memory. The scene was from two months after their wedding, so vivid that it seemed to be happening over again.

"Of course *you* won't be able to," she smiled mockingly. "Hugo will remove the wasps' nest. Much more of a *doer*, isn't he?" Even in her hatred, her voice was clipped to topiarised perfection. She stroked her round stomach. Willow was no expert, but he was sure that she was more than two months pregnant. Not that it made any difference other than for propriety's sake, because they'd never-

He opened his eyes and endeavoured to suffer the dust, but it was intolerable. He closed them again.

There was his older brother, Hugo, wasps' nest eradicated, standing in his garden, while Willow looked out of the kitchen window. His big brother was urinating onto his lawn, turning round and smiling at the kitchen window.

James opened his eyes once more. Ocular agony was preferable to that image.

Did Slade mean to kill him? Surely not. He tried to pull his wrists apart. There was a little give in the rope. If his ground his palms together and moved his hands from side to side then maybe ...

He gave up and closed his eyes again.

Then the birth. The birth of a child who couldn't be his. The first of three who couldn't be his. Hugo, hips thrust out, smoking a pipe.

The children looked like James, of course, because he was their father's brother, and he pretended that they were his. Elizabeth pretended they were his. She treated him with contempt, but she maintained the charade.

But everybody knew. The rest of his family. The villagers. Worst of all somehow, the staff. The only people who didn't know were the children themselves. Those children were the reason Willow hadn't killed himself. The children, and his cowardice. The gun, the knife, the sea - all seemed such sweet avenues of release until he considered the reality of the action. He came to admire those who had the fortitude to take their own lives.

It was almost a relief when the horse stopped and Slade dismounted, whacking Willow with his heel as he did.

Willow felt his collar gripped, then he whumped on the hard track. He landed on his tied hands, which hurt. He rolled onto his side, into a foetal position. He tried to pull his hands free again. The fall had not loosened his bonds, but not enough.

"I don't like your sort." Slade loomed over him. Through blurry tears, Willow saw a dangling knife - more of a sword.

"When you say you don't like my sort, do you mean English people or bounty hunters, or is it something else I've done?" Willow tried.

"Go on, keep talking. The more I hate you the easier this'll be."

"If it's because I'm English, then let me assure you that I'm no great fan of the English either. I know we used to rule here and that rankles, and-"

"We kicked your asses."

"Well, not really."

"Bullshit. I know my history. We whupped your lime-eating asses and sent you back across the sea like the arrogant, yellow-bellied, dough-faced-"

"We whupped our own asses," interrupted Willow, not sure why he felt suddenly brave. Perhaps, now he was definitely going to die, there was nothing left to lose. Whatever it was, it was liberating.

Thinking of liberating, his wrists were freeing up a little more. Perhaps, if could keep Slade talking, he'd be able to slip the bonds and - well, what? - well, at least he'd have a chance if he could use his arms.

"What the hell are you talking about?" Slade demanded

"You think that Americans defeated the British to win independence, don't you?"

"I know that."

"You're wrong."

"What the f-"

"Who comprised the revolutionary forces?"

"What?"

"Who were the people who joined together to make America's revolutionary forces?"

"Revolutionaries."

"Yes. And where were they from?"

"America." Slade announced confidently.

"Ah, no. That's where you're wrong. Your Indian fellow, he's from America. The revolutionaries were British. At the time of the Revolution, they were all British subjects. Many of them had been born in England."

"Bullcrap."

The Englishman's hands were nearly free. "It's not, and you know it. The Revolutionaries - Washington, Jefferson, Hamilton, and the rest of them - were British subjects living in America who didn't like their government."

"Well maybe, but-"

"*I'm* a British subject living in America who doesn't like my government. Consider it for a moment and you know it's true. I have much more in common with the Revolutionaries of the American War of Independence than you do."

"I do see the point you're trying to make," said Slade, "and it's about the most arrogant, stinking pile bullshit I ever heard. I'm not a cruel man, but now I *really* want to kill you."

He raised his knife.

Willow's hands were nearly free. "Wait!"

"What?"

"If you are going to kill me, please can you tell me one thing?"

Slade let the knife drop again. "Depends what it is."

"That seems reasonable." His hands would be free any moment. "I'm always surprised when anybody asks me to commit to something without explaining what it is first. How are you supposed to agree to any-"

"State your point or die now."

"Sorry. I will state my point. What I want to know is this: why are you Americans so obsessed with bottoms? It's *ass* this and *ass* that. Get your *ass* here. Take your *ass* over there. Your *ass* is mine. Or is it donkeys? Do you actually mean ass as in donkey?"

Slade glared down at him.

"It's bottoms, isn't it? I know it is. So why? Why the arse fixation?"

Slade raised the knife.

The bounty hunter gibbered. "Don't throw your life away! People saw me going into your saloon. Kill me and the sheriff will hunt you down!"

"I am the sheriff."

"Ah."

"Ah indeed, my Limey friend."

"But we're on the same side! I'm trying to bring a fugitive to justice."

"A fugitive." Slade let the knife drop again but his face hardened.

"Where would be if we let her kind walk free?"

"We'd be in the West, son, where we value freedom. Now lie back and think of merry old England."

Slade raised his knife.

"Look out behind you!" Willow shouted. To his amazement, Slade turned.

The Englishman yanked his hands free.

Slade turned back. Two handfuls of sand hit him square in the face.

The bounty hunter was up. He ran to the horse, swung himself up and kicked hard, almost giggling with the thrill of the chase and joy of success.

"Yee ha!" he shouted, as the horse shot off like a bee-stung hound.

Willow thundered away, grinning, happier than he'd been since he was a boy. He was away. He had won. Rule Britannia.

A loud whistle rang out.

The horse stopped as fast as it had started.

Willow kicked again and again.

The horse remained stationary. Willow looked over his shoulder. Slade, wiping the sand from his eyes, was walking down the road.

There was no point leaping off and trying to run – he'd be someone on foot trying to escape an armed man on horseback.

Using the height advantage up on the horse, Willow waited until Slade was right there, then kicked for his jaw.

Slade caught his foot and pulled.

Willow crashed down onto desert road. Slade pulled him up by the collar, then whacked him back down with a fist. His head swam. He blinked and tried to raise his arms, to hit back, to kick. But his strength was gone.

Slade dropped him. He lay, defeated. All his schooling, all that he'd learnt, was useless. Even being English wasn't going to help here.

"I said I'd make it quick," said Slade, taking a step back, "but now you've gone and changed my mind for me."

He swung his leg back. The next moment the Englishman felt his ribs explode.

He rolled over. His instinct was to burrow into the desert to escape the pain. He wondered what evolutionary ancestor that particular trait came from? Well, he thought, as another kick struck home, he'd be seeing God very soon, he could ask Him. Or perhaps evolution was a touchy subject with God?

Did everyone have such silly thoughts as they died, he wondered, until another kick slammed into his side and drove measured thought from his mind.

ACT ONE, CHAPTER TEN

Monk Business

"There's no need, you know, for the bigger chap to win a fight," said Mr Hillier-Edwards, who's not particularly large himself. "It's a shame your man … what's his name … Willow hadn't undergone Basic Training. He'd have shown that yahoo what's what."

"Perhaps he's still going to?" I asked.

"Ah, yes! A cliff-hanger! He's going to win that fight somehow, I would wager."

"It would be pretty stupid," said Mrs Hopkins, "if he died, given how much we've had to listen to about him."

"Indeed," said Julian, scratching his little beard, which he thinks makes him look wise. "He could be rescued by some sort of deus ex machina - perhaps a rock might fall from a cliff, or the aggressor - Slade - will walk backwards into a cactus or similar. Or perhaps an anglophile bandido could magically appear out of the desert. I hope not. It would be better writing if he's rescued by somebody or somebodies to whom we've already been introduced."

"What are 'epicanthic folds'?" asked Mrs Skillet, who hadn't been paying attention to the others' conversation. That's rude in some environments, but not in an old folks' home. Most of us are off in our own minds ninety percent of the time.

We talked about epicanthic folds - they're the flaps of skin over the inner corner of East Asian peoples' eyes that makes them look East Asian - in case you don't know and hadn't guessed - and whether one should be allowed to discuss a racial group's physical commonalities. Yes, why not, pretending they don't exist would be weird, said everyone apart from Mrs Terbangun. Mrs Terbangun *maintained that it was racialist to talk about what people look like.*

I understand that Mrs Terbangun probably has her heart it the right place. Kindness is important, but I've always seen that ignoring the obvious builds resentment and widens divides between groups.

Anyway, back to young me at the mine where, as I'm sure you remember, an elevator cart had fallen and smashed.

Dust settled as Loretta, Crane, and I stood looking at the collapsed elevator gear. I lifted my arms to un-gum my sweat-stuck pits and took a step to the left to escape the blinding sun-glare reflecting off a discarded can.

Crane tipped his hat back and took a step towards the shaft.

"Careful!" Loretta made a grab at him.

Crane pushed her hand away gently. "Don't worry, I'm really not planning to fall."

Loretta was such a scaredy cat, always seeing danger where there was none. The stout timber around the edge of the shaft was safe as a sidewalk.

I wiped sweat from my brow and watched Crane's inspection, wiggling my hips. My left butt was all tight and sore. That always happened when I ran too far and fast, but it usually went pretty quick.

Crane ran his finger over pale wood, exposed where the sun-darkened beam had broken. Some of the wood was splintered, as you'd expect from a beam that had snapped. But half the beam was neatly cut. Sawn through.

"Hmmm," said Crane, pulling his hat back and turning to go.

"Wait!" I grabbed his shirt. "That beam's sawn, isn't it? There's a killer, isn't there? Bumping everyone off! Who d'you think it is Crane? Can't be Silver, can it? 'Cause that's who they were trying to get with this!"

"We'll talk later." The lanky man loped off down the slope. Miles beyond him, the sun had reached the base of the mountains and the saltpan on the far side of the valley floor blazed white.

Loretta watched Crane go, lips twisted in a strange half-smile.

"Loretta, someone tried to kill Silver! For sure - look at the beam! What will we do, Loretta?

"I wouldn't be so excited about it." Loretta was touching the broken beam.

"I'm not excited!" I cried, bouncing on my toes. "But that beam's been sawed for sure! And recently, too. Pretty risky for the killer, but they knew that Silver was the only one who used it, and that he'd probably use it this morning, like he did yesterday. It's easier than walking down the hill and he's a lazy fatso."

"Eleanor! You should not talk about adults like that. Or children, for that matter."

"He is both lazy and fat, Loretta. It's just true."

"We all have our faults, child. It isn't ladylike to go about pointing them out."

"There's a killer on the loose and your big concern is me saying that a fat, lazy man is lazy and fat?"

"That's enough."

I scowled. "But there's a killer!"

"I'm sure there's an explanation."

"There is! One of us is a killer, bumping off everyone so they can keep The Prize all to themselves."

"But Denny and Indian Moses-"

"You think those were accidents?"

"Yes."

"No! Murder! Made to look like accidents. Somebody set those explosives that blew Denny's head in half, somebody pushed that cart that squished Moses like a June bug."

"And Happy Days Frida?"

That one frustrated me. "Well, that might not have been murder. Unless you can call it murder when a lion kills a person."

Loretta's beautiful blue eyes flashed, "Maybe the lion set the explosives and pushed the cart, too."

"Don't be silly. Lions don't like the dark. Just like you. That's how I know you're not the killer. You're the only one it can't be because you've never been into the mine."

"So, it could be you?"

"No, it can't be me because I know it isn't me."

"Would that be reason enough for a judge?"

"It should be reason enough. If the judge didn't believe me though, I'd just point out to him that I'd have a job pushing a grown man down a shaft if he didn't want to be pushed down it."

"Oh, I don't know. People can be mighty strong when they want to be. But let's say there is a killer and it's not you. Who is it?"

"Well, it can't be Crane, because he's nice. And he was surprised by the cut beam."

"He could have faked surprise. And people who seem nice are more than capable of doing nasty things. They say Napoleon was pleasant to talk to."

I stamped my foot. This was no time for teasing! "It's not Crane. And it's not Silver, because why would he try to kill himself?"

"To throw the junior sleuth off the scent?"

"Good point!" Loretta was still teasing me, but it was a good point.

"But you can save your detective work until later. Those dishes ain't going to wash themselves."

"I wish they would. I've got to look for clues."

"I'll tell you what," Loretta's smile just then reminded me of my mother's. "You can look for clues while I clear breakfast and do the dishes. When I'm done, I'll holler, and you can come help with the laundry. Deal?"

"Deal."

Loretta headed off down the hill, bottom swinging.

I wondered if I'd ever have a proper woman's bottom like that. Would it swing proper with my one short leg? But this was no time for silly musings. To work!

I inspected the beam again. Cut by a saw, yes sir, no doubt about it. And recently. But who was holding that saw?

I looked about for the tool. Strewn across the man-messed, sun-smashed hillside were nails and squashed tins, other bent bits of metal, and a lot of broken quartz. But no saw.

Moving slowly, with the sun baking my back, I searched for the saw in ever wider circles, then thought *what am I going to do if I find it?* It wasn't like I was going to be able to tell who'd used it, and I already knew the beam had been sawed.

So, looking for the saw was pointless.

I sat on an empty wooden wire spool. I was flummoxed. A zebra-tailed lizard watched me from a rock.

"Did you see anything?" I asked.

It ran off, all crazy legged. Did it mean me to follow?

No, of course it didn't. I'd find the killer in the same way a grown-up would. Believing a lizard could help was childish and this was no time for childishness.

I returned to the shaft to look for footprints. There were loads, mostly mine from when I'd been looking for the saw. I found what I guessed were Loretta's footprints, and maybe Crane's. Maybe there were some others. I don't know. It was hard to tell. I returned to my spool, fresh out of ideas. It was almost a relief when Loretta called me to help with the laundry.

"Have you heard of heat madness?" I asked Loretta, maybe an hour later. I was twisting a shirt around the big dorm's corner stanchion. There was no need to wring out the laundry quite so much - drying clothes was one thing the desert was good for - but wringing out was satisfying work.

"No, but I know what both those words mean, so I guess I've worked it out."

"I heard," I finished one shirt, tossed it to Loretta for hanging, then picked out another, "that a whole waggon train of people got so hot in this very valley that they all went heat mad and killed themselves."

"How?"

I hadn't heard that part of the story, so I had to make up answers. "Different ways. One of them tied his tongue to a horse's tail and whipped the horse. One of them cut off his own eyelids so the sun boiled his brain. One of them caught a tarantula hawk wasp, cut open his own stomach, and-”

“I get the point.”

“So that’s what it might be,” I said. “Heat madness.”

“I thought it was greed?” Loretta asked.

“Well, yes, combined with heat madness and … hello, what’s this?”

Crane was walking over the rise from Gila Canyon. We paused our laundering and watched him come. He had a sack in one hand and his face was grim.

I was a little scared. He looked very serious.

“What you got there?” asked Loretta.

He climbed the steps up to the big dorm’s veranda, upended the sack and let its contents clatter onto the wood.

It was two bars of wood, the shorter, stouter piece fixed into the other to make a ‘T’. Set in the stout piece were what looked a lot like four lion’s claws. They were dirty with black, sticky-looking goo and long hairs …

I realised.

“I knew it! I told you! There is a killer!” I picked up the weapon. Four lion’s claws were set into holes in the wood with resin. That was blood on them - Happy Frida’s blood. A murdered woman’s blood! Those very claws had ripped flesh - taken life! And not long before! The last person to hold the claw stick before me and Crane had been the murderer.

I held the weapon and tried to *feel* who’d held it before, tried to *feel* what it must be like to kill another person with something as primitive and messy as claws on a stick.

“I think you should put that down,” said Loretta, backing away.

I blinked. Loretta was beautiful, she was exotic, but she had no sense for the amazing. This was a really wild, special thing I was holding.

“But Loretta-” I started.

“Put it down,” said Crane, sounding mean for the first time ever.

I put it down.

“Where did you find it?” asked Loretta.

“Maybe a hundred paces along an adit, in a bucket in a pile of other buckets. I was looking for candles.”

“Do you know who left it there?”

"I have a theory," said Crane.

"Go on?" Loretta put a hand on Crane's arm, and they looked into each other's eyes like I wasn't even there.

"I think the killer …" Crane paused and looked from me, to Lorretta, then around, as I bounced on my toes, silently shouting at him to get on with it, "was Indian Moses."

"But he's dead!" I cried. How very disappointing. It was a bit boring if the killer was already dead. "How could a dead man saw a beam?"

"Hear me out."

He walked over to the dining table and took a seat, back to the valley. Loretta and me sat opposite. Even in the shade of the big dorm's veranda, I could feel the heat of the wood through my pants.

"Back in the town, Moses was … well, I don't know how to put this. He was a pretty man. Other men, who liked a pretty man, paid him to … I'm not quite sure how to-"

"He danced for men?" I asked.

"That is one way of putting it," Crane nodded.

"I thought only women danced for men?"

Crane shook his head. "Used to be there were no women in the West, not even the … dancers we have now. Men have urges. With no women around, those urges will take a different direction."

"You're saying all the Forty-Niners were backdoor men?" Loretta's eyebrows were so high on her forehead Eleanor was worried they might get lost in her hair. What was she was talking about?

"Nope, not all." said Crane. "Just a lot of them."

"I see," Loretta was nodding, "That explains the song I heard on the way out here:

All the young dudes are full of fear
That horny old studs a-filled with beer
Will suddenly prance,
Pull off their pants
And ride them hard in the rear."

Crane laughed. "What a charming, subtle ditty."

"Can we get back to Indian Moses?" I asked. I was a bit bored of these two flirting. And what was that silly rhyme all about?

"Sure thing. So, Moses used to dance for Silver. Moses probably didn't like that too much and wanted to kill Silver. So, he sawed the beam, maybe a few days back. Maybe even a week or more ago. But then the beam held when Silver used it. Something set if off this morning. Maybe the wind, maybe a fox."

"Foxes everywhere!" Loretta smiled at me.

I nearly giggled, but remembered they were talking about murder, and I was meant to be taking it seriously.

"And Silver killed Moses?" she asked.

"Probably. Or maybe it was dumb luck."

"But what about the others? Did Silver or Moses kill Happy Days Frida and Denny?" I could see no sense in either man killing either of the others.

"Moses," said Crane.

"But why?"

"Greed. He wanted The Prize to himself."

"Why do you think it was Moses and not Silver, Monk, or Masterton?" asked Loretta. "Maybe Moses did try to kill Silver, but that doesn't mean that he killed the others."

"That's true." Crane nodded, "but we know Moses was prepared to kill Silver, so it follows-"

"But you said Silver was going to kill Moses," I pointed out, "so he's a killer too. It could have been him."

"Yes," Crane nodded, "maybe, but I can't see Silver climbing all the way into the next valley to kill Happy Days Frida."

"I don't know," I shook my head. "He can move quick when he wants to!"

I wasn't sure that he could, but I didn't want him ruled out as a suspect. It was more fun to think it could have been any of those three varmints. I don't know why. Maybe it made me, Crane, and Loretta more of a team.

Loretta gave me a look then turned to Crane. "But it could have been either of the others. Maybe Moses tried to kill Silver. Maybe Silver did kill Moses. But why would Moses want to kill Happy Days Frida and Denny?"

"Greed, like I said."

"But Masterton and Monk - all of us, in fact - share that motive. You telling me that you'd hate to have The Prize all to yourself?"

"But we know Indian Moses is a killer," Crane countered.

"No, we don't. Even if he was, we don't know that he's the only one."

"Heat madness could have got everyone!" I announced. "We could all be killers!"

The adults looked at me.

"We should set a trap!" I declared. It was all very exciting.

Crane shook his head. "We should leave."

"We can't leave." Loretta looked at him coolly. "We all have our reasons for needing The Prize. Those reasons won't go away."

"Sure," said Crane after a while.

"So, what do we do?" I asked.

"I gotta go back into the mine," Crane climbed off the bench and stood. "I don't want to give them an excuse to reduce my cut, and besides I wouldn't mind finding The Prize myself. That way I know it'll get shared properly."

"Be careful," said Loretta, getting up herself and walking around the table to him.

"It's you two I'm worried about. Stay together. Loretta, take my gun."

He reached for his holster. Loretta reached a hand to his arm again. "I'll be more danger to myself and Eleanor it you leave that with me."

"I can use it!" I jumped up and reached out a hand.

"You wouldn't be able to hold it, let alone shoot it," said Crane. "It's very heavy."

"How about if I held it with two hands?" I asked, but Crane shook his head.

Crane loped off over the rise to Gila Canyon. Loretta and I finished the laundry then Loretta announced she was going to have a sleep, like she did every day. She told me to stay nearby.

I did as I'd been told for a bit, but then spotted a chuckwalla making his slow way across the cleared ground in front of the big dorm. I followed the chuckwalla to see if it would lead me to a secret source of water. Somebody had told me they did that. Not that we needed more water, the tank was still nearly full. But secret things were always worth finding.

The chuckwalla went a good way down the canyon - I'd never seen one travel so far - but then I lost it under a clump of desert holly not much bigger than the chuckwalla himself.

Now how did he do that? I wondered as I headed on, over the rise and into Gila Canyon, looking for more chuckwallas and hoping to see a Gila monster. It was ridiculous that I'd never seen a Gila monster in Gila Canyon. Behind, in the mining camp, Loretta slept on alone.

I walked slowly. This was the sort of heat that had killed all those people and given Death Valley its name. Maybe it was hotter than that? But if you moved slow, drank plenty, found shade when you could and rested every now and then, you'd be fine.

Usually I was okay doing that but today was different. It felt like I was cooking from the inside. I forgot about lizards and focused on getting out of the heat. I had to get into the mountain.

The first adit I came to was the blocked one, but I didn't need to go deep. Even ten yards in it was a hundred times cooler than midday Death Valley air. I peered in and sniffed. Sometimes coyotes went into tunnels to die, and I didn't want to meet one. And foxes, of course, were everywhere. Either one of those might give me a nasty nip if I trod on it in the dark.

But the only smell was rock, so I walked in warily, one hand trailing against the wall. I'd been down here with a candle and knew this tunnel was safe - no hidden shafts, saw wheels sticking out, or head-height dangling pulleys - but 'safe' in a mine still meant you had to be careful.

Twenty paces in I sat, rested my back against the cool wall and let the heat flow out of me.

I must have gone to sleep, because I was startled awake by a noise. A man was silhouetted in the glaring light of the entrance.

I'd have known that crow-like stoop anywhere. Masterton.

He was peering down the tunnel like I'd done. Was he checking it for murder clues and ailing coyotes or had he seen me go in?

"Eleanor?" he called. "Are you down there?"

His voice put me in mind of the wolf from the three little pigs story. I sat motionless.

"Oh, Eleanor, I know you're there, Eleanor. I saw you go in, Eleanor." He sure did like saying my name.

"So why you asking?" *What an idiot.* I stood up, meaning to head out past him.

"Stay where you are, Eleanor, dear, I'm coming in."

I'd sooner have chopped off my long leg than stayed put. I didn't know what he wanted from me, but I was dead sure I didn't want to give it. I picked up a fist sized chunk of quartz and crept towards him.

Masterton was moving in cautiously, one hand on the wall, testing the ground with each step. So, he was still sun blind.

If I could get round him before his eyes adjusted and he realised what I was doing … Five paces away, four, three … I ran for the gap between him and the rock wall, lightly and quietly as I could, gripping the quartz rock just in case.

He scooped me up like a shepherd scooping up a lamb, turned me around and gripped me in a tight embrace.

I still had my rock, but my arms were pinned. I kicked his legs. He shoved my feet to one side with a knee.

"Let me go!' I shouted.

"No need to struggle, Eleanor," I could feel his hot breath on my ear. "I just want to hold you awhile. It gets lonely. Aren't you lonely?"

"I don't think I'll ever be lonely enough to want to be held by you! I don't think anybody ever was, save maybe your ma!"

"That's what I like about you, Eleanor. You're feisty. I like the strugglers best."

His hand slipped round to clasp my bottom. Something hot and wet smothered my ear. He was licking it!

Yuk, yuk, yuk! That was too much!

I wrenched my hand free and slammed the quartz lump against his head, hard as I could.

He shouted and dropped me.

I was round him and running as fast as my messed-up legs would take me.

Heavy footsteps pounded after me.

I tried to run faster, but my left butt cheek chose that moment to have its worst spasm ever. Pain shot up my side and down my leg and I fell.

I scrabbled round onto my back. He was nearly on me. I threw the rock with all I had. It bounced off his shoulder and then his weight was crashing down.

He gripped me with his legs and punched me in the face.

I don't know if you've ever been punched in the face, but it is not like when you're play acting. You don't just rub your jaw and smile. At least I've never found that's the case, and I've been punched in the face more than most women, I would wager. It's the price of an adventurous life, I guess.

That was the first time, though, and one of the worst. I blinked and worked my jaw and I couldn't think and I couldn't see and I couldn't do anything.

My senses reordered. He'd pulled me onto my feet. I was stumbling along, butt cheek screaming in pain, jaw and cheeks feeling all askew, being dragged by the arm deeper into the mountain.

"What are you doing?" I shouted. My mouth felt all funny and sore. "What do you want?"

His only answer was weird grunting. Those horrible noises made me scared as I'd ever been. Was he going to kill me?

He stopped maybe fifty paces in. He held me tight, fingers hurting my arm, panting and grunting. I whacked at his arm, but it didn't hurt him. *I should have kept the rock!* I tried to kick him, but he held me out of reach.

When he'd recovered his wind, he pulled me towards him and I thought he was going to hug me again, but he pushed me over his foot and I fell onto my back. I dug my fingers into my butt cheek, trying to knead away the spasm.

"You hurt my head," he said. It was hard to be sure in the darkness, but it looked and sounded like he was unbuckling his belt.

"Well, I'm sorry about that, but you asked for it, mister. I'll do it again if you don't let me go." *I would have done it again right there and then, if I hadn't been all out of rocks.*

He was dropping his pants now. "You hurt me and you owe me."

"Are you going to kill me?"

"I wouldn't have done if you'd been game, but now ... Well, let's see how you do, shall we?"

I shifted away on my elbows, but he stepped onto my leg. I tried to wriggle free but that one boot on my knee held me firm. It didn't help that my butt was still shooting pain up and down my leg and my side.

"I ain't got no business with you!" I shouted at him.

"Keep a-squirming and a-talking, Eleanor. I love your sweet sassiness."

His pants were down now - I was pretty sure his underpants too. I didn't know what he wanted to do, but I didn't like it.

He squatted, gripped my hips and yanked, so I was under him. I pummelled his chest with both fists.

"Oh yes, Eleanor," he said, "keep hitting me." He leant forward and clamped a big hand on my neck. He stank of sweat and cheese. I dug my nails into his arm.

"Yes!" he cried. "Hurt me more!"

I wanted to hurt him more, I wanted to give him a hurt that he wouldn't walk away from. But the way he was sitting on me I couldn't reach him with my legs, one arm was pinned, and hitting him with the other one just seemed to make him happier.

I felt his fingers rummaging at my belt.

No! That would not do!

I whacked and whacked with my free arm, but to no avail. He wasn't talking any more. He was grunting like an excited pig and that was worse.

He pulled hard at my belt. Belt, pants, and all pulled down. My underpants were around my legs and my bottom was on the cool earth.

I writhed like a mad fish. A hand pressed down on my shoulder. His face came down near to mine and I bit him, hard.

He wrenched his chin out of my mouth "Oh, yes," he grunted.

He grabbed both my wrists, pulled my arms over my head, and gripped them in one hand. He circled my neck with his other hand and squeezed.

"Like that, do you?" he rasped, pushing his hips into me. I didn't like it one little bit, but with my throat crushed it was impossible to tell him.

He let go of my neck and reached down.

Then suddenly he was off me, lifting into the air like a rat whacked with a bat.

There was thud, a noise like a knife cutting into a steer carcass, a louder thud, then a long, sad gasp.

"Are you alright?" Someone asked. Crane.

I felt silly, lying there with my pants down. I hoicked them up. Strangely enough, my butt had stopped its spasming in all the excitement. "Yeah, I'm all right. Did you kill him?"

Crane didn't answer. He reached a hand to help me up.

On my feet I straightened my clothes. My shirt had been twisted right round and two of the buttons were missing, so there'd be sewing to do.

Crane lit a match, and then a candle.

Masterton was slumped back against the wall in the dark, his head hanging weirdly to one side and his neck gaping open like a new mouth.

"Thank you," I said.

"Anytime, miss. Are you hurt?"

My neck was sore, breathing was a struggle, my head was pounding, and my face was smarting where he'd punched me, and my butt and leg throbbed.

"I'm fine," I said.

"Good. There's something I want you to do for me."

"Sure."

"Don't tell anybody I did this."

"But he was attacking me. You had every right to kill the varmint!"

"Just don't tell anyone, all right?"

"All right."

"Good. Now let's go."

He turned.

I stepped over Masterton's legs. "Crane?" I called.

"Yup."

"Can I have a hug, please?" I couldn't remember when I'd needed a hug more.

"Sure."

I leapt into Crane's arms and clasped on tight. He smelled of soap and leather - and a bit of sweat, too, but in a good way. He made to put me down, but I didn't want to let go. He straightened with me still clamped onto him, wrapped an arm around, and walked out of the tunnel into the light.

ACT TWO

ACT TWO, CHAPTER ONE

The Right Hook of Mormon

Mrs Terbangun, Mrs Hopkins and the rest were uncharacteristically subdued after last night's reading. Possibly because it was so long, but I think it was because most of them are women. I suspect they've all received unwelcome male attention of varying degrees along the way, from the irritating to the horrific. Mercifully, Masterton's attack was the closest I've ever come to being raped, possibly because I carried a gun for the rest of my time in the lawless West.

Mr Hillier-Edwards surprised me - as much as anything surprises me these days - by catching up to me in the corridor.

"I'm very sorry for what happened to you. Men are a disgrace, and I'd like to apologise on behalf of all of them. Masterton got what he deserved. If I had my way, all men who attack girls - or women - would suffer the same fate. We caught a few in the war. They ... well, let's say they got what they deserved. Good night."

Two generations of British and American men have suffered terribly and witnessed appalling depredations this century. You pass them every day in the street without knowing. I headed upstairs, wondering not only what horrors Mr Hillier-Edwards had suffered in the war, but what horrors he'd been forced to commit. I've only ever killed people who deserved it. I can't imagine being made to kill a stranger simply because greedy, power-hungry men have launched a war.

Now I'm back at my writing desk and ready to return to the West. We're not going quite as far as the Fabulous, but to the road where we left James Willow under the boot of Sheriff Ossian Slade.

A shot rang out.

Here is death, Willow thought to himself. He let himself fall away, tumbling through the clouds, ready to meet God.

Everything that had happened was Divine Purpose, and now, surely, he'd discover what that purpose was. How would God explain his humiliation? How did Willow's misery fit into the Heavenly Scheme? Would God Himself explain, or did he delegate such tasks to minor officials with clipped moustaches and angel's wings?

There was shouting. Willow had not expected brashness in heaven.

"I said walk away, mister." It was a voice the Englishman hadn't heard before. American, but not the uneducated drawl of the standard Western American. It was more liked the educated East Coast yapping of the Clemenses, but higher pitched and elderly. It did not sound like a rescuer's voice.

"I am a sheriff carrying out the law. Move along, sir." That was Slade. He sounded commanding. The Englishman would have moved along.

"I am imbued with a higher power than man can give." declared the weedy voice. Another shot ricocheted off a nearby rock. "The next one's in your gut if you don't get on your horse and ride away."

What a well-trained horse to stand there while bullets are fired mused the Englishman. *Or, more likely, frontier horses were as used to gunfire as English horses were to church bells.*

Willow opened his eyes. Slade was standing above him, fingers waggling over the butt of his holstered pistol.

He lifted himself up on his elbows. Ten paces down the road were a cluster of women, children, cattle and one horse, all looking from him to the man they'd interrupted in the process of kicking him to death. His rescuers were the Mormons they'd passed that morning.

Standing forward from the others was a small, skinny man well into his sixties, maybe even with a toe in his seventies. He was clean-shaven and wore a neatly pressed brown waistcoat over a shirt that had seen better days. Apart from the rifle pointed at Slade, he was pretty much the opposite of threatening.

"I'll give you to the count of three!" the old Mormon yelped.

"How about we fight for him?" Slade said with half a smile.

"That's a funny idea, mister! You must have forty years on me, and you're double my weight at least!"

"I'll give you first hit."

"How would that work?"

The bounty hunter looked from Mormon to sheriff. "Hang on a minute, this is my life you're dealing with here, and-"

"Quiet, you," Slade kicked him with the side of his boot. "I can see you're a man of God, old timer, and I guess you think you're doing the right thing here. I respect that. Also, I know you don't want to kill me. Am I right?"

The Mormon didn't say anything.

"Shoot him!" Willow the bounty hunter yelped. "He was trying to kill me for being English!"

"So, I'll put my gun where I can't reach it," Slade ignored Willow, "then hold my hands behind my back. You get first hit, anywhere you like apart from the privates. Then, if there's any fight left in me, we duke it out. Last man standing gets to do what they want with this sorry lime-juicer."

"I do not belong - oooof!" Willow began, but Slade kicked him again.

"Two hits," said the Mormon.

"You got yourself a deal, mister." Slade took out his pistol and walked away, presumably to place it on a handy rock. Handy rocks were one thing the western desert was not short of.

The Englishman stared at the Mormon.

He was a little old man!

Slade was a head taller and, as the Mormon had observed, at least double his weight. What the Devil had the Mormon agreed to? Slade would shrug off two punches from the decrepit old geezer, then pick him up and pull his limbs off.

Slade paced down the road towards the old man. Willow hauled himself painfully to his feet, looked about, and saw where Slade had left his gun. He took a pace towards it. He wasn't too proud to shoot the sheriff in the back.

"Don't even think about it, mister!" One of the Mormons - a young woman - had a rifle trained on him.

"Whose side are you on?" he asked.

"God's," she replied.

Well, there you go. Difficult to argue that one.

Mormon and sheriff squared up, or at least stood as square as two people of such differing shapes and sizes could. Willow was put in mind of David and Goliath. It was a shame this David didn't have a sling.

True to his word, Slade clasped his hands behind his back. *They were a strangely honourable people out here*, thought Willow. Would he have behaved so decently? It was hard to know. Although he'd planned to shoot the sheriff in the back less than a minute before, so he probably wasn't the most decent man this side of the Atlantic.

"I warn you," the Mormon yapped up at Slade, "I mean to hit you with all I've got."

"So long as you don't hit my balls, whack away. The harder you hit me, the less bad I'll feel handing you your whupping after."

The elderly Mormon nodded, pulled back his right fist, bent his knees and coiled his frame around, like he was winding himself up. He was bendy for an old fellow. He whispered a short prayer, then leapt round like a Jack Russell terrier, uncoiling as he flew upwards, flinging his arm in a long arc and slamming his fist into the sheriff's jaw like a well-practiced sledgehammer hitting a railing spike.

Slade rocked on his heels for a moment as if too surprised to fall, then toppled backwards and whumped heavily onto the dirt.

Willow ran over. The Mormon shook his fingers then blew on his knuckles.

Slade was out cold. The Englishman raised a boot above his erstwhile captor's face.

"No, son," said the Mormon.

"He was going to kill me! God would approve."

"Calm yourself. I'm sure he had his reasons."

Willow put his foot back on the dirt, secretly relieved. He hadn't wanted to kill Slade, he'd just felt like he ought to.

"That was amazing. How did you …?"

"I was a prize fighter," the elderly Mormon said. He didn't look or sound like a prize fighter. "Featherweight," he added, as if reading Willow's mind. "Some things you don't forget. How to hit a man in the face is one of them, I guess."

Late that afternoon they stopped in a gulch and made camp on the alluvium, shaded by a low, red cliff on the long side of a dry meander. Nobody had talked to the Englishman all day and he'd returned the favour. They hadn't seemed to mind him tagging along. Since there were heading in the same direction as his coach, he reckoned the coach would have to pass at some point. So far, he'd been unlucky. He could have headed back towards the town, but on the one hand, the coach may have already left by a different route, and on the other, he didn't want to be alone in this world of madmen and animals that could kill you.

While the Mormons busied about making camp, he walked what would have been upstream. Wondering how long it had been since water had made this streambed a stream, he spotted a darker patch under an overhang and bent to investigate. Three red-spotted toads were crouching on the damp but cracked mud, blinking at him with hostility and a little apprehension. Bidding the amphibians good day, he went on his way.

He found a broad rock under the dappled shade of a small-leaved tree and sat on it. Speedy little birds flitted about. A jackass rabbit shot away for about half a second, then stopped and eyed him from the shelter of a creosote bush some ten feet away, apparently convinced that, if he stayed still enough, he wouldn't be seen.

The dry stream was one of those surprisingly green spots in the desert where you could almost begin to enjoy the countryside. The Englishman watched a variety of animals appear, go about their business, and then head off to whatever was next on their agenda.

There were certainly an awful lot of birds, mammals, and lizards - more than one would see sitting by a stream in England. Who would have thought that the supposedly barren desert would host more wildlife than his homeland's sylvan paradise? Or perhaps lack of foliage simply made it easier to see animals here?

Wildlife wasn't the only way that England compared unfavourably. Willow had been brought up to believe that the English were the best, that an Englishman was superior to any other in the world. However, everyone he met in the West was his equal - if he was being generous to himself. Generous to a point of deluded stupidity.

After a while, a child appeared with a steaming bowl and a spoon, left them on a rock, and padded off back down the dry stream without a word.

Willow ate. It was a vegetable stew; utterly delicious, but probably the saltiest thing he'd ever had. He guessed the Mormons of Salt Lake weren't short of that mineral.

He was wondering whether he should make an effort to go over and talk to his hosts and saviours, and whether he was even allowed to, when the old Mormon who'd punched Slade came wandering out of the dark with a steaming tin mug in each hand. He passed one to the Englishman, then held out his spare hand.

"I'm Cyril. Cyril Callahan," he said, as they shook.

"Willow," said the bounty hunter. "James Willow."

"Tell me about yourself, James Willow," said Callahan, settling next to him.

"What do you mean?"

"Start where you were born, and how that led to you being here now."

"It might take a while."

"I have no prior engagements." Callahan's squeaky voice was at odds with his relaxed manner, and his ability to fell huge men forty years his junior with one hit.

Oh, why not? thought Willow.

"I was born in a village in Oxfordshire, in England. My father had made some money in India and bought the village's manor. I was the third child of four. I had brothers ten and eight years older than me, and a sister a year and a half younger."

"It sounds idyllic," said Callahan.

"Does it?" The image of Christmas lunch filled Willow's mind, as it so often did. He was looking in on a warm family scene. His sister was holding a Brussels sprout aloft on a fork and spinning a whimsical yarn about it.

Two well-fed, handsome young men were roaring with laughter. A pair of ruddy-faced parents were chuckling warmly. Willow was laughing too, but his laugh was fake. His sister's antics were not funny. The staff, stood around the edge of the room dressed in black and white, were chuckling along too, more part of the family than James ever had been.

"I was the third son," Willow continued to Callahan. "I lacked the confidence of my brothers or the charm of my little sister."

"Ah," Callahan was looking into the middle distance and nodding. "Even a privileged childhood can be a lonely one."

"I liked my own company. I'd walk the fields and read. I became quite the master of the pianoforte."

"You sound like that type of Englishman who's got a bit of an education on him."

"I was sent away to school."

"Where you were just as lonely, I'd wager."

"I enjoyed my school days." He had been lonely. And bullied. Horribly bullied. He tried not to remember those difficult years.

"And then?"

"Then came Elizabeth."

"You fell in love?"

"She was beautiful and fun and clever. I wouldn't have dared talk to her. She approached me at a dance."

"What do you think she saw in you?"

Willow looked at the Mormon. That was a strange question. Possibly an insulting one, but the old man's face was so free from guile that Willow answered with the truth that he'd long denied to himself.

"She saw advancement and money."

Willow expected Callahan to protest like an Englishman - *Oh no, I'm sure there was more to it; surely your wit and intellect must have played the greater part, blah, blah, blah, platitude to try to make you feel better, blah, blah, blah, self-deprecating story to show he'd also been wronged by a woman, blah, blah, blah, noise to avoid the horror of embarrassed silence.*

But Callahan simply nodded.

A fat, brown lizard came marching along the streambed, saw the men and stopped, then headed as if on tiptoes towards the rocky bank, where it disappeared into a crevice.

Willow shook his head, remembering the early days with Elizabeth. Trips to Oxford, picnics by the Thames. Laughter and smiles, touches on the arm that promised physical tenderness once their union was sanctified. That one brief kiss on the lips in the dark one evening when they were parting that had left him giddy, unable to walk away for minutes.

For him, it had been a period of genuine joy. For her, he now understood, it had been an act. Knowing that she'd never loved him did not make it any easier. It didn't make him love her any less. The abominable treatment after they were married, the acts that might have driven a braver man to suicide - did, in fact, drive him to suicide as far as his family were aware - didn't make him love her any less.

"The problem was," he continued, "that I didn't actually have any money."

"Parents cut you out?"

"They never cut me in. They believed sons should make their own way in the world."

"A sound philosophy."

"I'm sure, and I have tried not to be bitter. I would have liked a little help, though. My brothers made their way easily enough. After university, they joined my father's business, took it over and expanded it. Unfortunately, when I left university, they had no position for me."

"They could have found you something, surely?"

"They told me I was too clever for any employment they might offer. The family business, they said, wasn't ready for me yet." Willow sighed. "I clung onto that 'yet' and convinced myself that my family had conspired to encourage my betterment. Perhaps, I thought, my parents and brothers expected me to join the East India Company to experience life and business before returning as the golden, prodigal child and swelling their modest enterprise into an empire to rival the East India.

"It took me an embarrassingly long time to realise they didn't expect anything from me at all. They hadn't conspired. It wouldn't have crossed their minds to discuss my future. They didn't give two figs what I did. So,

I didn't do anything. I read, I travelled to London, attending lectures and observing the world, fooling myself that I was educating myself before choosing a career. In fact, I was doing nothing. I had no money and no prospects. Better men might have been goaded into action by such a situation. I ignored it and did nothing to improve it."

"Planning to live on family money?" asked Callahan.

"I didn't have any. I wasn't even due an inheritance - that's all going to my eldest brother."

"But Elizabeth didn't know you were penniless?"

"She did not."

"And you didn't tell her."

Willow closed his eyes. He'd known what she was after, all along. It had taken him a long time to admit it, but he'd known. He'd hoped she'd learn to love him and forget about the money … No, it was worse than that. He hoped she'd be trapped by the marriage. Once they were united before God, she'd be his, money or no, joined with him forever. Then she'd learn to love him. She'd have to. They would have to have children, which would cement their love. That was the purpose of marriage.

He could not have been more wrong.

"On our wedding day, at the drinks reception before dinner, my eldest brother Hugo elucidated my position and prospects to Elizabeth." He could picture the scene perfectly. He pictured it at least once an hour, every day.

Hugo, red faced, moustache wet with wine, leaning in too close.

Her hand on his arm. His manly arm, thick as James' leg.

Hugo looking up at James and, smiling like a toad, whispering into his beautiful bride's ear, holding his youngest brother's gaze as he ruined his life.

That was the moment the world changed. The moment that separated the two parts of his life.

Elizabeth had looked about, seeking him out, nostrils flaring, face flushing. She found him. Her eyes narrowed into flinty hatred. And stayed like that. From that moment on, he'd only ever seen her smile and dazzle again when she was talking to other men. Mostly when she was talking to Hugo.

That very night - their wedding night - she'd ... He usually managed not to think about their wedding night. He wiped his eyes. "Sorry, sorry, I-"

"Save the details, I get the picture," Callahan nodded grimly. "Misery and humiliation drove you to America."

"And pennilessness." Willow shrugged. "I am the catch of the century."

"God has tested you."

The old man was the first sympathetic ear Willow had found in his entire life. "It's hard to love a God who'd punish me so."

"His ways are, indeed, mysterious, yet there is purpose to it all. There are many who suffer a great deal more than you, James Willow. You will not appreciate the gifts of your youth and health until you have lost them, but these are greater by far than any amount of money. Any wealthy old man - or woman, for that matter - would swap all their material gain to return to their youth."

Willow nodded. He didn't see the use of health and youth to a man shunned by his family and the only woman he could ever love, but he didn't want to seem disagreeable.

"Why have you come West, though?" asked Callahan. "You seem more suited to the East."

"You mean I seem weak and incapable?"

"Let's say urbane."

Willow sighed. "I was penniless. I made some money in New York-"

"As a tutor? You speak like a tutor."

"No. As a bathroom attendant."

"Oh."

"Indeed. Actually, the tips were good. I think the Manhattan gentry felt sorry for me. I made a great deal more than I would have done as a tutor. But there wasn't much room for advancement, short of attending ever larger bathrooms, I suppose, so I headed south to see what I could find. It was there I saw the woman I'm looking for, although I didn't know it at the time."

"You fell in love with another woman?"

Willow laughed. "Oh no, not at all. Although the woman I found is certainly striking. Shortly after I saw her in the flesh, I saw her again on wanted posters. She's a murderer. Her bounty will purchase a smallholding or set up a business, so I set off after her."

"But you don't even have a gun!"

"I did. I had an Allen pistol. Slade - the sheriff you punched - took it."

"An Allen's not a gun. It's a liability."

"So I heard after I'd bought it."

"How do you plan to bring her in?"

"I plan to find her and take her to the nearest sheriff's office."

"And she'll just come along, will she?"

"To be honest, I haven't given much thought to the actual business of apprehending her. So far, I have focussed on finding her. I had thought I was doing quite well."

Callahan stood. Behind him stars shone like sequins on a black dress. Bats had taken over the insectivorous duties of the flitting birds. An owl hooted.

"Come on," said the elderly gentleman, "I'll find you some bedding."

The following morning, Willow found Callahan on the far side of the dry gulch, brushing the Mormons' one horse. Man and animal were fringed in gold by the sun rising across an endless plain of grit and scrub. The horse was tacked up with a saddle and bridle, which it hadn't been the day before. Who was going to ride it, Willow wondered, and where had they got the kit from?

"Thanks for everything," he said to Callahan, holding out his hand.

"Don't thank me yet. I ain't finished giving you things. I want you to take Delores here."

Willow looked around. The only living creatures in sight, other than a coyote slinking about in the mid distance, were himself, Callahan, and the horse.

"Not your horse! I couldn't!"

"I'm giving you my gun, as well," said Callahan, unbuckling his holster. "Colt Navy. It ain't no Allen. People will take you seriously when you point this at them."

"I can't take these things."

"I want you to have them." Callahan looked up at him, grey eyes shining. "I done a lot of things in my life, Willow, not many of 'em good. I mean to get square with God before I die. So, I want to give you some money as well. Take it, please. You'll be helping me if you do."

Delores looked like a good, strong horse, and the gun looked fearsome. And he needed money.

"Well, if you're sure it will help you …"

ACT TWO, CHAPTER TWO

Tempest

Mr Hillier-Edwards had a heart attack in the night.

He went to hospital in an ambulance. I saw the blue lights through my curtains as I wrote but hardly skipped a beat. One has to be blasé about people popping their clogs here in Hell's antechamber, or one would spend one's life in misery.

I hadn't known it was Mr Hillier-Edwards, of course. I was surprisingly upset when I found out. I thought I was a pragmatic old bird. Mr H-E has had a good long life – or at least a long one, I have no idea whether it's been a good one – so it's ridiculous to be upset that he might die. Of course he might! Any of us codgers might die at any moment. That's the point of the place. I might not live to the end of this sen - urghhh.

Just kidding.

Mr H-E's heart attack is, apparently, mild, but the last codger who had a "mild" heart attack never came back, so I am not holding my breath for my new friend's return. I shall miss him.

I thought about waiting for him before carrying on with the reading. But if there's anything that's going to jinx his chances of coming back, it's waiting for him to come back. And maybe he'd like me to catch him up with private readings as he recovers.

On a completely different subject, there was a snobby little happening in yesterday morning's bridge drive. We play bridge because it's posh. "Posh" in

England is a pleasingly wide-ranging word. You can use it to describe a queen living in a palace, or someone who prefers a slightly more expensive biscuit with their tea. The difference between posh and snobby is something else I learnt on this side of the Atlantic. Posh is kind of okay. Snobby means looking down on others, which is despicable.

I am aware of the irony that I look down on snobby people.

Anyway, we play bridge because it's posh. Bingo would be more fun, but our fees are far too high to allow something as common as bingo to sully our lavender and urine-scented games hall.

At the end of the first rubber, Mrs Bull clambered to her feet and said, "I'm just going to nip to the toilet."

I don't think I've mentioned Mrs Bull. She's the only one with a regional accent. All the others speak with a posh accent (that useful word again). Mrs Bull has a Yorkshire accent. She's a kind and good woman, but she seems nervous of the posher lot. I guess it's because she's not posh herself, but one must of course be wary of deciding others' motives.

Mrs Hopkins shook her jowls and announced, very much loud enough for Mrs Bull to hear as she left, "By golly, how I hate the 'T' word!"

"Mrs Hopkins," I said, when Mrs Bull had gone. "Imagine that Jesus is visiting and wants to choose a friend from between two people. Person One uses the word toilet. She learnt that word growing up. It's the word her parents and her people used. Person Two looks down on Person One, genuinely judges her less valuable, because she says toilet. Who do you reckon Jesus would prefer, person one or person two?"

"The person with manners, I expect!" Mrs Hopkins snapped back. Like I may have said earlier, you might as well butt your head against a cliff as try to change an adult's opinion, but seeing Mrs Bull embarrassed got me riled.

Anyway, let's go back to the mine, where the word "toilet" would have been far too la-di-da to describe the shithouse where we did our business.

Silver perched in a shaded scoop high on the edge of Gila Canyon.

A former Death Valley denizen had blasted a gap in the steep canyon side, flattened the ground, and carried a couple of stools up there. Silver didn't know when, or who, or why, nor did he care. The mountains up and down both sides of Death Valley were filled with strange little structures and nooks that men had built or dug or blown. The heat made men do weird things. Some men. It didn't make Silver do much.

He wasn't much for doing things. He liked to sit.

After a while, Eleanor came hobbling down the canyon. Even walking slowly and crippled as she did, there was always a happy dance to her step. He couldn't help but smile. She was a lovely little girl, he guessed.

Her face was injured, he noticed, then immediately forgot without wondering why. He wasn't one to trouble himself with others' problems.

She didn't spot him, even though he wasn't more than twenty yards above her. People didn't notice even a big man when he sat still. Animals didn't notice you neither when you didn't move. A jackass rabbit would hop right up, sniffing away, and get the surprise of its life when your shotgun blasted its head clean off. One time he'd shot one and the headless body had sat there for a good while, squirting ever smaller squirts of blood up into the air.

Silver had laughed for ten minutes at the silly rabbit.

Of course, a jackass rabbit was rotten eating, along with everything else in this cursed land. A sailor had once told him that if you looked through a glass, you'd see a world of colour and wonders under the drab, grey sea. Desert was the same. Nothing that was any good to anyone on the surface. But if you could put your head under the ground and look about, you'd see gold, silver, and diamonds, and all those other good things that could be dug up to give a man the life he deserved.

Eleanor stopped and squatted to peer at something. Lizard, probably. She was always looking at lizards and other ugly critters. Silver didn't care two shakes of salt for animals. The only animals worth any attention were the ones you could eat, or the ones that could eat you.

In the dry gully below, Eleanor peered into an adit. She looked about herself, checking there was nobody around. She looked right at Silver and didn't see him. He smiled again.

The girl took a candle and something else from her pack - locofoco matches, probably - and headed into the tunnel. *What was she doing in the blocked adit?* he wondered. He'd follow her in a while and find out. Maybe she'd found something he'd want.

He could kill her, he mused. Increase his split of The Prize all the more. There were so few of them now that two camp servants were a luxury. Perhaps, if she stayed in that tunnel a while he'd follow her and make sure she never left. He didn't really want to. It was hot and he was tired and killing even a child was an effort. Then again, when he thought of how much money he'd make by claiming his share of her share …

Was it time yet to reveal The Prize, he wondered? He knew where it was of course. He closed his eyes and thought back to the morning that had changed everything.

Silver was in the mine office, fixing the paperwork. It was tedious, and he was looking for an excuse to give up on it. So when it darkened suddenly, he hauled himself up and trudged outside to see what was afoot.

As fresh a breeze as he'd known in Death Valley was blowing down Fabulous Canyon. Black clouds were swirling like a mustering army of the damned over the mountain that towered above the mine. It was already raining up there.

It was more serious than a spring shower. This was flash flood weather.

He headed over the nearest tunnel to raise the alarm and get everybody above ground. He didn't want to lose any men. Finding new workers was weary business. He opened his mouth to holler but closed it without shouting when he heard someone running towards him. He turned, hand on his gun.

It was Swift. He chuckled. The ironically named Swift was not the running type. He was sweaty, red, and panting like a fat man arriving at a first-come-first-served pie giveaway.

"Silver!" he managed. His far-apart and frog-like eyes were bulging, he was so wet with sweat it looked like he'd spent the morning underwater, but he was smiling. "We found the mother-lode!" Swift was foreign, from somewhere in Europe. Silver liked neither the man nor his accent and tried to avoid talking to him. But this sounded interesting.

He looked about. Nobody else in sight. The fifty or so other miners were underground. He lowered his voice all the same. "What do you mean?"

"The mother-lode is what they call a large strike of gold," said the European, as if talking to someone who'd never been near a mine. He'd been a teacher or something back in hurdy-gurdy land and thought he was better than all of them. Silver had been a whisker away from shooting the know-it-all varmint pretty much every time he'd ever had to speak to him.

"I understand the word." Silver's teeth were tight. "I am asking for more information." He was straining to remain patient, but his hand drifted all on its own towards his pistol. It was amazing that this man had survived so long in the West, where a man might shoot you in the gut for looking at him funny.

"Yes, that's clear." Swift gave a dismissive little shake of his head, as if Silver had just wasted his time explaining. "I was blasting out a passage with Bynum - Andy Bynum." Silver didn't know the name. He only remembered Swift's because the man was such an asshat. "And we uncovered a seam of ore laden so much with gold that it's not a mile off pure. Millions of bucks worth I tell you, Silver. Millions."

Swift leant back, grinning like a man who's slept with your wife and knows you can't do anything about it.

"Millions?" Pure gold seams were about as common as fire-breathing lizards.

"I know rock, Silver. There are tests you can do," Swift explained, as if Silver had never seen a rock in his life. "The edge we've uncovered is more than a million dollars' worth. But the seam goes further. Much further. There are ways of judging"

"I know how to reckon a seam!" Silver snapped. This man was more annoying than gout.

"Sure," Swift smiled, as if humouring a child. "So I think this seam is bigger than the Nipton lode and that was-"

"Twenty-seven million," Silver interrupted.

"Thirty-two, including the secondary seam found a month after the first."

Silver ground his teeth. "Who else knows about it apart from Bynum?"

"Me."

Silver's hand went to his gun. He couldn't help it. Swift didn't seem to notice.

"Who else was in the tunnel, other than you and Bynum?" he asked.

"Only Bynum and I are in that tunnel today."

"Should be other men down there. Rule is you stay shouting distance of at least one other group. Break the rules, lose pay. Them's the rules."

Swift looked pained. "Bynum and I are ... friends. We like being not near the others. But I tell you this with no worries because no person will worry about a poxy fine when the bonus from this strike is divvied."

"All right, fine. Show me the lode." No matter the size of the lode, Silver resolved, Swift wouldn't see a penny's bonus from it, either by a creative working of the books or something a little more fatal.

"You must call up more men," Swift commanded. "The more that we have-"

"I understand mining, Swift. I want to take a look first, see what we need."

"There is no need for you to look, I have told you."

"Take me to it."

Swift rolled his eyes, shook his head, sighed, then said "fine, follow me."

Swift headed off. Silver glanced upwards. It was even darker at the top of the mountain. A flood was more than likely, but he had some time. He wondered about getting the men out before he went to look at the lode. It would be harder to keep Swift's find quiet if everyone was teeming about topside. The mine probably wouldn't flood. Sometimes the blackest clouds didn't produce much rain, he told himself.

As he followed Swift down-canyon, a wind swept over them like a damp, lacey curtain. He looked up again. It had only been moments, but the sky was darker still. An idiot could see that an almighty storm was about to break, and underground was the last place that anyone should be, but Swift was still heading for Gila Canyon, wholly oblivious to the danger from above.

Oh yeah, the man was a genius.

Silver followed Swift into an adit and along a candle-lit passage. A man was waiting a couple of hundred paces into the mountain – the other guy, presumably. Silver had already forgotten his name. Next to the other guy was a seam of ore more laden with gold than Silver had believed possible.

He had never seen anything so beautiful. "Are you sure it's gold?" he asked, stepping back a couple of paces. Both men went to poke at the seam, talking over each other to proclaim the quality of the strike.

Silver unclipped his holster.

He shot Swift in the back. The other guy turned and took a bullet in the chest.

Silver jogged back along the tunnel - first time he'd run in a good long while - and out.

Up above, the mountain was a holy hell of swirling purple and black clouds, lightning flashing but, strangely enough, no boom of thunder. Nothing to alert the miners.

A drop of rain big as a carpenter bee struck his forehead.

The narrow gulches that ran down the mountainside to the salt pans below were testament to ferocious flash floods. He'd seen mud six yards up the slick rock sides of slot canyons. Dry gullies became raging torrents in a matter of moments. Tunnels under the ground would fill just as quickly.

There would be no escape for anybody caught underground by the coming flood.

He had to get the men topside.

He headed to the nearest adit and gripped the leather cord dangling from the alarm bell.

And then let go of it.

He stood, heavy raindrops whacking into the ground all around him and onto his hat.

If this lode was half the size of the Nipton strike, shared between fifty, it was a lot. Enough to live well for a good few years. But it wasn't live-like-a-king-forever money, not shared between fifty.

Kept to one man or shared by just a few, then maybe it was. Maybe it was own-your-own-ship money. Maybe it was it was own-a-team-of-young-men-to-do-your-every-bidding money.

Rain was drumming on his hat now.

It was a big decision.

Before today, he'd killed three men, all in self-defence. Self-defence was what he was calling it, anyway.

But Swift and the other guy hadn't been self-defence. He'd done it without thinking. It had been instinct. And where did instinct come from? Surely it must come from his maker?

God had made him kill Swift and his friend.

And what was instinct – or God - telling him now?

Silver strode back up the canyon, pondering God's mysterious ways.

Rain bucketed down. The path up to the mine buildings was a stream. Silver had never known a deluge like it. He stumbled the last few yards into the shelter of a veranda, pulled his sodden hat from his wet head and stood panting.

The mine buildings were perched on a ridge between two canyons, safe from the flashiest of floods. Rain hammered down on the roof and around, but there was a deeper, louder rumble. Already, just minutes after the rainstorm had struck the camp, he could hear flash floods racing down the mountainside like waterfalls.

He went into the office to get his rifle. Some of the miners might escape and head for the safety of the buildings. Silver would make sure that they didn't escape God's plan.

Silver shook himself back into the present. Had he really killed fifty men to keep them off The Prize? No, that had been God's work. Who was he to question the plans of the Almighty?

He looked up the high, dry mountain, then back to the blocked adit that Eleanor had headed along. What was so interesting down there? He heaved himself off his stool. Would God want the girl dead? He'd have to wait and see.

*

I hadn't got a proper look at Masterton's corpse with Crane there. Nothing wrong with looking at dead bodies, of course. It's important to take an interest in the world. But not everybody gets that. So I went back on my own to have a proper inspection.

I lit a couple more candles and placed them around the horrible man's corpse, then squatted a pace back. He was sitting against the wall, jaw hanging, face kind of collapsed, a great stain on his chest.

Dead. All the same bits as before - same teeth and hair and heart and skin - all not working now because someone had opened up his throat. Weird how easy it is, I mused, there in the dark tunnel, to take away someone's most precious gift, and how impossible it is to give it back.

I hadn't liked him a whole lot in life; his darting tongue, his slimy gaze and his way of standing so close to you that the air felt like it was made of snot. But now … Now he was only a thing, less important and less dangerous and less alive than a cactus. Just a pile of clothes with meat in it.

I hopped in closer and poked a finger into his cheek. It was like cold putty. I poked his open eye. It felt like putty with a dried skin over it.

I picked up a candle so I could see right into that eye. Was he looking out at me from Heaven? Or Hell, more likely? So, if he was in Hell, what was happening to him right at that moment? Was there a demon poking his ass with a red-hot fork?

Footsteps made me turn.

There was no mistaking the silhouette. Silver was waddling along the tunnel, taking up pretty much the whole of it. There was no way past him, and no way he hadn't seen me squatting there with five candles on the burn.

"Hello!" I said.

"Hello, Eleanor." He took off his hat, scratched his head, and looked at Masterton. "Who killed him?"

"I don't know," I said. "Accident, maybe?"

Silver bent over to take a better look. I made to bolt, but he took my forearm in a pudgy-fingered but unshakeable grip. He straightened, letting go of my arm but blocking my escape. "He slit his own throat by accident?"

"Maybe." I couldn't help but laugh at the idea.

Silver looked appalled. A lot of adults are not comfortable when you laugh next to dead people.

"It's a good place to get away with a murder. If I hadn't seen you go in here he might never have been found."

"I guess."

"But you knew he was here."

I didn't know what to say. I couldn't deny it.

"So, you know who killed him."

"I followed a fox in here."

"Tell me or you'll stay in here with him."

"Do you mean you'll kill me?"

He nodded. Silver was not a complicated man. But he was a big one and a strong one. I was in a right fix. I didn't want to get Crane in trouble.

"It was Monk." I tried.

"When did he do it?"

"Yesterday morning."

"I was with Monk all yesterday morning. So it must have been Crane."

"I meant yesterday afternoon."

Silver smiled. He was stupid, but he wasn't that stupid. He turned on his heel and headed out of tunnel.

I looked at Masterton. He stared glassily at something behind my head - a flying demon come to cut him to shreds then glue him back together and do it again, maybe.

"Now look what you've done," I told the dead man. "You no good, damn, dirty, greasy varmint!" I hoiked up spit into my mouth, then decided better of it. It was one thing to bad-mouth the dead, but even Masterton didn't deserve to be spit on. Or maybe he did, but I reckoned God was probably a bit to pernickety to approve.

Silver emerged. The heat thickened the air. It was hard to breathe and hard to move. That made it harder to think. So, Crane was the killer. Silver sniffed. He wasn't surprised. Crane might try to paint himself as good and decent, but he wasn't. Nobody was. There were two types of people. People who looked out for number one, and people who pretended they weren't looking out for number one.

Crane wanted The Prize for himself. So, Silver would have to kill

137

Crane. A pain in the ass, but it would have to be done.

He'd have to get the gold with only Monk's help. He nearly chuckled. He'd headed back to town because he needed help to get The Prize from under the ground, separate it from the quartz, then take it to the bank in town. Denny, Indian Moses, Happy Days Frida, and Masterton were dead, and Crane was about to be. So, he had only Monk for help, plus an almost useless girl and a wholly useless woman. That wasn't much better than doing it on his own. So going to the town to get help had been a waste of time.

You live and learn, he thought. Only one person you can trust and that's the one looking back at you from the mirror.

He made his way slowly but confidently down the baking canyon. Years of traversing the vertiginous terrain of the valley had given him some of the grace, if none of the pace, of a Bighorn.

He'd find Monk where he'd left him in a lower adit and take him to start on The Prize. It would probably have made more sense to kill Crane first, but Crane was in a tunnel further up the mountain and Silver didn't want to walk uphill in the heat unless he absolutely had to.

Besides, it might not be so easy to kill Crane. He was tough. Silver was strong and he was big, but there was no point kidding himself that he wasn't a whole lot older and fatter than he'd once been. His reactions weren't what they were, and his aim had never been good, particularly under pressure. If he drew on Crane, he'd probably end up shot himself.

No, he wasn't going to take Crane. He'd get Monk to do it.

The New Town

Julian didn't spot that Swift, the annoying miner killed by Silver, was based on him. Ironically perhaps, know-it-alls never know that they're know-it-alls.

One of the biddies asked me how I knew about Swift and Bynum's discovery of The Prize. I told her I was omniscient and left her standing there with a limp cucumber sandwich in her hand, opening and closing her mouth.

I am getting a bit too mean these days. It's the writing. I hate people telling me I've got things wrong, or questioning anything at all in fact. Maybe I should stop reading it to them. Maybe I could publish it anonymously.

And - the cucumber sandwiches in this joint sum up British cuisine. Done well, a cucumber sandwich is surprisingly edible. But cucumber sandwiches are only ever done well by people making them for themselves. Cafés, restaurants or old people's homes don't seem to every try to make them tasty. Worst of all, they make them too early, so the bread goes soggy.

Over in the US, the general attitude of a restaurant or caterer seems to be, "We genuinely hope you enjoy this. We like it ourselves and we've put a good deal of time into perfecting it." If your average US diner made a cucumber sandwich, you can bet they'd try and make it the best goddam cucumber sandwich this side of the old Mississippi.

The British catering philosophy is "This is the least possible effort we thought we could get away with. You want something better, make it yourself."

Mr Hillier-Edwards is improving, they say, now sitting up in bed. But that is, you guessed it, what they said about the last one who didn't come back.

However, there's no point thinking the worst. I'm going to beaver away so that there's plenty for him to read, trying to distract myself from thinking about Mr Hillier-Edwards lying in hospital and possibly ceasing to be. He may be dead as I write this. I don't know why it's upset me. I guess I must quite like the old geezer. And, if I'm honest, it reminds me that I'm going to die soon. I'm not ready. I'm not scared. I'm annoyed about missing things. I want to see what happens and I don't want to stop being me.

Doreen knocked on my door and interrupted my distraction writing to tell me that I was missing breakfast. I told her I wasn't missing anything. She told me I had to come. I asked her to find the rule book and bring it back to me open at the page which says I have to go to breakfast. She tutted, went away and didn't come back. It is a long time since I gave a fig about tuts.

Delores walked the long, dusty trail uncomplainingly with James Willow perched on her back.

The Englishman had not ridden for a long time. His thighs chafed like wildfire and muscles ached from neck to toes. His lower back, which had troubled him before, had been fine until his legs had started burning, but now it was all bent up from trying to keep his thighs from rubbing. He would have complained, but the horse was the only living creature in earshot, and he felt bad bemoaning his own situation to a companion who was, in every sense, doing all the heavy lifting.

Indeed, he could have dismounted and walked, but he was battered and bruised from his beating, and being uncomfortable didn't seem as bad as trudging through the dust.

The horse plodded though drab desert. Pert-hipped coyotes peered from stony perches, stern tortoises glared, and skinny jackass rabbits eyed them nervously from behind spindly bushes.

Most of the humans they saw were pony express riders, galloping towards them in furious determination, pounding by with no more acknowledgement than one might give a cactus, then thundering off out of sight and sound. Even their mounts didn't deem Willow and Delores worth a glance. They zipped past with their long faces set in expressions of ferocious equine self-importance.

In his coach, the Clemenses had told him about the pony express. They'd mocked the riders' pomposity and heroic reputation of course, but at the same time they'd seemed impressed by the riders themselves, and by the marvel of carrying information so quickly over so many miles.

The chief concern, they'd told Willow, was weight. The riders were selected for their slightness, then forced to eat meagre rations and drink just enough to survive. The carried missives were written on paper so thin that it almost didn't exist. The express riders weren't allowed a gun because guns were heavy. They were commanded to ride right on through any trouble. One had apparently ridden in between the opposing factions of a gunfight a few weeks before, because going around them would have added to his journey. He'd come through unscathed. If a pony express man was shot, however, his orders were to ride on without complaint.

Willow didn't take to the pony express. They took themselves far too seriously. Would it really have slowed them down to respond to his cheery halloos with a tipped hat or a nod? However, he was grateful for their regular watering stations, where both he and Delores drank long and joyfully, and he could purchase fodder for them both with the money from Callahan the Mormon.

The afternoon after leaving the Mormons, Englishman and horse approached a heavy-wheeled wagon pulled by four oxen. It was laden with white stone that glinted in the bright sun. On either side walked a man, each with a hand resting on the cart. Both wore dusty dusters and dusty wide-brimmed hats.

Shaken mentally as well as physically by Slade's beating, Willow felt a little sick at the sight of the broad-shouldered men. But there was only one road, they were going a great deal slower than Delores, so there was no choice but to catch up and overtake.

Over the rumbling of the wagon, the men didn't hear Delores's hooves until they were almost upon them. When they did, both men jumped round at the same time. Willow tensed, expecting drawn pistols and a hail of hot lead.

"Halloo!" shouted the chap on the left, smiling with his

arms outstretched.

The other swept his hat from his head and bowed deeply.

The oxen plodded on, but it didn't seem to bother the men.

"Good afternoon," said Willow.

"Isn't it?" said the bower. He had the cheeks and grin of a well-fed baby. "Isn't it just the finest dang afternoon there ever was?"

"Sure is, pard'!" said his friend.

"What's that in your wagon?" asked Willow.

"That, sir," said Baby Face, "is the finest dang ore that you'll find this side of Frisco."

"There's enough gold in that there ore," added the other, "to make a golden hat for every lady in this beautiful land."

"And have enough left to sole their boots with gold!" claimed the other.

"And make them a gold road to walk along from Denver to Detroit!"

They smiled up at him, clearly expecting a response.

"Aha!" Willow replied. "Good stuff!"

"Goddam amazing stuff!" said the smiler. Then, suddenly not smiling, he added, "'Pologies for swearing, sir," he muttered, "I'm excited is all."

"Please, don't trouble yourself," said Willow, "it couldn't matter less."

The smiler's beam returned. "You a goddam gent, sir!" He slapped his leg, releasing a cloud of dust from his filthy trousers. "And there I go again! I'm so sorry, but I am plain gold crazy."

When Willow had seen the size of them, their beards and their skin tanned like saddle leather, he'd thought they must be rough, grizzled men, hard as the rock they dug. Now he'd looked in their eyes, he saw that they were little more than children in men's bodies, out on a great adventure and about as happy as anyone he'd ever met.

Their joy was contagious. He left them reluctantly, but riding straighter in the saddle, despite his thigh burn. Delores seemed to share his newfound confidence and walked with a stronger, faster gait.

A while later, he began to pass the strangest trees on either side of the road. They were short and thick-limbed, their trunks and branches were furry, and each branch was crowned with a ball of green spikes. Not one of these odd trees was the same as the next. Here was one with only two branches, raised like the spiky, green-mittened hands of a surrendering man. Over there was one with maybe fifty branches, its spiky leaves like fifty green fireworks exploding together. It was a riot of arboreal oddness. They were more extraordinary and interesting than any English trees. Why had he never heard of them?

He and Delores caught up with more ore carts accompanied by two or more men, and lone miners with stuffed backpacks, all headed the same way along the increasingly worn road. Some of the carts were drawn by oxen, some by mules, but God might have made the walking miners from the same mould on the same day. They were all bearded and tanned, few older than thirty, and almost all possessed with the same fiery joy that had so delighted Willow in the first two. Willow wondered if there were any happier group of people in all of the world.

Most were of European origin, but there were a good number of Chinamen, Africans, Mexicans, and Indians too. It took Willow a while to notice their ethnic differences, perhaps because in every other way they were so similar. Here were a band of brothers, united in the joy of adventure and the promise of fabulous wealth. It lifted Willow no end to pass among these wonderfully cheery men.

The image of Elizabeth's shrewish, hate-filled face poked from of the shadows of his memory every now and then, but the next set of broad grins from happy miners dissolved his misery back into the mist.

The road was busier and busier. The nearer trees were coated with dust. The excited men crowed about the value of claims, hauls and strikes, and teased each other good-naturedly. They greeted Willow heartily. Finding he had no mining chat, they moved on. They weren't being rude. The Englishman simply wasn't part of their thrilling world.

As he rode on, Willow became convinced he could feel the ground vibrating. Soon he could hear a pounding and rumbling from the far side of the mountains. Was it an earthquake?

"You worried about the thunder, sir?" asked a nearby miner. The deeply tanned man had broad cheeks and the sing-song voice of a Mexican. His enormous eyes and thick eyebrows made him look more like a beautiful woman than a male miner, despite the dusty kit and beard.

"No, not worried. Just wondering what that noise might be?" He hoped the disconcertingly good-looking Mexican could hear it too.

"It's the mills, sir. Can you hear those louder beats? Boom! Boom! Boom!"

"I can."

"Those are stamp mills. Goddam weights of metal lifting up," the little miner raised his short arms, "and *smashing* down onto the ore." He slammed his hands down onto imaginary rock. "And hear you the rolling thunder?"

"I do."

"Ball mills. Also for the smashing of the ore. These are goddam balls of metal, in a goddam spinning metal drum." The Mexican whirled his stubby arms. "Ore goes in, balls smash! Everything you can hear is collaborating in the extraction of the good, good gold. If you are interested in mining, sir, I have claims for many more feet of ore than I could myself ever mine. I will sell some to you for a great deal less than they are worth and you will never work again!"

The Englishman assured him that he quite enough feet of claim already, thank you, and rode on. He thought about the Mexican's offer. The prospect of never working again was an appealing one. The only proper jobs he'd ever had, bathroom attendant and glass scrubber, had not filled him with joy. But he had few dollars and no idea what a foot of ore was.

The next miners offered him more feet of ore, and he nearly said yes. They were very convincing. After that, just about everybody he passed tried to sell him feet of ore. *If everybody is trying to sell me feet of ore,* thought Willow after a while, *then it's just possible that these feet aren't that valuable after all!*

Pleased by his business acumen, he rode on with a self-congratulatory smile, nodding hello to miners and rejecting offers of ore with knowing good cheer. He realised that it was the first instance in a very long while that he'd smiled for more than a passing moment.

He liked this hot land of happy miners. When he'd claimed his bounty, he resolved to tarry a while and see what he could find.

The broad valley passed between two high bluffs then there, to the north, was the town. It was as large as an English county town, even though it couldn't have been more than a few years old. Brick buildings in the centre gave way to wooden structures sprawling across the land to the edge of a bowl of hills. The hills themselves were pocked with rectangular, dark doorways, each bibbed by a fan of debris, some with trellis-mounted rail lines leading from the darkness.

The miners and their carts and their backpacks continued to the west, to the noisy mills. Other men streamed from the mills, heading northwards to the town. Willow joined the latter throng, riding past corrals of cattle and horses, outlying sheds that looked like they'd been knocked together in a matter of minutes, and a landscape strewn with building debris and discarded tins shining in the bright sun.

As he neared the town, the clamour of hallooing miners almost blocked out the hellish crashing of the mills. The smell of hot men, rotting food, and dung was eye-watering. Other than the dazzling tins, everything - men, horses, buildings, carts, and carriages - was brown.

"Delores," Willow said to his horse, "it is not just location that will prevent this settlement from wresting North Oxfordshire's Best Kept Village Award from Fenny Compton this year."

"You!" someone yelled above the clamour.

Willow looked about himself.

"Yeah you! The stiff on the horse!" The shouter was the oldest person Willow had seen all day by some margin, and also the first woman. She must have been sixty-five, but she strode towards him with the strength of the rural dweller. "Stable your horse with me. I'm not the cheapest, but I won't rob you. Some of the rest will, some of 'em won't. Take your chances elsewhere if you like."

Willow looked up the road into town, then back to the woman. "I thought I'd just take her along with me and-"

"No horses in town. It's too busy. Imagine if all of these was riding." She gestured at the teeming throng. She had a point.

He left Delores and a good bit of the Mormon's money with the stablewoman, and headed into town.

The broad road became a proper high street and wooden sheds gave way to flat-fronted, brick-built edifices. The first store he passed was a delicious-smelling German Konditorei with boards outside proclaiming "Apfelkuchen" and "Bienenstich." The aroma was a welcome break from the standard stink of a Western town.

There were candle shops, banks, hotels, a jeweller, a theatre, a church, fire companies, a hurdy-gurdy house and more. Willow's smile widened. What a town! All sprouted up in a just a couple of years from the rich manure of the gold hunting diaspora. There were new mining towns in England, but these American versions seemed so much brighter, vibrant, and less depressing. Perhaps it was because the men here were independent workers who really thought they were going make a fortune, rather than labourers slaving all hours in hellish conditions for subsistence wages so that the mine's owner's daughter might buy another horse.

The crowd was mostly miners, but there was also a scattering of well-to-do looking women in dresses. There were men in suits, presumably bankers, accountants, and other money men making fortunes from the fortune seekers. There were butchers, bakers and undertakers. Willow recognised a pony express rider who had passed him heading the other way the day before, and wondered how he'd got there.

In front of a three-story bank were a string quartet, a dozen dancing children and half a dozen drunken miners stamping out a hornpipe. A giant with a magnificent moustache and pistol grips like bulls' horns came strolling along like a lord inspecting his estates. The crowd cleared like a bow-wave before him.

"Who was that?" Willow asked a passing miner, once the moustachioed swaggerer was well out of earshot.

"Dead-Eye McClintock. He's killed thirty men," the miner nodded with wide-eyed reverence, as if Dead-Eye had healed thirty blind people, then hurried by.

Willow walked on, stopping outside a building that confused him. The saloon, Pandora's Chest, was opulently elegant or eye-poppingly vulgar, and he couldn't decide which. There was more bright paint and general shine than one would find in the whole of Buckinghamshire, but the building had a welcoming appeal. He'd put a foot on the first step when shouts rang out, followed by screams, the sound of galloping hooves and a long, loud "*Yippee!*"

Two riders came careering down the broad street. The throng disintegrated into individuals running and diving for verandas. "Yippee!" rang out again. It was the lead rider - a woman's voice, if Willow wasn't mistaken! Dust from pounding hooves clouded over the scrambling pedestrians, adding dirt to endangerment.

People scattered all around, but Willow stood his ground. He didn't know why. Was he subconsciously seeking suicide?

It seemed the lead rider must hit him, but hooves dug in and the beast wheeled round.

The rider *was* a woman. She steered her mount to the steps of Pandora's Chest. She wore blue, tough-looking trousers, a black shirt, and a black hat. Willow had never seen a woman in trousers before, nor, for that matter, had he seen a pair of trousers quite like these. You could see the shape of her legs as clearly as if she'd been naked.

Willow realised his mouth had dropped open as he stared at the rider. Not the best of looks. He closed his mouth and raised his eyes, flushing.

The extraordinary woman looked straight back at him with shining blue eyes and half a full-lipped smile for just a moment, then turned to the other rider.

"That's one hundred dollars, Bub!" she shouted, "One hundred dollars!"

To Willow's surprise, since horses weren't allowed in this part of town and everyone had been endangered by the irresponsible race, the dispersed crowd reassembled to cheer and congratulate her.

She swung a long leg up and over the saddle and dismounted. She headed straight for Willow, leading her horse by the reins, blue-clad hips swinging.

He blinked.

She swept her hat from her head. For some reason, he'd expected a cascade of wonderfully clean and brushed blonde hair. Her hair was blonde, but the strands that weren't sweatily plastered to her forehead stuck out in all sorts of angles, like straw from a hastily fabricated scarecrow. She was still lovely though - tanned, firm skin and a white-toothed smile that shone with the joy of being one of God's healthiest creations.

Willow gulped, nodding like an idiot as she approached, then nearly passed out when she handed him the reins of her horse without looking at him. He took them without thinking. She strode past. The crowd followed her, chatting and calling.

"Did you ever see such a thing!" exclaimed a breathless and smartly-dressed woman.

"Who could ever tame her?" another asked.

"She's not for taming!" a miner excitedly declared. "A man doesn't take her. She takes him!"

Willow held the horse until as stampede into the Pandora's Chest saloon, passed around him, slowed to a trickle then petered out, leaving him alone.

Cheers and laughs rang out from the building, but the street was quiet. He looked at the horse and the horse looked at him with a *well, what?* expression.

There was a hitching rail. Willow tied the horse and took a step towards the saloon. He very much wanted to talk to the striking racer. Informing her that he'd secured her horse was surely a strong conversation starter.

He put a foot on the saloon's step for the second time and paused.

It would be busy in there. No doubt all those sycophantic worshippers who'd swarmed after her would make it impossible to gain an audience. It would make much more sense to leave her to her admirers for now and come back later.

He lifted his foot from the step, bade the horse farewell, and headed on through the town.

ACT TWO, CHAPTER FOUR

Kindness of Strangers

Mr Hillier-Edwards arrived back from the hospital a little before lunchtime yesterday. He's not up to the stairs yet, so he couldn't come to me, but Doreen told me I was the first person he asked to see after his daughter left. She showed me to his new ground floor digs.

He didn't look tip-top, but much better than I'd expected. He assured me that he was well enough to attend my evening reading, and asked whether it was possible to spend the afternoon catching up on the chapters that he'd missed.

"Shall I read them to you?" I asked. I was immediately embarrassed by my offer.

"Oh no, no, no, that's far too much fuss. I'm really very capable of reading to myself. Please spend the time writing more of your wonderful story. If you'd like, of course. It's not for me to order you about ..." He petered out, his cheeks a little pinker than before.

"Shall I fetch your manuscript?" asked Doreen in her matter-of-fact way. I must confess, I hadn't realised she was still standing there.

Mr Hillier-Edwards waited until Doreen was out of earshot and said, "I think that heart attack was meant to bump me off. It certainly felt like it was trying to." He chuckled, as if he was talking about something amusing that a child had said, rather than an agonising and surely terrifying attack. "But I said no thanks, not yet! I need to stay on this physical plane until I've heard the end of Mrs Salmon's wonderful story."

I told him that he had a while to wait, as this was the first book about my Western adventures in a series of ten.

"I'll do my best to stick around."

We both laughed.

"In case I don't though, would you please be able to tell me how Crazy Horse had his revenge for the massacre at Sand Creek? It doesn't sound like the others are interested since they haven't brought it up and …"

"I could tell you now, if you like. I'll probably be done by the time Doreen's back. I don't remember enough to make it a long story."

"That would be marvellous, thank you."

Mr Hillier-Edwards relaxed into his pillows a little and closed his eyes.

"Well, like I said, it's all complicated. Presenting it neatly as Crazy Horse's revenge is a bit pat and probably wrong. But here's the story.

"The massacre and mutilation of women and children at Sand Creek was portrayed to settlers and people back east as a great victory over the savage Indian, but the western tribes knew what had happened. It united many as never before, notably under an Oglala Sioux called Red Cloud. One of his lieutenants was a strange and brilliant young Oglala called Crazy Horse. I could write a book about him. Maybe I will one day."

I meant that. My one regret from all this writing is that I didn't start it earlier. Now it's something of a race against the clock.

"Two years after Sand Creek, in 1866, a young buck called Captain William Fetterman rode into the west. He was billeted at Fort Kearney, in the heartland of what the Sioux considered to be their territory. It hadn't been their territory long, the Sioux were invaders too, but that's a whole other story – like I said, it's complicated.

"To cut the complication short – Fort Kearny was under a sort of arms-length siege by the newly united Sioux, Northern Cheyenne and Arapaho. It was very dangerous to leave the fort. This didn't worry Fetterman, who said that he could whip the whole of the Sioux nation with eighty cavalrymen.

"The commander of Fort Kearny, whose name escapes me, was wary of Fetterman's arrogance. He ordered the captain to never leave sight of the fort, and particularly to never pass over a rise to the north called Lodge Trail Ridge. Carrington – that was the commander's name. Colonel Carrington. He

received much of the blame for what happened, but he shouldn't have done.

"One day, some soldiers were attacked by the Sioux. Fetterman was sent out with - by some amazing coincidence - and perhaps proof that, if there is a God, He has a sense of humour and He's not a very nice dude – eighty cavalrymen. You remember what Fetterman had said about eighty cavalrymen?"

"That he could whip the whole Sioux nation with that number."

"Correct, well listened Mr Hillier-Edwards."

"Thank you, Mrs Salmon."

"The Indians often tried a bait and run tactic in battle. A small number would flee, tempting the pursuers into an ambush. It rarely worked, because it was about the first thing they warned you about when you crossed the Mississippi. But it worked on Fetterman.

"He ordered his eighty to pursue the cheeky, no good, weak and easily whippable Indians over Lodge Trail Ridge. On the other side were a couple of thousand warriors from all seven tribes of the Sioux, plus some Northern Cheyenne and Arapahos, led by young Crazy Horse. It was his plan, and it worked.

"The soldiers were surrounded, killed, then scalped and mutilated. Eighty-one soldiers were slaughtered, with about ten Indians killed."

"I thought there were eighty?" asked Mr Hillier-Edwards.

"Eighty-one including Fetterman."

"Of course."

"As usual, it was something of a pyrrhic victory for the Indians, because it gave the army further motive and excuse to persecute them. Just over a decade after the Fetterman Massacre, Crazy Horse was dead and the Sioux were tamed."

"It's all so very sad."

"It sure was."

"There were men like Fetterman in the War. Thank God none of the Fettermans I knew had any power, and we knew not to promote them. By and large, people underestimating Jerry or the Jap only got themselves killed."

There was a knock on the door. Doreen was back with my manuscript.

I left Mr Hiller-Edwards reading, and headed up to continue with the story of Willow in town, in which we'll meet my mother.

James Willow the bounty hunter walked between a hotch-potch of elegant and sordid buildings. Smart looking shops stood imperiously next to tent saloons and cribs - tiny, wooden, one-person houses that contained a sleeping mat and not much else.

Between one of the tent saloons and the street was a swimming hole full of bearded men. Half were standing around the side, facing inwards, with their elbows on the pool edge, watching, whistling and cheering, as the other half wrestled.

"Two-dollar boom boom?" asked a voice in Willow's ear, startling him.

A Chinese lady, handsome, and perhaps a little older than Willow, had materialized behind him. Willow would by no means call himself a man of the world, but he could guess the meaning of *two-dollar boom boom*.

He felt hot and not a little faint. "A kind offer, but thank you, no," he managed.

"Why you in Tenderloin?" she asked, more interested than challenging.

"Tender loin?"

"Tenderloin. Here. Money boon boom place. Start three streets back. Other side that street, no Tenderloin."

Willow followed her pointing finger. Now that he was looking for it, it was about three streets back where the buildings changed from brick to tent and wood.

"Is it really two dollars?" he heard himself asking. He wasn't sure why. He'd never slept with a whore. Or anyone, for that matter. He imagined looking into a mirror and saying "I am not a virgin." It was tempting.

"Two dollar basic. Tip extra." She raised her eyebrows. "Pay more if you like to do more." She treated him to a smile that would have had an English vicar climbing a tree. Willow felt a stirring, which he strove to ignore.

"You might be able to help me." He reached into his satchel for his wanted poster and showed her the picture of his quarry.

She gave it a long look, lips pursed, then nodded and looked up at him. "Two dollar."

"Surely a little information is worth less than your virtue?"

She laughed so long she had to wipe her eyes, which answered the question. When she recovered composure enough to speak, she repeated herself. "Two dollar."

He gave her two dollars.

"Never seen her," she said.

Willow blinked.

"What? So why did you ask for ..."

"You pay to ask question. I answer. You got what you pay for."

Willow looked at her. She held his gaze.

"Well, I'm not sure that this is totally fair," he managed. "You certainly implied that you had information and where I come from-"

She slapped his chest to interrupt him. "I'm joking, fool! I see everything here. She come. Now she gone."

"Where?"

"Don't know."

He shook his head again. Two dollars was a lot.

"But I know someone who does know."

"Who?"

"Two dollar."

Willow sighed and reached into his satchel again.

She slapped his hand. "Stop, fool! You too free with money!"

"But you asked ..."

"Haggle, fool! You should not have given me the first two dollar." She rolled her eyes.

"I see. How about one dollar?"

She looked at him as if appalled, then smiled as if she'd spotted something she liked. "Follow me."

He did.

"Do you want the dollar?" he asked but she didn't seem to hear.

She headed up the street, then through the entrance of a tent saloon. Perhaps fifty percent certain he was about to be murdered, Willow followed.

He was just in time to see his Chinese friend leaving through the back flap. He passed through, tipping his hat at the smattering of men at tables, who ignored him. The tent was thick with cloying, sugary, floral smoke that was both repellent and alluring. *Like horse piss on straw*, he found himself thinking; not the smell itself, but the aroma of horse piss on straw was something else that he found both disgusting and appealing.

Leading away from the rear of the tent saloon was a sandy alley lined with wooden and canvas cribs. The strange smell was not as thick out here, but it still filled the air. He'd only heard stories of it, but he knew what the smell must be. Opium.

The Chinese lady stopped outside the last crib on the left. While the others had doors, this crib had a portiére, if such a fancy word could be applied to the torn flap of canvas hanging across the opening.

"Lizzie!" shouted his guide.

They stood in the heat and the smell. His guide studied him, and he studied her right back. Her lips were wider and nose more prominent than he'd expected from the caricatures of Chinese people that he'd seen in newspapers. Her brow was broad, and her head seemed too large for her bird-like frame. Her dark eyes looked at him coolly with, or so it seemed to him, the paradox of a cheerful mockery of the world coupled with experiences of horrors and hardships that Willow would take a thousand years to encounter (or so he thought at the time).

Feeling about as comfortable as a long-tailed cat in a room full of rocking chairs, Willow opened his mouth to say that perhaps nobody was in, but his guide held a finger aloft to indicate that he should wait.

"Wha-at?" came finally from the flapped crib. It sounded like the crib's inhabitant had been roused from deep sleep. "You got me a john?"

"No. Not john. Man here looking for dark lady who you saw. Don't tell him you didn't."

Scuffling came from inside. A delicate hand pulled the canvas flap aside and a woolly blonde head peeked around it. It blinked at Willow, blue eyes tearing up in the sun.

"I leave you now," said the Chinese lady.

Willow reached for the dollar, but she was gone before he could find it.

"Thank you!" he called after her.

Lizzie stepped out of her crib, followed by a strong waft of perfume and, if Willow was right about that smell, opium.

He'd had something ready to say but couldn't recall what it was, because his mind was knocked asunder by her beauty. He had not expected to see anybody attractive in this town, and perhaps it was because he had seen few women in the last few weeks, but now he'd seen two and this woman took his breath away even more than the horse racer. She was pale, paler than anyone Willow had seen in a long while, but her eyes were bulging - "exophthalmic," as the phrenologists would say - and she was skinny to what must have been a dangerous degree. The way those eyes held his made him want to weep for all the delicate loveliness and sorrow in the world.

The rider's beauty was a force to be afraid of. The opium-smoking whore's beauty was a wonder to fall in love with.

The world, thought Willow, was never simple.

"Well?" she asked. Her voice was smoky and tired.

He showed her the wanted poster.

She looked at it, then back up at him. Something shifted in her expression, as if she and Willow had battled and she'd lost.

"I need money," she said.

"Do you know where the woman is?"

"I asked her to go after Eleanor. Eleanor's my daughter. She's ten. Or maybe eleven now." Lizzie's eyes filled.

"Where?"

"I had to send Eleanor away, you see. I sent her with Crane. He's the best of men, but I thought having a woman there would help. I should go to her. I've-" tears brimmed over and raced down her cheeks, "I've got myself trapped."

She stood with her eyes closed, shaking with gentle sobs. Willow looked about. Beyond the crib, in an area of debris-strewn wasteland, was a large pig chomping on a big orange and black lizard. The front half of the lizard hung out of the pig's mouth, legs waving. tongue flopping and eyes blinking as the pig munched its back legs and pelvis.

It was not all beauty in this town.

Willow waited until Lizzie stopped crying and said, "I didn't know that Loretta was ..." She looked at the wanted notice wide-eyed and shook her head as fresh tears sprang.

"Well … she is." Willow felt foolish. He had a strong urge to hug this crying beauty, to rock her and comfort her, but he was bound by years of stiff conditioning.

"I plan to bring her back," he said.

"Will you bring my daughter back, too?"

"I can try."

Lizzie's shoulders slumped even further.

"Um. I mean, yes, of course. What does she look like?"

"I'm sorry," Lizzie Salmon put a delicate hand on his arm. "Don't get her. I want her back, but she has to stay until the work is done. I will go to get her myself. I will. Soon. I just need to … I need money. Do you have money?"

"Will you tell me where they've gone?"

"Will you give me ten dollars?"

Willow gulped. He had only twenty dollars left. "I will," he said as the Chinese lady shouted *Fool!* in his mind. But he would need to toughen up an awful lot before he could haggle with a beautiful, destitute woman weeping over the daughter she missed.

"Come inside," she said, turning and stooping.

The crib was lit only by gaps in its planks, but the sheets on the mattress were clean and a happy little china doll in a blue woolen outfit looked down from a shelf. It smelled of opium, but it was a much lighter smell than the fug in the tent and mixed pleasantly with aromas of perfume and woman.

Lizzie sat on the bed and patted it for him to sit next to her.

"The woman you're looking for is at a mine called the Fabulous. It's a couple of miles up Fabulous Canyon on the eastern slope of Death Valley. You'll have to go into the main valley, then south. I'm not sure how far, perhaps a dozen miles, maybe more. Eventually you'll find a large stamp mill. There's an aerial tramway leading from the stamp mill up into Fabulous Canyon. Walk up under that. The road is broken, so you can't take a cart. But would you have a cart?" she looked at him, eyes just a little mad. "No, you don't look like the cart type."

"Right." said Willow, trying to picture the directions. "Into the valley, south to the stamp mill, then east under an aerial tramway. I'm not entirely sure what an aerial tramway is, but I'm fairly sure I'll know it when I see it. I know what a stamp mill is, but I've no idea what it looks like."

Lizzie looked at him as if he'd suddenly started talking about the likelihood of life on the planet Mars.

"I'm sure I'll work it all out," he reassured her.

Her expression settled.

"Yes, that's right. Oh! And take a lot of water into the valley - much more than you think you need. That's very important. And don't dally."

"Why not?"

"It's hot there. Too hot."

"It can't be any hotter than here."

"Oh, it is. Much hotter. People die all the time."

"From the heat?"

"No, they get kicked to death by butterflies."

"What?"

"Yes, the heat. Weren't we talking about the heat?" For a moment Willow had seen the vivacious woman encased within the opium trap, but then the cloudy shell closed up and she lowered her eyes.

"Why would anyone be mining there?" Willow asked.

"They have a reason. It's why I sent Eleanor. I hope she returns soon so I can continue her education and make her more than I've ever been," she explained, then continued in a voice so quiet that it was almost a whisper, "that's what I told myself when I sent her, but really I wanted her out of the way so I could be alone with my drug and my shame."

"It's opium that has you trapped here?" Willow asked.

"No, it's a team of magic bees." The real Lizzie was back for a moment, then she deflated. "It's expensive. I have only one way to make money. I don't want Eleanor to see. I don't make much money because I'm too skinny."

"Why don't you just stop buying opium?" Willow suggested.

She laughed through her nose. "You know, that's sound advice. Maybe I'll follow it. Tomorrow, perhaps. You should go now. Unless ..."

She slid her gaze to him, widened her eyes, and pursed her lips.

"What?" he asked.

"Are you a sporting man?"

"A sporting man?"

"Yes."

"I played some cricket at school, but I wouldn't say I was-"

"No." She put a hand on his leg. "Are you looking for business? Are you a john?" She attempted to sound and look like a sassy whore, but it was pathetic. He much preferred her insect-based humour.

She was a great deal more adorable than Willow might have imagined a whore living in a pigsty could be. To have taken her up on her offer would have been to defile her. He did want to sleep with her, but on the night of their wedding, in the highest room of a castle in the mountains with silk curtains billowing, the moon shining and possibly eagles soaring by, accompanied by the whisper of the wind and the rumble of distant thunder. Not in a shed, surrounded by rubbish, and accompanied by the slurping crunches of an enormous pig eating a terrifying lizard.

He took her bird-boned wrist between his fingers and lifted her hand away.

"Of course." Her head dropped.

"I don't think you're too skinny. I think you're beautiful. It's just I'm not - ah – a john."

"Sure," she said.

He laid fifteen dollars out on the bed and left her.

He turned in the doorway to say farewell, but she didn't look up.

James Willow headed from the Tenderloin into the centre of town. The mining metropolis swirled noisily around him. With much on his mind, he hardly noticed it. The Fabulous Mine. In a canyon off the ominously named Death Valley. He was nearing his quarry and, hopefully, the beginning of his fortune. But what would he do when he found her?

Cyril Callahan the Mormon had asked him that question, and he'd not yet addressed it. But it was vital. Seeing the female horse racer had made him worry even more. He had imagined that the wanted woman would immediately concede to natural male authority and the rule of law. In this wild West, that attitude was hopelessly naïve. It was possible that she'd fight. If she was anything like the racing woman, it was very possible, he had to admit, that she would hand his arse to him. She might shoot him before he'd even introduced himself.

There was an answer, though. He'd spotted it earlier.

He bobbed through the crowd like a rowing boat through a choppy sea. He passed a group of men fighting and hardly noticed them. He arrived at a stout brick building. The sign announced the sheriff's office.

He pushed the iron-studded wooden door. He'd expected it to be locked, but it swung open on oiled hinges.

Once his eyes adjusted, he found himself in a broad room. The far side was filled with two barred cells, both empty. Across from the cells, a man sat behind a desk, boots on the desk, white hat over his eyes, apparently asleep. He wore a white suit with gold fluting. Behind him was a huge black iron safe.

Willow walked back outside, checked that the sign really did say "Sheriff's Office" and not "O'Malley's Theatre Troop," or similar, and walked back in. It was hot as a pottery oven in there. Heavy brick and small windows hadn't been the ideal architectural decision for the climate.

He coughed.

"Yup," said the man without moving.

"I'm looking for the sheriff."

"You found 'im." His gravelly accent was familiar.

"You're English!" He wasn't English like Willow. Willow spoke the English of clipped lawns and clean, clever-looking dogs. This man's accent made Willow think of knives in foggy alleyways and badger baiting.

A finger lifted to tip the hat back, revealing a thick but trimmed black beard and dark eyes on a wide face.

"Yup," he said.

"My name's Willow."

"I'm Marshall."

"Oh, I thought you were the sheriff. I don't fully understand the diff-"

"I am the sheriff. My name's Marshall."

Willow thought for a moment. "Well, that's extraordinary. What are the odds?"

"Astronomical, I imagine," said Marshall, flatly.

"And I'm English, too!"

The sheriff sighed and held Willow's gaze longer than was comfortable. Eventually he said, "Whoopee for you."

Willow blinked. "Two fellow countrymen, miles from home. Does that not give us a bond?"

"Don't get too excited about being English round here. Go outside, throw a stone and you'll hit an Englishman. Some of them you'll want to have a bond with, some of them you wouldn't piss on if they were on fire. I don't know which you are yet, so why don't you tell me why you're here and we'll see? I should warn you now, though, it's your business I'm interested in. I don't care two rats' cocks whether you're from Bristol or Ancient Mesopotamia."

"*Two* rats' cocks?"

"What?"

"It's an interesting measure. If you don't care two rats' cocks, does that mean you do care one rat's cock? And how many rats' cocks *can* one care? If the maximum that one can care is two rats' cocks, then caring one rat's cock would mean that you are, in fact, relatively invested in the issue."

Sheriff Marshall regarded Willow flatly, as if he was waiting for a verbose and irritating child to get to its point.

"Sorry, I've spent too much time with two brothers who worry about things like that. Here's my business."

Willow slapped his wanted notice onto the table and stood back.

The sheriff swung his booted feet off the table, sat up, looked at the notice, then up at Willow. "And?"

"I know where she is. It's not far. Help me get her and I'll give you one quarter of the bounty."

Marshall chuckled.

"What's funny?"

"You are. Do you know how much *money* there is in this town? I can make double this," he tapped a big finger on the wanted poster, "before breakfast, without leaving this desk."

"But she's a criminal! You're a sheriff!"

"I am. And-" A shot rang out. From its volume, the gun had been fired not more than a dozen yards from the sheriff's office. "And there's more than enough crime in town to keep me busy. I don't need to go looking for it."

Willow stared at the sheriff. He did not look busy. It didn't look, for example, like he was planning to investigate a shooting *right outside his office.*

Marshall half-smiled. "Look, I do quite like you. You've got a kind face. You seem to have morals and that's rare round here. That's a decent piece there," he pointed at the Colt Navy revolver on Willow's hip. "Point it at this lady," he tapped the poster, "and she'll do what you tell her. Bring her back here. I'll lock her up and pay you the bounty."

Willow looked down at the gun on his hip. It frightened him a little.

"Used the gun much?" asked the sheriff.

"Not a great deal."

"Do you mean never?"

"I do."

"Where did you get it?"

"A man gave it to me."

Marshall didn't pry. "Take it to Jones the Gun, seven doors north of this place. He'll make sure it's in good working order for a fair price. He's a Welshman, but that doesn't matter. Some Welsh'll rob you, some won't."

"Thanks!"

Willow left, stood for a while working out which way was north, then headed seven doors in that direction.

Jones the Gun took the Colt Navy, emptied the bullets, spun the cylinder, flicked it back into place, pulled the trigger a few times, put the bullets back in, and handed it back, butt first.

"That's one goddern solid weapon you got there, mister." Jones might have been Welsh, but his accent was as American as they came. "Well looked after, well-oiled, and fully operational. If you come second in a gunfight, it's your fault. Good day to you, sir."

"Thank you," Willow replied. "How much ...?"

"I did nothing to it. You don't owe me nothing."

The Englishman considered correcting the double negative for a moment. Instead, he thanked the man and left.

He headed along the high street with a spring in his step. Sheriff Marshall might not have helped him, but he had been kind in a way. And the Jones the Gun could have fleeced him. Could have told him the barrel needed replacing, or that the whole gun was a write-off that wouldn't ever fire again and bought it off him for half a dollar, then sold him a broken one for five.

Willow's education might not be much use here, but there were decent people who could help him until he learned the ways of the West. Then he would help others. Buoyed by refreshed confidence in the kindness of his fellow man, he bounded up the steps into Pandora's Chest.

It was hot and crowded with people very similar to the miners he'd encountered on the road. In fact, he recognised a few of them. The drinkers were mostly Caucasian, but there were quite a few Mexicans and a smattering of Chinese and Africans. All seemed to be competing to see who could talk the loudest.

It was a backslapping, whiskey-swilling, loud-laughing, manly man's sort of place.

He turned to leave.

"Willow!" A voice rang out, unmistakably English with just that one word.

He paused.

"I'll be damned if that's not young James Willow! What the deuce are you doing here, man?"

He didn't want to turn. He knew that voice. Robert Morris. His school torment. Willow had been the smallest boy in his year. Morris had been one of the largest. Willow had been on none of the sports teams. Morris had captained most of them. Willow would have loved to say that the child had been all brawn, but Morris had trounced Willow in every exam, too. God, in his goodness, had seen fit to put Willow and Morris in the same school house, so they were together almost all the time, day and night.

Defeating Willow in every way hadn't been enough for Morris. He had beaten him regularly, often with an audience of braying boys.

He took a step towards the door. This was not school. There were no rules. He could walk out. He could leave the town that night. He didn't need to see Morris.

"Little Willow! Don't be shy! It's a joy to see you! Come and have a drink!"

Willow pictured the beginning of his final year. Willow, newly a prefect, was supervising the new boys' prep in their high-ceilinged common room, surrounded by life-sized paintings of bearded men on horses. He was telling the boys a story about an explorer's heroism, heavily implying that he himself was going to become just such a hero when he left at the end of the year. These were new boys; they didn't know that Willow was pathetic and to be persecuted. He thought he might foster a reasonable relationship with the new chaps, based on respect, patriarchal decency and tales of derring-do.

Morris marched into the prep room, all noise and bravado. Willow tried to joke with him, tried to show the younger boys that he was friends with this boy-man. Morris pulled Willow to his feet, slammed him down over the table, pulled down his trousers and underpants, put him over his lap, and slapped his bare backside until he cried. He'd left him snivelling. The little boys had laughed. Willow could not look any of the new boys in the eye from that day on and they'd mocked him openly for the rest of that hateful year.

And there was more. The private bullying. The humiliation of being used like a woman. And worst - worst of all - he had not hated being used. He'd sought it out and allowed it, nay, encouraged it.

James Willow had pushed those memories so deep into the back of his mind that they'd almost disappeared, but here they came flooding back, overwhelming him. He could feel the pain in his arse. He could feel the pleasure. The sickening guilt flooded as he started to harden.

Willow stood, breathing deeply, battling back through the memories to the present. He became aware of people in the bar staring at him. Morris was saying something else, but Willow couldn't hear.

Sheriff Marshall hadn't given two hoots when a shot had been fired in the street outside his office.

That's one goddern solid weapon you got there, mister.

Willow placed a hand on the Navy Colt revolver's grip and turned, smiling.

It was Morris and it wasn't Morris. It was his erstwhile bully's face, but surrounded by bushy hair and a beard, and transported onto a body even more massive. His chest was like a bison's, criss-crossed by what must have been the widest, most bullet-stuffed bandolier in the west. Willow might have a Navy pistol, but Morris had a couple of naval cannons strapped to his huge thighs.

The big man's smile faded when he looked down at Willow's hand on his gun.

No point waiting, thought Willow. He had endured years of persecution from this school hero, his bullying older brother Hugo impregnating his wife, and Elizabeth herself, hating him and goading him. All his shame and pain swirled into a mess of anger and a thirst for retribution that had to be quenched, now.

He drew.

Or at least he tried to draw.

His gun stayed where it was, because he'd forgotten to unclip the holster.

He wrenched at the weapon while Morris threw his head back and laughed the laugh that rang in Willow's nightmares. He fumbled at the clasp as Morris strode towards him.

He was no nearer getting the damn thing out when Morris gabbed his bicep in two fingers and squeezed.

Willow yelped as Morris lifted his hand clear of his gun, then held his arm high. Willow punched at him with his other fist, but it was like punching a tree.

Morris slapped him a couple of times about the face.

"Anybody fancy a ride on this pretty little thing?" Morris boomed in that posh bully-boy accent Willow remembered so well. "He's not as pretty as he used to be, but I'm sure he'll push back just as hard. I've never ridden a pony who loved it so much."

The crowd whooped and Willow flapped and flailed, but he couldn't do a thing. He was back at school. But this time he didn't want it, not at all.

The grip on his arm tightened and another hand gripped his belt.

"Who's first?"

"What, *here?*" asked a sensitive soul.

"Why not! The young lady doesn't mind, do you Willow?"

Ridiculously Willow found himself considering whether he'd rather have it in private or public. *Not at all* was the hands down winner.

"Do you chaps know what?" said Morris, "I think I'll have first dibs. Before he gets too messy."

CRACK!

For a moment Willow thought God had done something useful for once and Morris had been struck by lightning. The hold on his belt and arm released. He fell onto his feet, and straightened.

Morris was staggering backwards, hands on his throat, purple faced.

There was a rawhide whip wrapped round his neck. Holding the other end was the lady who'd won the horse race. She still wore the blue trousers and black shirt, but she'd washed her hair so that it framed her tanned face with shining gold.

It was better than divine intervention.

She tugged the whip and Morris fell. The whip was wickedly tight. It looked like Morris was trying and failing to close his open mouth. His eyes were like red-veined boiled eggs, his tanned flesh darkening every moment. Willow was seriously worried that she might kill him.

The rider in blue trousers strode towards her victim.

Morris's hands fell away from the whip, flapping like a baby chicken. The rider gripped his hair with her free hand. Willow thought she was going to uncoil the whip and send him on his way, lesson learnt.

But no.

She yanked his hair with one hand and the whip with the other. There was an almighty crack.

Still holding the dead man's hair, she uncoiled the leather whip and let Morris fall forwards, whumping onto the boards.

She coiled the whip in flash and clipped it to her hip.

"Someone clean that up," she pointed at Morris's corpse. He was big as a dead bear.

The killer looked at Willow.

"Thanks for tying up my horse," she said.

ACT TWO, CHAPTER FIVE

Lies

Doreen brought the manuscript back to my room when Mr Hillier-Edwards had read it.

"I hate to be a bother, and do say if you'd rather I didn't," she said, "but could I borrow the manuscript so I can catch up, too? I only started coming to the readings recently, so I've missed all the beginning. I'm getting the bus home tonight, but I'll get Gary to pick me up in the car tomorrow so I can take it if that's alright? I'll ask him to drive me in and bring it back the next day."

"Of course you can borrow it, and I don't mind at all if you take it on the bus," I said

"Oh it's not the bus, it's the walk the other side. It goes for rain for the next couple of days and I wouldn't want to spoil your papers."

"How long is the walk?" I asked.

"Hour to an hour and a half, depending on how fast you go. Under an hour if it's cold or raining hard, or both."

"In the dark?"

"Your eyes get used to it, and I have a torch in case."

"And an umbrella?"

"I had one, but it broke in the wind the other day. I'm glad, to be honest. Umbrellas are more trouble than they're worth."

"Why doesn't your husband get you from the bus stop in your motor car?"

"Gary goes for a pint or two after work. A man needs his time with his

friends. I better get going, if that's ok? I've got tea to prepare."

"Of course!" *I was embarrassed that Doreen felt she needed my permission to leave, and I felt guilty for snapping at her when she'd tried to make me go to breakfast. I must try to be kind to everybody. Everybody has problems.*

Everybody at the mine certainly did ...

Monk was emerging from a tunnel when Silver found him.

"We ain't never going to find The Prize." Monk took off his hat and threw it on the dirt.

Silver did not like Monk's permanent smile. Even now as he griped and stooped to scoop up his hat, his white teeth shone through a crescent of drawn lips. No. He did not like that smile. He did not like the man. But he didn't need to like him. He needed him to help collect The Prize and that was that.

Hat retrieved, Monk stared at Silver expectantly. There were two types of people in the world, Silver mused. People who did, and people who needed to be told what to do. Silver was the former, Monk was the latter. It was just the way it was. No point getting worked up about it.

"I know where it is," he said.

"You know where what is?"

"You know what I'm talking about." Giving up the secret of The Prize stuck in Silver's craw. He couldn't say it straight.

Monk's eyes narrowed above his grin. "Why you telling me now?"

"Masterton's dead."

"Snake had it coming. The world's a better place without him."

"Crane killed him."

Monk's gun hand relaxed and the grin changed into a genuine smile. "Thought as much. I knew he was the killer."

"Worked it all out, had you?"

"I knew it wasn't me. So it was you, Crane, or Masterton. Reckon you're too fat to pretend to be a lion. Masterton's dead, so I guess it's not him. So that leaves Crane."

"You're a regular genius."

"So my ma always said. Tell me where The Prize is at."

"Follow me."

"What about Crane?"

"We'll deal with him later."

Lorretta asked me about my bruised jaw. I wanted to tell her that a slimy varmint had punched me and Crane had killed him dead, but instead I told her I'd run into a beam in the dark of the mine. I'm pretty sure she believed me.

We prepared and served dinner as if everything was normal. But it was pretty far from normal.

Me, Loretta and the men sat under the dorm veranda, even though the sun had dropped behind the western range a while back. Usually, the men moved the table out at night to get the breeze, but that evening they hadn't bothered. I guess they had other things on their minds.

Silver and Monk stared at Crane. Crane focussed on eating. He did a reasonable job of looking like he didn't have a care in the world, but the back of his neck was bright red.

Loretta fussed about as if she could make everything all fine by pretending it was all fine. I was so glad she was there, a calm support to me. She'd look after me, I thought, if the others all shot each other to death.

Loretta didn't ask where Masterton was, which I thought was odd, and nobody else mentioned him. But you could see that Silver knew, and that he'd told Monk. I felt sick to my knees and my elbows. I *shouldn't* have told Silver that Crane killed Masterton.

But what choice had I had?

I should have told him why he did it. I should have explained that Crane killed Masterton for a darned good reason, and it didn't mean he'd killed the others. But I couldn't bring myself to say the words. It was like I was ashamed for what Masterton had tried to do to me.

I hoped Silver and Monk didn't plan to do anything horrid. I prayed they weren't going to kill Crane. He was the only good man in the mine. I should have told him that I'd told Silver, so he'd be ready to defend himself.

There was a shovel propped against the hut's corner stanchion. It had been there since I got to the mine. If I picked it up, I could have whacked Monk and then maybe Crane could have killed Silver.

But they wouldn't kill Crane, would they? Surely they couldn't? Crane had a big revolver on his hip, and I was sure he knew how to use it. I was pretty sure he'd been in at least one war. The way he looked sometimes, he'd seen things. Maybe done things. My ma said every man in the West had dark in his past. "What about the women?" I'd asked. "Oh, most of them have had a time of it too," she'd said, with a very strange look on her face.

"I'm going up the hill," said Crane after dinner. I guessed he meant to sleep in one of the cribs further up the mountain. He left, walking backwards, fingers hovering over the butt of his gun.

Monk and Silver watched him go.

"Why didn't you shoot him?" Silver asked Monk when he'd gone.

"Why didn't you?" grinned Monk.

"Because I told you to."

I looked at Loretta. She raised her eyebrows. Monk and Silver were carrying on as if we weren't there. They were so stupid.

"He had his hand on his gun all dinner," whined Monk. "And I reckon he's quick. Why don't we forget about our plan and cut him in on The Prize? There's enough of it and he don't deserve no punishment for killing Masterton. We should reward him if anything."

Silver shook his head. "He killed the rest. He won't stop."

"Crane didn't kill anyone!" I blurted. The men looked up at me as if I was a zebra-tailed lizard who'd started talking.

"Apart from Masterton, that is," I added.

Loretta was giving me a funny look too.

"What do you know about who killed who?" asked Monk.

"Masterton killed Happy Days Frida, Denny, and Indian Moses," I claimed.

"How do you know?" asked Silver.

"Masterton told me," I lied.

"Why would he do that?" Silver looked like he was taking me seriously, but he looked mean, too.

I was going to have to tell them. I had to, to save Crane. But then I thought of a lie which was kind of the truth. "That tunnel you found me in. I went in there exploring and Masterton followed me. He said he was going to kill me, and I asked why and he said he was killing everybody because he wanted The Prize for himself. Then he attacked me. But Crane seen him follow me, so he followed Masterton. Masterton attacked Crane too. Crane didn't want to kill him, but he had to. So, Crane did kill Masterton, but Masterton attacked him first. And me too. It was a rescue and it was self-defence all in one. He had a double reason to kill Masterton."

"Why would Masterton attack you and not just shoot you?" asked Silver.

I looked down.

"Well?" Monk grinned.

"Don't press the girl," said Loretta.

Both men looked at Loretta. It felt like time had stopped.

"We need to know what happened," said Silver.

Loretta put her hands on her hips. "You know why he attacked her. She doesn't want to talk about it." I'd never heard Loretta like this.

Neither had Silver, by the look on his face. "All right," he said.

"So, you're not going to kill Crane?" I asked, giving Silver my best *please can I have what I want* eyes. He wasn't all bad.

"I didn't say that."

"We going to kill him or give him a medal or what?" demanded Monk.

"Could be the girl's right about Crane," Silver mused. "She's a clever one. Could be he's a good man and he can share The Prize. Could be the girl's lying. Like I said, she's clever. I'll sleep on it."

"Crane knows we're out to get him. He'll leave in the night. Or more likely come for us."

"Only if he can find us. Don't know about you but I'm going to sleep in the tunnels. I'll set up a wire or two so I'll hear him if he comes."

"What about the ghosts?"

"I'm more worried about flying lead than flying spirits."

ACT TWO, CHAPTER SIX

In Tequila Veritas

Mrs Terbangun asked if I'd remembered Silver's reasonableness correctly.

"A man who'd left fifty miners to drown could not have a spark of decency in him!" she declared.

"'Itler liked dogs," said Mrs Bull, in her Yorkshire accent, reddening. I'd never heard her speak without being spoken to.

"That is not true," Mrs Terbangun announced.

"You know that, do you?" asked Mrs Hopkins.

"Hitler was a racialist. He could not have liked dogs."

"That's rather the point, innit?" said Mrs Bull. "Just cause you're one thing doesn't mean you're t'other."

"That's very true," said Mr Hillier-Edwards. "Sometimes men who seem the most gentle make the most enthusiastic killers. And I have heard that the scoundrel Hitler did like dogs. In fact, I think he loved all animals. He was a vegetarian, don't you know. And he was certainly racist. Although he did like some races." Mr H-E chuckled. Surprisingly dark sense of humour on the genial old chap. I like that.

"Yes, he likes the good races," muttered Mrs Hopkins.

"What did you say?" demanded Mrs Terbangun.

"Do you really think that all races are the same?" Mrs Hopkins pouted like a trout and raised an eyebrow.

"Of course!"

"But, just the other day, you said the Pakistanis are very hard workers."

"Well, they are!

"So the races are different!" Mrs Hopkins was triumphant.

"I ... no"

"I think," Mr Hillier-Edwards chimed in, "that Mrs Terbangun means that all people have the same value. Reminds me of a Pakistani fellow in my regiment. Excellent fellow. We were in North Africa and -"

I slipped out, signalling to Mr H-E that I was off to carry on with my writing.

Doreen took the manuscript this afternoon. She missed the reading because her husband didn't want to pick her up any later than he had to, but I said she could borrow it afterwards.

James Willow followed his rescuer. The crowd of drinking miners separated before the blonde whip-killer without otherwise acknowledging her, like the press of cattle parting as the farmer crosses the yard.

"Miss!" Willow called, "Miss!"

She stopped and turned. Again, without looking or pausing their chatter, the saloon's patrons shuffled about to create a clearing for them in the press of bodies. Willow did not think it was in deference to him.

She was a little shorter than he was, which surprised him. She'd seemed taller. Her cheeks were somewhat hollow, but this only emphasised her high cheek bones, strong chin and large nose. Her face could not be called feminine, but her beauty could not be denied.

"Thank you," he said.

"You're welcome." She turned away.

He reached out a hand to grab her shoulder but then thought better of it. Instead, he trotted after her like a terrier. "Please, let me buy you a drink," he said to her back. "It's the least I can do."

She turned again and gave him a look that might have curdled cheese. "Given what I just saved you from, yeah, you're right. One drink *is* about the least you could possibly do."

"I'd give you the world, but I own very little of it." He patted his pockets. "Would you like my hat?" His leather hat had been a proud, perky affair when he'd bought it back East, but sweat and sun had wilted it into something that looked and felt like a long-dead bat.

"I'm all good for hats, thanks."

"So, a drink, then?"

"Nobody needs to buy me drink. Pandora's Chest is my bar."

"You're Pandora?"

"Why would you think I have the same name as my saloon?" The smile was gone. Her hand went to the whip.

"I just … Sorry."

"I'll forgive you. Especially because, by the strangest coincidence, my name is Pandora." She held out a hand, smiling again. "They call me Pandora Catastrophe Jones. I don't like the Catastrophe nickname much, but 'Calamity' was taken."

He shook her cool hand. "I'm James Willow. I don't have a nickname."

"You nearly picked one up this evening."

"Yes."

"You could have been James 'The Mine' Willow."

"Thanks."

"On account of how many men had been in your dark-"

"I understand the derivation."

Pandora didn't exactly smile, but her mouth softened and her eyes brightened. Those eyes were very pale; more turquoise than blue. Willow fell in love for the second time that day.

"I'd prefer 'The Eagle,' or similar to 'The Mine.'"

"You're no eagle, Mr Willow."

"Is 'Wise Owl' taken?"

"Would it suit you? Are you wise?"

"I suppose not." He really wasn't.

"I do believe that there is a tree called the pussy willow." This time the corner of her lip twitched almost imperceptibly, as if to suggest that she could smile.

A few nearby miners snorted a laugh. So, they were listening.

"James 'Pussy' Willow. Or does James 'The Pussy' Willow sound better?" She raised one large eyebrow. Her eyebrows were dark blond, darker than her golden hair. Did this mean her hair was coloured? Willow did not know.

"So, Pandora Catastrophe Jones, are you related to Jones the Gun?" Willow thought a change of subject might suit him.

"Jones is a common name out here. And everywhere else, far as I know."

"Sorry."

"But Jones the Gun is my pa."

Willow thought of the gunsmith. If there was a family resemblance he couldn't bring it to mind. "He's a good man."

She tipped her head in agreement, looked into his eyes for a couple of heartbeats then asked, "Are you?"

Willow pursed his lips. *What a question!* Pandora regarded him coolly.

"I used to think so," he said eventually.

Her pale eyes burned right into his skull. A rivulet of sweat escaped his hat and trickled ticklishly down his forehead.

"Maybe I'll let you get me that drink after all," she said eventually. "You can tell me how you got bad."

Willow glanced around. It felt like everyone in the room was watching the newcomer talking to the beautiful whipsmith.

"Aren't you worried the sheriff will come?"

"Why would I worry about him?"

"Because you ... rescued me?"

That eyebrow again. "How long have you been in the West?"

"I think I got here today."

"This is a new town, James 'The Pussy' Willow. It has a new bone orchard with thirty-two graves. Guess how many of those are murdered men."

"Thirty-two?"

"No. "

"Thirty-one?"

"No. Thirty."

"I see," Willow was relieved to stop guessing. "The other two?"

"One's a murdered woman; one's an executed man. The executed dude killed the woman. Nobody gives a gopher crap if you kill a man out here. Opposite, as a matter of fact. There's a phrase people use when they see a newcomer - 'has he got his man yet?' they say. It means has he killed anyone yet."

"Gosh."

"Have you got your man yet?"

"I have not."

She nodded, as if he really might have done. "When you do, make sure it's not a woman. People round here love a man killer, but they hate a woman killer. Which puts me on a peachy perch. They say it's a man's world out here. But it's a woman's world if you do it right. Being beautiful also helps."

Willow looked around, wondering if there was a revolver pointed at him right then, a bullet primed to pierce his soft flesh. He did not want to be somebody's 'man.'

Pandora read his mind. "Stop fussing, Pussy Willow. You don't really have to get your man, and it is considered indelicate to kill a man who isn't on the shoot."

"On the shoot?"

"You don't seem that dumb, greenhorn. Work it out." With that, she turned. The press of people parted as she walked away then coalesced behind her.

She'd said that she wanted to hear his story, so presumably she wanted him to follow her.

"Excuse me!" he said, "Excuse me!" and slowly made his way through the manly throng.

Deeper into the saloon it was noisier, smokier, louder, and the very air felt drunker. Pandora arrived at a corner table. The two men occupying it saw her coming, stood, tipped their hats, and left.

Pandora took the seat with its back to the wall and looked up at Willow. He hesitated and opened his mouth but could think of nothing to say. She smiled and nodded to the other chair.

As he sat, a man with a complicated moustache arrived with a bottle and two glass tumblers. He uncorked the bottle, poured clear liquid into each tumbler, clonked the bottle down next to them, and left.

Willow expected Pandora to snatch up the tumbler, down its contents in one impressive gulp, then slam it down with an 'Ahhhh!' But she lifted it calmly and sipped, eyes never leaving his. He followed suit.

He sniffed hard, managed not to cough, then looked at the tumbler. "What is this?"

"Cactus juice."

"It's … interesting."

"Mexicans call it tequila."

"Because too much of it is going … to kill ya?"

Pandora didn't even smile. She scanned the room as if checking all was well, then fixed him with the same look that a rattlesnake might have given an overweight mouse.

"Tell me how you came to be here, James Willow."

He was glad she'd dropped 'The Pussy.' "I left England to seek my fortune."

"Something go wrong in England?"

Willow sighed. "It did. It's true. I didn't leave to seek anything. I left England because I had to leave England. But I'm glad I came here. I love the desert, and I love the optimism. There are no old people here to tell the young what to do."

"Maybe that's why everyone's killing each other."

"Well, that's not great," he agreed.

They talked some more. Interestingly, the more he drank, the smoother the tequila became. He became cleverer and wittier, vaguely aware that he might have been repeating himself a little, but so clever and witty that it didn't matter. Pandora became more and more beautiful.

She filled his tumbler again and again. It wasn't until he tried to lean forward that he realised the tequila's potency. His body came forward tickety-boo, but his brain was left behind, confused to be naked and out in the air like that.

When Willow's brain had managed to flow back into his head, he saw that Sheriff Marshall had appeared next to Pandora, speaking quietly into her ear.

"It's rude to whisper," Willow said. To the killer and the man who condoned killing. Apparently, his brain hadn't fully resettled itself.

Pandora gave him a look.

"I wasn't whispering," said Marshall, "I was talking quietly. Not my fault it's loud in 'ere."

"I suppose that's … all right, then." said Willow.

"Why, thank you." The sheriff went on talking quietly and Willow was glad for the excuse to sit back. Sitting back was less confusing.

"So," said Pandora Catastrophe Jones a little while afterwards, "Lizzie Salmon told you where to find the woman you're looking for."

Willow nodded, far too drunk to be worried about how Sheriff Marshall might have known that. "She's at a mine on the side of Death Valley."

"Which?"

Willow paused. Reason and caution paddled through the mists of his mind like two lost ducks on a foggy sea. "Why do you want to know?"

"I can help you." Her tone suddenly remined Willow of his wife. His wife! He was all the way out here in an alien world, but as far as the law and God were concerned, Elizabeth was still his wife.

"Did I tell you about my wife?" he asked.

"Which. Mine."

She sounded frightening. She was going to try to claim his bounty. He'd already told her too much. "It's called the …" what was it called? He remembered, then struggled to think up a plausible alternative name. "The Magnificent. You go into Death Valley and turn north."

"I know the Magnificent. It's a mile east of town."

"Oh. Yes. I got the name wrong. Directions are right, though. It's north in the valley for sure. And it's called the …" *Tickety-boo? Spiffing?* "It's called the Badger." *Badger? Where had that come from?*

"The Badger?"

"Yes"

She looked at him long and hard. "All right," she said, eventually. "You got a mule?"

"I've got a horse."

"Death Valley's too hot for horses."

"Could I travel at night?"

"If you want to be lion food."

"It's a good horse."

"The best horse might reach the valley floor before it dies. You need a mule and a lot of water."

He frowned. "Where would I find a mule?"

"I could find you one. But everyone wants one, so the price has gone loco."

"Loco?"

"Up."

"I see."

"I could probably find you one for a hundred dollars."

Willow looked at the table. He had five.

"You said you had a decent horse?"

"An excellent horse. She goes by the name of Delores."

She nodded. "And let me see that revolver."

Willow left town early the following morning, walking next to a mule laden with supplies and more water than a team of twenty men could surely need. He was glad it was still dark because the very idea of sunlight nearly made him vomit. If he'd hadn't been drunker than he'd ever been the night before, he'd have stayed in bed swearing that he'd been poisoned.

It was easy to follow the first half of Lizzie Salmon's directions - *take the road westwards out of town, when you get to the base of a valley wider than any valley you ever saw before, turn left.* Even in the dim pre-dawn light, the road was an unmissable white line running westward, on and on, into the hazy distance.

The wonderful Pandora had given him a room for a night, or at least a bed shielded by hanging sheets in the cavernous dorm shed behind her saloon. He told himself he'd never expected more. She was a vision of competence and Western savvy. He was a bumbling foreigner fleeing a sorry past and heading towards he knew not what. And besides, he was married.

He missed the reassuring weight of the revolver strapped to his leg. Pandora had assured him it was nigh impossible to hit an aggressive snake with a bullet from a pistol, especially if you'd already proven that you couldn't even get it out of its holster when you needed it. A stout stick, she'd claimed, was better defence against any of the various animals that might take an interest in him.

He hadn't been convinced. He was particularly afraid of coyotes. The Clemens brothers had said that they weren't dangerous, but he'd had a bad experience with a dog, and he didn't like the way coyotes looked at him.

But then he'd drunk more tequila and he'd given her his revolver.

He'd ended up exchanging his revolver and Delores for a mule and supplies. It had seemed like a marvellous deal at the time. Now he wasn't so sure.

He remembered to look for a stout stick to fight off the local critters. He was not overly hopeful. Dusty rocks and desiccated shrubbery stretched away to the mountains on both sides of the track, with nary a tree in sight.

The sun emerged over a ridge behind him and made long shadows of the desert vegetation and his own hatted figure. His mule's shadow's ears were crazily long. Up ahead, the leather-clad backs of early rising miners glowed golden, and their kit flashed like rubies. The air was fragrant and warm. The surrounding scrub was green and gold in the dawn light, not the silvery monochrome that they'd be later when the sun beat down like the vengeance of an Egyptian god.

Willow's hangover, much to his surprise, morphed into the good-spirited kind, when one just feels a little slower and happier. He felt well-rested, the road was good, and he could have waked a thousand miles.

"I'll call you Elizabeth," he told the mule.

The beast plodded on, seemingly unmoved by its change of name.

ACT THREE

ACT THREE, CHAPTER ONE

Chasing the Dragon

Mrs Hopkins approached when most of the others had shuffled out at the end of last night's reading. "I've been thinking about … toilets." I raised an eyebrow. "I don't like the word. I still find it difficult to say. But that doesn't mean I should think less of people who do say … who do use that word. You were right. I've apologised to Mrs Bull."

I was a tad annoyed. I've long claimed that I am too old to be surprised, and I've long believed that people don't change. But Mrs Hopkins proved me double wrong last night.

Mrs Hopkins isn't the only cheerier soul. Mr Hillier-Edwards has been gadding about and chatting to me and the other biddies like he's running for mayor. His heart attack seems to have given him a new lease on life. Something's making him happy as a newly paid cowboy at a hoedown, anyway.

I don't have much else to say at the start of this new act. I'm not sure why I'm making it new act. I suppose everything's in place ready to roll towards the finale. There's a lot of trouble to come, but we will get to an end, and we'll find out who the killer is. Have you guessed? Do you think it might be me? That would be funny. What will you do if I confess to murders seventy years ago on the other side of the world? What would the police do?

Lizzie Salmon picked her way across the wasteland of tins, splintered wood, and other flotsam strewn about the island of human trash that they called the town. Nearby, a pig was digging up a rat's nest while another pig ate a rat. The local hogs were more like lions than pigs. She was worried they might eat her one night.

Some nights she was so sad she wished they would eat her.

She reached the point she'd been aiming for, where there was no trash and the desert looked liked it had for thousands of years. She stood, hot tin coffee cup in her hand. The surrounding hills were yellowy-pink in the pre-dawn light. Soon the sun would attack, blasting into bright colourlessness the plants and rock and all that scurried across them.

If she ignored the grunts and snuffles of the pigs, and focussed her gaze on the lovely hills, she could pretend that she was the wife of a good cattle man, in the prairies east of the Rockies. She'd heard there was wonderful cattle country there, further north than the endless, dreary scrubland she'd crossed to get West.

Her parents had done their best to make an honest living in the slums of New Orleans. Honest work did not pay well in that town in those days. Nor, now Lizzie thought of it, in any towns or days she'd ever known. Her father had taken the jobs he could get on the docks and her mother had spent her days teaching Lizzie letters, geography, math, and music on the old piano in the honky-tonk a few blocks away.

Lizzie had been a pretty girl and an early developer. Other boys and some men had been interested in her as long as she could remember. The glances and comments had amused and pleased her when she had a home and parents. She played up to it. She stole powder and lip paint from the apothecary store, pouted in the mirror and then on the streets.

Her mother hated it.

Then her mother died.

Then her father drank, got sick, and lost his mind.

She saw him looking. She knew it was coming. The moment he laid a hand on her, she fled. She'd never seen her father again. She heard by chance later that he'd been killed by a dancing bear, after accepting a wager that he could beat the beast in a fist fight. She'd laughed along with the man telling the story, until he'd said the name of the drunk fool who'd lost his money and his life.

Lizzie walked all night around the edges of the city, avoiding people.

But morning brought hunger and she'd sought help.

She found Slim Peter, a horse trader's wrangler. He was in the city to drop his boss's proceeds at the bank and pick up supplies. His boss always gave him the town run, she learned later, because he looked so poor no bandit would ever think he was carrying more than a bean.

He'd spent the night drinking and whoring and was in fine spirits. He bought Lizzie breakfast and she rode in his carriage. Before she realised what she was doing, she was west out of the swamps and into horse and cattle country and had left the only place she'd ever known. She lied about her age. Slim Peter asked her to marry him. She'd never had such a fine time and she'd been happy to oblige.

The wedding never happened.

The boss of the horse trader's yard was Luke Declan, a fat man of fifty years or so, dressed in white. He'd lost the fingers on his right hand to a horse when he was a boy and lost his wife to an alligator when he was a man. Some said he'd helped that alligator find his wife.

The widower Luke Declan took a shine to Lizzie and asked her to move into the big house. She said she'd have to ask Peter, but when she went back to their shack Peter wasn't there.

She never saw him again.

She didn't look for him too hard. She'd been going off him anyway. Later she realised that Luke Declan must have killed Peter, or had him killed, more likely. She'd tried to feel bad about that, but she couldn't. It had happened, it wasn't her fault, and there was nothing she could do to change it. No point getting all tied up about it.

Luke Declan told her he was too old to have relations with her, but he liked looking at her and wanted her to share his bed. This she did and, good to his word, he never pestered her. Later, Lizzie met many men his age and older who were all too keen to have relations with her. She wondered if the horse had bitten off more than Declan's fingers.

All was fine for a while. The other women in the house hated her, but she was used to women hating her. The men were kind.

One late night they were playing cards below while Lizzie lay on her big bed. There came a thudding on the stairs. A man with a ring of white hair crowning his head and a moist roll of fat around his neck waddled into her room.

"I won your virginity," he drawled drunkenly. "In a game of draw poker," he explained on seeing her confused look.

She couldn't remember what had happened next. Maybe because it happened so many more times.

It started slow, maybe once a month, on card nights when Declan lost. Then he started selling her to people who visited and it was weekly, then people started visiting just to see her and it was twice, three times a day. Sometimes more.

Declan took money from the men downstairs and she never saw a cent. Some men fell in love and brought her gifts. She liked the first few ribbons and mirrors, but soon she had a box full of them. She tried to give them to the other women. The other women spat at her. All of their men - husbands and fancy men both - slept with Lizzie regularly.

Some men offered to take her away from it all. When the first one she liked asked her, she asked Luke Declan if she could go with him. She never saw her suitor again. Declan's wranglers and workers doubled as a little army and all the lawmen within fifty miles were kin or friends. All of them had visited Lizzie to boot, so weren't about to abet her departure. Only a fool would try to take her.

A fool came along.

Keith Reed was huge limbed and crazy as popcorn on a hot stove, with a head smooth as a bullet, and a bag full of gold that he'd got from who knew where. She'd climbed from the bedroom window one moonless night. Reed was waiting below with two fast horses. There'd been shouting in the dark, then shooting, but they got away.

She didn't find out about the bullet in Reed's gut till later. He never mentioned it and she didn't think to ask.

They travelled west, living off the land, avoiding people, and sleeping under the stars. Lizzie liked to think that it was Keith Reed who'd made her pregnant with Eleanor on one of those beautiful, starry nights. She never tried to calculate the dates that might prove it was one of the many, many men who'd visited her in Declan's room.

In her fantasies, they found some land and bought a herd of cattle with Keith's gold. He built a ranch and shot wolves. She farmed a larger and larger patch of crops to feed their growing family. Neighbours - none closer than a couple of miles - were good and helpful. They all came together at Christmas, ruddy faced from tramping through snow, feasted on goose, and got happy drunk - not shouting, shooting and sleeping with whores drunk.

In reality, Keith died of his gunshot wound a couple of weeks after they fled, protesting to his last breath that he'd never been shot at all.

Lizzie took Keith Reed's gold, set herself up in a boarding house in a Texan town, and got a job as a teacher in the school. The job lasted as long as it took for her pregnancy to show. She stayed in the boarding house and had her baby alone.

Mother and child were pariahs in that good Christian town. The Jesus-loving folk turned their noses up at her in the street. Women would walk in front of her at the grocer's store line as if she wasn't there. When the grocer deigned to serve her, he explained that he was doing it for the good of the baby, not for her, a Hell-cursed slut mother.

When the baby was old enough to travel safely, probably a little before, Lizzie left and headed west. Keith's gold ran out. No Christian school would hire an unmarried teacher with a child. One family took her in as domestic help, but the local pastor came and had a word and she and little Eleanor were shooed out of the door the following day.

Not far off starving, and her little girl sick, she returned to the first profession she'd known. It was the only way to feed her daughter. She travelled from town to town with the child whom she loved more than all the world, teaching her as much as she could, whilst shielding her from her money-earning activities as much as she was able.

A few men fell in love with her, some even said they would take Eleanor, too. But they were cowhands and miners, reliable as sparrows, and every one of them moved on without so much as a farewell.

Then she met the Chinese women and their opium. The sweet smoke wafted her off in a boat lined with cotton cushions across a warm sea to an island of smiles. She knew happiness for the first time since her mother died.

She was sensible. One could be, she told herself. She saw addicts, but they were weak fools. They didn't have Eleanor to keep them straight. Opium was a treat for Lizzie, like cake on a Sunday.

But her new female friends encouraged her. Emerging from the happiness of an opium fug, she realised how unhappy she was. And why should she be unhappy? Did Eleanor want an unhappy mother? Would Lizzie's own dead mother want her daughter to be unhappy?

The treat became a habit, then a requirement more necessary than food.

Her savings went in moments. Or maybe it was months. Close attention to the calendar was an early casualty of opium addiction. She built up debts that she'd never be able to pay and kicked herself when she realised that she'd trapped herself just as neatly as Declan had trapped her back East.

Luckily, she knew exactly how to escape her self-loathing and desperation.

Opium.

Eleanor had been so good. When Lizzie came back woozy and useless, Eleanor would settle her and spoon soup into her mouth.

Then she'd sent good, honest, loving Eleanor away.

The smiling man had asked for sport on credit, but she wouldn't do that. He offered to take her daughter and return her with a share of a great fortune. He told her about The Prize, and said they needed someone to help look after the camp.

Lizzie told herself that she'd done it for Eleanor's future, but truth was she couldn't bear the girl's goodness anymore. She couldn't stand those big, clever, unconditionally loving eyes welcoming her home from a night's drugged-out whoring.

She told herself that Eleanor owed her for all the food and board and schooling she'd supplied. She knew that was a lie. Eleanor had not chosen to be born. Lizzie's role as a mother was God-given. If you were a heathen or one of those intellectuals who didn't believe in God, then parenthood was nature-given. Point was, from any standpoint Eleanor's existence was Lizzie's responsibility. Her daughter owed her nothing. She owed her daughter everything.

Even while sending Eleanor to the mine, trying to feel awful about it, she'd been excited about how much more time she'd have with opium. She'd felt awful about that too, but, obviously, not awful enough. She'd put her drug before her daughter.

As a sop to her conscience, she'd persuaded the smiling man to take someone else along to keep an eye on Eleanor - Crane, the only decent human she knew in the town. She'd got talking to him one day in the store and he'd carried her groceries home - or at least to the edge of the Tenderloin, where she'd insisted on taking them.

He'd asked if he could get her a drink, and she'd thought he was an idiot who hadn't realised she was a sporting woman. But she'd gone for that drink and soon realised that he wasn't after sport. She reckoned he must like other men. Those good Christian folk declared that men liking other men was an abomination, maybe even worse than having a child out of wedlock. But Crane didn't seem so bad.

She came to trust him. They met most days to chat. How could she mind if he lusted after his own sex? It didn't harm anyone. How could God hate it, she wondered, since God had made Crane? In fact, she kind of preferred him that way. It was refreshing knowing he didn't want anything physical from her - or Eleanor, for that matter. Her little girl was old enough now to attract leers from the vilest of the vile.

So, she'd been more than glad when Crane agreed to join Eleanor on the expedition to the Fabulous. He'd seemed only too pleased to go. She'd wondered what he'd been running from, but she'd never asked, and then she'd smoked a pipe and forgotten.

With Eleanor gone, Lizzie left the house and moved to a crib. It was all she needed. She could charge men the same in the crib as she had in the house, and pay off her debts more quickly with the money she was saving on rent. That was the theory. Fact was, she now had more time and more money to spend on opium.

Now every morning started like this. Standing outside, before it became too hot to stand in the open, looking at the hills and resolving to leave. To find Eleanor at the mine, head back East, claim to be a widow and find work as a teacher. Maybe even find a decent man. Maybe that would be Crane. They could say Eleanor was their kid. Didn't matter if Crane didn't want to lie with her. She'd done enough of that for ten lifetimes.

But when the sun rose, her resolve sank. Misery flooded in and she told herself she'd have just one pipe to help with the day. Packing up would be easier, she reasoned, after a pipe. Then one pipe became two and the next thing she knew she was waiting for the sun to rise, sore in the nethers and promising herself never to do it again.

She sighed and turned to return to her crib, to dig out the a few new-earned nuggets of gold that she could exchange for pipes in the den.

She found her way through the cans and the trash, past the pigs.

There was a man leaning against her crib. No, not a man, but a woman dressed like a man and standing like a man. Pandora Catastrophe Jones, saloon owner and all-round super woman - the woman who Lizzie could be if she could stop the opium.

"Howdy Lizzie," said Pandora.

"Howdy. What can I do for you? You want to start sporting like a man as well?"

"Tell me where you sent your daughter, the black woman, and James Willow." Her face was hard.

"Why?" Lizzie blinked, surprised by the question.

"I'll count to three." Her fingers went to her whip handle.

"I sent them to Denver."

Pandora's face stayed set but her eyes glittered. "Thanks for the information. To show my gratitude, let me buy you a pipe."

Lizzie blinked. They both knew that a couple of pipes would have Lizzie telling Pandora anything she wanted to know. Whatever that was, it wasn't good. "Not good" in the West meant murder.

A shoot-out might kill Eleanor.

On the other hand, opium.

"I'll get my hat," said Lizzie.

ACT THREE, CHAPTER TWO

Quick Silver

Julian assured me that it was the right place to start a third act. I told him I would rest easier in my bed knowing I had his approval.

"Would you like me to edit the work so far?" he asked.

"What exactly do you mean by 'edit'?" I asked. "Do you mean check for spelling mistakes?"

"No, no that happens at the end and would be a waste of my skilled time. Typically, a novel's principal editor will suggest larger scale changes – characters that need more fleshing out or less fleshing out, plot points that don't coalesce convincingly, chapters that could be omitted or need a wholesale – "

"Oh, thank you so much," I interrupted innocently (I am not a good person) "but I already have three editors."

"Who?" he asked, reddening.

"Why, Mr Hillier-Edwards, Mrs Bull, and Doreen."

"Ah!" he cried. "They are what we call Beta Readers. They give unprofessional advice. It's fun for them to feel they are involved, but they are not actually useful. I will be giving educated pointers which will actually improve the work."

I pretended to consider it for a moment, then said "No thank you."

"I see," he said, deflating.

I felt bad. But I put work into this book, and I value their opinion over his a thousandfold. He's a different generation and I don't think he has any empathy. I don't think the young do, these days. They think that they're right and the old ways are stupid. But the young are wrong, and the new ways are *stupid. I daresay the old said the same when I was young.*

Having said that, Doreen is a good egg and she's certainly not old. I suppose it's the educated young who are the problem, because someone's made the mistake of telling them they're intelligent. Maybe they are, but they sure are dumb too.

I do hope Mr Hillier-Edwards, Mrs Bull, and Doreen all agree when I ask them to be editors. I'm going to look pretty silly if they don't.

And on with the book. We're going to pay another visit into the mind of Mr Silver.

Halicore Silver had slept in places a whole lot worse than a tunnel with a bundled rug for a pillow. But he was older now. Everything was harder. Even lying on the floor was a process. Time was he'd just lay down. *I'll lie down* he'd have thought, and the next thing he'd be lying down. Now he had to lower himself to the ground like a near-dead prize bull being hoisted down onto a cow.

There was a time - sometimes it felt like a thousand years ago, sometimes it felt like yesterday - when he'd slept on the plains, no pillow, and his only cover an old duster.

Three years he'd hunted the men who'd attacked the homestead and slaughtered his pa and brothers, hoping to find his ma and his sisters alive. He'd always known that they'd died within days of being taken, maybe hours. Finding his mother's severed arm on the edge of their property would have been clue enough for most men. But Silver had had nothing left but to search for them.

It had been a lonely, meandering trek across storm-pounded prairies, tribe to tribe, fort to fort, homestead to homestead. He been lied to and cheated so many times that he learned to lie and cheat. He'd been misled and used so many times that he'd learned there are no bonds between people. Everyone acts in their own interest, always. Anyone who doesn't is a fool who's not long for this world. Even the preachers and the good, smiling wives were out for nobody but themselves.

Difference was, Silver couldn't be bothered to paint a veneer on his character anymore. He was too tired to lie to himself and the world.

He pictured drowned miners. That boy - Gurnick — straight blonde hair sat like an acorn's top on that smooth, hopeful, always smiling face. That old joker - Silver couldn't remember his name if he'd ever known it - skinny but with a gut like a pregnant woman's, never took a thing seriously.

Silver felt nothing. They'd have done the same to him in a heartbeat. Any man would have let ten times as many die for a tenth of the gold.

It would be his soon. He'd head back East, buy a big place - near enough to a city and far enough away from it, too.

He closed his eyes against the light of his candle and listened to the mountain. The rock was alive, he'd learnt that, only it moved slowly. If you stayed still enough, you'd hear -

Click!

A revolver hammer, nearby in the dark. He lay still. No point leaping up. Not that he could leap up, not anymore.

"Hello, Crane," he said.

No answer.

"How did you get round the traps?"

Still no answer. Silver fancied he could hear Crane breathing, but it could have been the sighing of the rock.

"Kill me now, if that tickles you," he continued, "but you'll never find The Prize. I know where it is. Split it with me, Monk, and the ladies. It's still enough to make you for life."

Silence.

"Greedy, huh? Can't say I blame you. How about I help you kill the others, then show you where it is, and we go sixty-forty. Sixty for you. What do you say?"

Nothing but crushing silence, punctuated by a distant drip. Had Crane gone? Had he drifted off and dreamt that revolver's click?

"Final offer. I'll kill the others, seventy you, thirty me."

"Get up," said a voice in the darkness. It wasn't Crane's.

ACT THREE, CHAPTER THREE

Betrayed in the Desert

I have my editors.

Mrs Bull, Mr Hillier-Edwards, and Doreen all agreed immediately. Then they all insisted that there wasn't a word they would change. I'm sure they'll think of plenty after a brandy or two — we agreed that I'd pay them in booze. We're going to meet in the evenings after I've finished the book, instead of going to creative writing club. If nothing comes of it, I'm sure I'll still enjoy drinking and chatting with my friends.

Friends. There's a strange thing. I decided when I got here that I wouldn't look for any new friends. I've had plenty in my time, and I wanted to spend my last few years with my memories of them. But I guess sometimes friends find you.

Last night's chapter was the shortest by far. I think Julian was relieved. He got to talk about writing for what seemed like an awfully long time. A few people left shortly after he started, which I thought was terribly rude. While Julian wittered away about who knew what, I went back to the West in my mind, and had a go at planning out the rest of the book.

James Willow walked next to Elizabeth the mule. He kept a vague eye out for the stout stick which Pandora had assured him would be weapon enough against coyotes and rattlesnakes. Given the lack of trees, he was fairly certain he wasn't going to find one. In the end, he picked up a cricket ball-sized rock and felt a little safer.

The road was clear, firm, and dry as his wife's eyes. Willow began to climb out of his hangover and enjoy his pre-dawn walk. But then the burning ogre sun reared over the horizon and smothered man and mule under a blanket of pounding, wasting heat. Man and mule slowed. Soon he'd drunk so much water that he was wondering whether what had seemed like far too much was actually not enough.

They had their first view of Death Valley around midday. Willow's first view, anyway; he couldn't vouch for Elizabeth the mule, but by the way she also stopped and stared open-mouthed, he guessed it was her first time too. That, or sun and tequila had fried his brain into bestowing too much speculative ability on a mule.

Willow had had no idea that places like Death Valley existed on God's otherwise green earth. The mind-bogglingly vast valley was surely the realm of some mighty over-god who might gobble in one swallow the little English god of pretty churches and gentle valleys.

The valley's base blazed white in the sun, stretching on and on and on. The highest point of the far (very far) side had snow on it, even though where Willow was, high up on the opposite side, it was the hottest day he'd ever know.

Rising from the side of the vast Valley he was currently descending was a yellow, red, and black mountain. Its summit was corkscrewed, as if some great hand had reached down and twisted the rocky dough right round as it baked. If that corkscrew mountain had been in England, it would have been pride of the county, a major tourist attraction and known by every schoolchild in the land. In Death Valley, it was just one of hundreds of huge, bizarre, geological wonders. The land was so vast that the twisted mountain itself, although mountain-sized, was no more than a pimple on Death Valley's lower slopes.

And were those sand dunes he could see in the distance?

And all of this was but a small part of the American West, where countless more marvels awaited his discovery.

No god would have created this insane land, Willow decided. It was a place of devils. But wonderful devils. Devils, dare he think it, to be worshipped.

He marched on, so struck with awe that he forgot the heat for a good hundred paces. He almost smacked his own forehead when he realised that he also hadn't thought about his wife Elizabeth at all, all day, even though he'd named the mule after her (naming the mule after the person he wanted to forget, he now realised, had not been his brightest decision).

Realising he hadn't thought of his wife, of course, made him think of her. Sickening shame and guilt bloomed from his gut, yet again.

Willow stood, looking into the vastness. He turned around slowly. There was no other human soul for miles.

He pictured his wife. He pictured Hugo. He pictured the dead bully Robert Morris. He pictured the Mormon-punched Ossian Slade.

He closed his eyes, breathed heavily through his nose for a good thirty seconds, then opened his mouth wide and roared as loud as he could.

He screamed and roared, arms lifted, turning slowly, pouring out his rage at the mountains, the valleys, the dirt, the rocks, and the whitening sky. He paused to suck in breath, then screamed and roared again, as long as he could, as loud as he could. Then he did it again.

Finally, he stopped, blinking. The mule was eyeing him with a mix of surprise and concern.

"I'm alright," he said. "Sorry."

He was pretty sure Elizabeth rolled her eyes.

He walked on.

Did he feel different after his extraordinary display? Perhaps. The shame and guilt had deadened, replaced by a paradoxical sense of unimportance and purpose. He simply didn't matter. He was a speck in this huge valley, and this huge valley was a speck in the world. If he didn't matter, his guilt and shame didn't matter. Freed from that burden, he could get on and make something of the rest of his life. He didn't need to be Willow, the loser cuckold. He could be whatever he made of himself from this moment on.

His past did not matter, but his future could matter.

He would begin by bringing a criminal to justice, earning a decent sum of money for once in his life, and returning a child to her mother.

Perhaps next he would rescue Lizzie, the beautiful sporting woman, from her drugged life amongst the pigs? Yes, he'd take her and her child on his new adventures. Who cared that she'd been a whore? Her past, like his, did not matter. There was nobody here in this wonderful, beautiful new world to judge them.

He strode on, chin high.

Soon he was trudging, chin low, because it was too jolly hot to strut. But his resolve remained. He did not need to be his past.

The valley's floor was a great deal further than it looked, which was, perversely, what he'd expected. This was a morning of paradoxes.

Impossibly, the day became hotter. It was hotter than he'd known it could be outside of a furnace. Or possibly inside of one, too. He felt a new sympathy for pottery.

Finally, at the base of the valley, was a clutch of sheds and a great many cans, some shining, some rusted dull, like shingle on an ugly beach. The settlement looked deserted. Only the stupid, Pandora had assured Willow, remained in the valley in summer. Summer! The word didn't fit. This wasn't summer, it was Hell.

He poked his head into the first shed, rock held aloft. There were six beds with thin mattresses, a desk and six chairs messily arranged around what might have been called, at a stretch, a dining room table.

He took two tentative steps into the shed. There was a rattle in the darkness.

He darted out and stood, sweating even more than before, watching the door, waiting for a charging snake and not sure what he'd do if one came. None did.

All was silent. He might have been the only human for twenty miles, maybe more. It was a strange, not wholly unpleasant feeling.

"HELLO!" he shouted. His voice echoed softly back.

He had another roaring and screaming session. By God, it felt good. Whatever he did after he'd collected the bounty, he'd find time to be far enough from everyone else to make all the noise he wanted.

He realised that he could be naked and nobody would know. He undressed and piled his clothes neatly on one of those handy rocks. He walked about for a while, avoiding sharp stones. One a whim, he scooped up some grit, rubbed it onto his chest and did some more hollering.

Elizabeth the mule, the only other large living creature nearby - he hoped - stood and blinked at him from the shade of a shed, as if she'd come to expect this sort of behaviour from humans.

Suddenly very tired, Willow dressed and found a dormitory shed without rattling inhabitants. He lay on the bed furthest from the door, looking at the desiccated wooden ceiling. He thought about being scared of rattlesnakes, coyotes, lions, bandits and women, but he couldn't be bothered.

He woke at first light. Outside, it was relatively cool. Elizabeth was nearby, munching at who knew what. He passed water and looked about this alien, majestic world.

The vast valley was calm as a deserted cathedral. Its base was still shaded, but the sun's rays reached the mountains to the west, illuminating them heather-purple. Death Valley, Willow decided, was a place of God after all. He took a deep breath. The air was warm and clean. And that was how Willow felt now, standing there, warm and clean, another little creature in the vastness. Part of the vastness.

He opened his mouth to roar again but closed it. He didn't need to roar any more.

Elizabeth his wife was in his mind again, but she was far away and he couldn't hear her insults. She had no power here.

"Come here!" he called to Elizabeth the mule. "Let's find the child and the beginning of our fortune."

The mule stayed put so he went to her to find his breakfast.

"How about we call you Pandora?" He asked, as he rummaged through a pack. "That's a much better name."

He was pretty sure the mule shook her head in weary dismissal.

"No, you're right. It's bad luck to change a name."

An hour later, Willow's newfound confidence and love for Death Valley had taken something of a knock. He was beginning to suspect he'd need to scream again at some point.

A wind had not so much whipped up as come stampeding down the valley from the north. It filled his ears. It filled his head. He could only just hear himself shout. He knew because he'd tried. The gale was blasting into his rear, which was something of a blessing as it helped him along, but its ceaseless roar and sting of sand was near intolerable.

It took him a surprisingly long time to realise that wrapping his spare shirt about his face and ears made life a lot more bearable.

He and Elizabeth trudged along, heads down.

Head south on the eastern side of the valley. Turn left at the stamp mill and follow the road up a canyon until you find the mine.

Such was the second half of Lizzie Salmon's instruction. He knew the purpose of a stamp mills. He knew the difference between a stamp mill and a ball mill. However, he did not know what a stamp mill looked like. Or a ball mill, for that matter. He'd assumed he'd know one when he saw one, but now he was beginning to question that assumption.

Sometime after noon, the wind died in moments, as if a god or devil had pulled the Gale Cease lever.

Blinking with relief, he looked at Elizabeth as if to say *I'm glad that's over*. Elizabeth regarded him cooly, seemingly unmoved.

"Be like that." Willow said, looking around, now that looking around was possible. To the east the foothills were the yellows and reds of autumn leaves. *Quite stunning*, he thought. Up ahead was a building.

"Is that a stamp mill, Elizabeth?" Willow asked.

The mule didn't answer, but surprised him by heading off towards it. It was the first time she'd headed off without waiting for him to start.

Willow plodded on behind. Before long, he missed the horrendous wind, because now heat filled the valley like far too hot water in a gigantic bath. In moments, his clothes were sodden with sweat. Not long after that, he could have wrung sweat out of his belt.

They reached the building. It could have been a stamp mill once, was his assessment. It had a concrete base and it contained iron cogs and tanks. Willow had expected a huge weight which could be raised and dropped to pummel ore. There was nothing like that here, but perhaps there had been before, or perhaps Willow had misunderstood the workings of a stamp mill.

There was quartz scattered about. Willow knew that quartz was the ore from which gold and silver were milled, although he didn't understand how that actually happened. There *was* a track running east into the mountains, as Lizzie had described.

"What do you think, Elizabeth? Is this our stamp mill?"

The mule shrugged, or at least Willow was fairly sure she did.

"I rather agree. Perhaps it is, perhaps it isn't. However, we are in no specific rush, we have plenty of supplies, so let's head up the trail a little and see if we find a mine."

The track led up a vast fan of jagged alluvium into a broad valley floored with colourful pebbles. Over perhaps a mile, the valley narrowed into a ravine a few paces wide, with high cliff walls. It was cooler and silent in the shaded rock corridor. Willow was reminded once again of ecclesiastical buildings.

"This, Elizabeth, is what I believe they call a slot canyon, carved by water over millennia."

The mule looked at him.

"I know what you're thinking," he continued. "Water, here? Surely the wind has more effect on the landscape. But no, even a wind like this morning's has little erosive agency compared to a flood. Even heavy rainfall just once every century, would, over the countless millennia, carve ..."

Willow continued to expound on theories that he'd learnt at the Royal Geographical Society. Equine Elizabeth seemed as uninterested in his geological musings as his wife Elizabeth had been.

The flatter, sandy rock floor of the canyon was much easier going than the slog up the alluvium. He could walk calmly rather than trudge desperately. Contentment flowed back into Willow's limbs and mind. It was hotter than a forge, but he had a lot of water. If one walked slowly enough, the heat was bearable. The land was a mystical marvel. The folds of rock, the strange formations and their bizarre colours, appealed to him greatly. Would all land look like this, he wondered, without soil and plants concealing the rocky beauty?

He pretended he was Adam, exploring the newly created world alone.

Was he wrong to implore God not to make an Eve?

He found several mining tunnels - dark doorways into the rock that looked like passages to a secret world - but no actual mine. Willow wasn't sure what the Fabulous mine looked like, but he was fairly certain there would be buildings, pickaxes and men with beards.

The canyon wound on, opening to a gravel-floored, shrub-strewn valley busy with butterflies, then tightening again. To Willow's surprise, man and mule came round one curve and found a stream bubbling along the rocky ground. How could there be a stream? Surely it hadn't rained for months.

Elizabeth took a sniff at the water and backed away.

"What you don't understand, Elizabeth," said Willow, "is that this water is about the cleanest you will ever come across. The rock acts as a filter, you see, removing impurities. No doubt you've never drunk water so clean, and that's what's putting you off. Now we are carrying water, but you never know much we'll need. So, it makes sense to drink our fill here. Then we'll fill our empty canteens."

He pulled his tin cup from the baggage on the mule's back, crouched and plucked a few stones aside to create a pool of diamond-clear water. He filled his cup then drained it in three big swallows.

It did taste a bit odd.

He filled the cup again and sniffed it.

It smelled, if he had to put a finger on it, like disease. Should rock-filtered, super clean water smell of disease? Probably, he had to admit, not.

He elected not to fill the empty flasks just yet.

"Perhaps we'll follow the valley a little and get our water from this stream's source," he said. He felt nauseous. Anything bad in the water would take a few hours to affect him, so the feeling of sickness was nothing but lily-liveredness. He told himself to buck up.

Around the next bend the canyon came to an end, at least for Willow and Elizabeth. Fifty paces ahead the passage was blocked by a wall of rock as high as a tall tree. A thin waterfall trickled down its face. Willow knew with his first glance that it was utterly unscalable.

Elizabeth stopped.

"Come on!" Willow called. He wanted to investigate the base of the falls. The mule wouldn't budge. Willow shook his head, then noticed that there was a smell; a stronger version of the whiff in the water.

Suddenly, he knew what he was going to find. He forgot Elizabeth and walked along the stream.

The smell strengthened with every step until it was a veritable stench.

In the shallow pool at the base of the waterfall were two naked, dead men. They were very dead. Their eyes, guts and private parts were gone, but there was still meat on their frames, dried like jerky in the air, wet and waving like white-green seaweed under the water.

It was as if scavengers had feasted on the men until they had become poisonous, then known to stop.

The water from the waterfall flowed around, through, and under the corpses. There could be no doubt that the water flowing on down the valley was tainted.

Willow looked back at Elizabeth. *I told you so* said her eyes. *Can you explain the filtering effect of the rock again?* asked the twist of her mouth.

He staggered to the edge of the canyon so that Elizabeth wouldn't have to see and vomited, choked, and vomited again.

He picked his way back to Elizabeth between bushes and over rock, drank some clean water from a flask, returned to the canyon edge and vomited some more.

There was no way up the waterfall, and in fact, now that Willow stopped marvelling at the mystical, wonderful landscape like an air-headed child, he had to admit there was no road into the canyon and there never had been. It was probably an animals' trail. And what he'd decided to call the stamp mill really hadn't had a stamp in it.

Then he remembered - Lizzie had said there was an aerial tramway running from the stamp mill up the valley. There'd been nothing like that, nothing man-made at all running up the valley.

He slapped his forehead. What an idiot.

How could he have forgotten about the tramway? Was it the heat? Or was it his new-found confidence that he was a proto-hero about to blossom, and not the sort of loser cuckold who'd march miles up the wrong valley and poison himself?

He crunched back along the canyon, crying a little.

At least it was downhill out of this side valley to Death Valley itself, he told himself after a while.

He giggled.

He'd made a mistake. *Two mistakes*, said the human Elizabeth who lived in his mind, *you wasted time and you poisoned yourself.*

Bugger off, he told her.

People made mistakes. They learned from them. He was fine. There was no deadline for finding his bounty and retrieving the child.

He did feel foolish for drinking the contaminated water. Had it been in his stomach long enough to poison him? Food poisoning took a few hours to take effect. He guessed it was the same with whatever sort of poisoning you got from essentially licking two decaying corpses.

Head lowered, shielding his eyes from the glare, he was almost on the riders before he saw them. Pandora had told him no horses could bear this heat. He guessed these four hadn't heard that.

He squinted at them. There were two tall men, a fat man, and a thin man. He almost giggled. It was like the start of a music hall joke.

Then he saw that the slender man was a woman. Pandora. She was riding Delores. One of the others was the English Sheriff Marshall. He didn't recognise the fat man or the second tall one.

"Hello?" he called. *Why had they followed him? Had he left something behind?*

The four riders reined in and regarded him as if he was an old broken wagon or similar mildly interesting finding.

Willow walked on towards the waiting riders, feeling foolish and out of place. Feeling foolish and out of place was his usual reaction to meeting other humans, so that wasn't too much of a surprise.

The tall stranger - broad-chested as well as tall - was clean-shaven and dark haired, with a face like a side of beef. Strapped to this face were, rather incongruously, a pair of eyeglasses. He sat looking at Willow, lip curled, like a maid regarding a fresh dog mess on a recently cleaned step.

The fat man had a wispy beard, a cheery, red face, and eyes a little like a startled horse's, giving the impression that he was both amused and a little unnerved by the world.

"Hello!" Willow tried again.

Silence. He wished one of them would say something.

Beef-face took his pistol from its holster, pointed it at Willow and said, "Shall I kill him?"

Willow retracted his wish.

"No," Pandora replied, then, to Willow. "There's been a change of plan. You will give us the mule and your supplies and go back to town. We're going to the Fabulous. You're not."

He looked around. He still hadn't found a stout stick. He'd even dropped his rock because he'd felt so happy and peaceful in the beautiful desert. Although the stoutest stick wouldn't be much help against four guns. Probably more than four. Tough types like these no doubt had little pistols in ankle-holsters and other concealed weaponry. Those saddlebags were probably full of guns.

He turned to Elizabeth the mule, as if she might help. She looked back at him as if to say, *I just carry stuff.*

"If I give you everything you gave me in return for my horse and gun, will you return my horse and gun?" he tried.

Pandora laughed. "I'll leave you a big canteen of water and a couple of biscuits. That will get you back to town."

"What if I refuse?"

The gunshot made him jump. He hadn't seen Marshall draw and raise his revolver, but now it was pointed at him, barrel smoking. He took a speedy inventory of his body and limbs. He wasn't holed. It was obviously just a warning shot.

"Damn, missed." said the sheriff. The cad had to tried shoot him! A fellow Englishman to boot!

The fat man opened and closed his mouth in apparent despair, looking from Marshall to Pandora to Willow.

Beef-face laughed. "You couldn't hit the ground with your hat in three throws!"

"I bet you can't get him with your first shot."

"Watch me!" Beef-face raised his gun.

"Stop," said Pandora. "There is no need to kill the man."

"I don't give a dried owl crap what there's a need for. I don't like the snooty bastard," said Sheriff Marshall, taking aim again.

Willow jinked one way and then the other, thinking to make himself a difficult target, while also aware that he may be jinking into the path of a poorly aimed shot. But he couldn't just stand there.

The first bullet whacked into his shoulder like a kick from a horse. He spun about and fell.

Another shot rang out, then a report like a whip crack.

"Wow, Pandora," said Beef-face's voice.

Willow opened his eyes. He was lying on his back. Stunning, hot pain burst from his shoulder. He managed to lift his head.

The sheriff was missing. The fat man was looking from Pandora to Marshall's riderless horse and back again, mouth open. Beef-face was looking at Willow and chuckling.

Pandora was coiling her leather whip. "Are you hurt bad?" she asked.

Marshall was lying on the dirt, still. It looked an awful lot like Pandora had killed Willow's fellow countryman with her leather whip. He felt his jaw dropping.

"Willow, are you hurt bad?" she asked again.

Willow touched at his shoulder and lifted blood-stained fingers away. "Yes. Sorry. It seems I've been shot."

"Trust an Englishman to apologise for getting shot." Pandora slid off her horse, slung a leather satchel across her shoulder, and strode across the dirt towards him. She crouched. She was sweating, so she *was* human, but she smelled fragrant and musky, a thousand times better than any sweaty man.

She prodded a finger into his shoulder, below his wound, then directly on it.

He yelped.

"You'd think a sheriff would be a better aim," she concluded as she stood, reaching into her bag. "You're nicked, not shot."

Willow looked at his fingers again. *Lot of blood for a nick*, he thought.

Craster Bellamy shifted on the red velvet cushion that he'd borrowed from a saloon in the Tenderloin. Not Pandora's Saloon. He wasn't a clever man, but he wasn't stupid enough to steal a cushion from Pandora. Riding this far, the pillow didn't help much. His ass hurt. A lot. Had done for a month now, worse all the time. He hoped it was piles.

He stroked his beard while Pandora treated the Englishman's shot shoulder. The other Englishman lay dead. Bellamy was English himself by blood, but he'd been born in America. He knew little about his parents' homeland and he felt about as English as a Gila monster (he knew enough about England to know they didn't have deserts or Gila monsters).

He was terrified that the pain in his ass was cancer. A man in town with a sore butt had gone to the doctor and found he had prostate cancer. The doctor told him he had just weeks to live. The sick man had responded by walking through town and shooting everyone he didn't like the look of. He didn't get far. It's hard to go on a rampage in a town where everyone's got a gun on his, or indeed her, hip. Although, mused Bellamy, it's a lot easier to go on that rampage in the first place if you have a gun on your hip. Universal gun ownership had its pros and cons.

Bellamy hadn't been to the doctor because he didn't want to hear he had the cancer. He dreaded dying because he could not countenance the idea of never seeing his wife Betsie again. He should never have left her, and he felt sick with longing every time he pictured her worried face. The plan to spend a year away and come back gold-rich had seemed sound. He'd looked forward to the adventure. He'd enjoyed it for a while. He made some money mining but then he spent it all because everything out here was so expensive, even if you avoided the whores, gambling and liquor, as he did.

He'd go back down the mines one day, he told himself, but he'd been telling himself that for a while now. He told himself that he stayed topside because people weren't finding much anymore. Fact was, he was scared of being underground. Mines collapsed and people died. It happened. Some of the people who dug mines were complete idiots. He should know. He'd dug mines with no idea what he was doing.

Where they were headed now - the Fabulous - there'd been a flood that drowned fifty men. Even before he'd heard about the Fabulous, he often wondered what it would be like to be drowned in the dark underground. It was an experience, he decided, that he'd rather avoid.

So Craster Bellamy paid his way working for Pandora. He'd been part of things he wasn't proud of - hurting people and worse. If he ever did get home, it was going to be difficult to tell Betsie the tales of his adventures. He was going to have pretend he'd become the silent, brooding type with dark but noble secrets, like a man back from war. With any luck he'd be heading home soon. Pandora had told him and the other two that there was a fortune to be made on this job. With his share, Craster could go back to Betsie. Providing Pandora didn't kill him, of course. She did have a habit of killing people. Sometimes she helped them though. She was a contrary one.

Pandora finished up her nursing and mounted her horse with the Englishman's mule's lead rein in one hand. Without a word she turned her horse down-canyon. It was the signal to go. She didn't give orders much, just expected her hired men to do what they were meant to do. Bellamy appreciated that. All the male bosses he'd worked for gave orders all the time. They liked to remind everyone - including themselves, he guessed - that they were in charge. Pandora didn't feel that need. It was the first time he'd worked for a woman, but if they were all like Pandora he'd look to work for ladies in the future. If the pain in his ass didn't turn out to be a cancer that was going to kill him before summer was over, that was.

He rode up to the Englishman. Pandora wouldn't mind like most bosses would. She gave you rein so long as you got your work done.

The Englishman looked up at him unhappily. The bullet wound - little more than a cut through the top of the shoulder - was about a mild as a bullet wound could be. But Bellamy had never seen anyone happy after getting shot.

"You'll be fine, pard', it's not so far to town," he said to the sad man in what he hoped was a reassuring tone. "Life's all about knocks that you come back from."

"So they say," the Englishman replied. "But I haven't come back from many of mine yet."

"Everything will be all right in the end, son. If it's not all right, it's not the end."

The Englishman smiled back weakly. "Thanks. That's actually quite reassuring."

Bellamy rode away. He thought about what the Englishman had said about not coming back from his knocks and it depressed him. If this pain was cancer knocking at his ass then he wasn't going to come back from it, and everything was not going to be right in the end. Or in his end, as a wag might say.

He felt bad leaving the melancholy Englishman, too. Whichever way you looked at it, leaving a wounded man in the desert was not a Christian act. Sure, Pandora had left a canteen with just about enough water to make it back to town, if nothing else went wrong, but she could have left him his mule and the rest of his water. That would have given him a much greater chance of making it back alive.

Yup, she was a contrary one. She was a tolerant, respectful, even kind woman, who'd kill you the moment you stepped out of line.

Fortunately, Bellamy had a trick to lift his misery. He closed his eyes and pretended he was an eagle, flying high above and looking down on silly little men like himself and all the others.

And so, Craster Bellamy journeyed on, body on his horse following Pandora and the other hired man, mind flying high above, watching two men, a woman, three horses and a mule plod through the hot desert, on their way to find a fortune at the Fabulous.

Willow sat on a rock watching the three ride away down the alluvial fan to the main Death Valley. They'd taken everything apart from a canteen of water and a small sack of biscuits. Elizabeth the mule looked back as she was led away, with what Willow liked to think was a regretful sigh. The three humans didn't turn, even the friendly one with the beard. Friendly! He was one of the gang who'd taken everything Willow had and left him miles from nowhere. It was funny what passed for friendly out West.

When they were almost gone, he stood and walked over to Marshall. The dead man's head was at a horrible angle. He guessed Pandora must have flicked the whip around his neck and jerked hard. She certainly was a dab hand at killing big, nasty Englishmen, and much stronger than Willow thought women could be.

They'd taken the sheriff's gun, and Willow couldn't see anything else of use on him. He didn't want to go through the dead man's pockets. He considered kicking the cad, but it was too hot.

Suddenly it was far too hot. The world whirled. He bent double, hands on hips, panting like a dog. He needed water.

He fumbled the canteen into his hands. He managed to remove the lid before his mind whooshed into unconsciousness. He tumbled over onto the stony ground and lay in a heap. The canteen landed with its base propped neatly upwards on a nearby stone and all the water glugged out.

ACT THREE, CHAPTER FOUR

Spades are Trumps

"Too long" was the consensus on the previous chapter. Two toilet breaks were needed. Chapters that are too long are easy to fix, I'm guessing. Surely one just finds the middle and inserts a new chapter heading. So, I have a plan. I'm going to make some chapters too long, so my aged listeners can complain that the chapter is too long, instead of more challenging comments like "I don't believe in this character," or "actually, you'd be safe drinking water that had washed over a corpse."

Last night's other comment was from Doreen, who said she hadn't known there'd been so many English people in the Wild West. I left Mr Hillier-Edwards explaining how Britain had built America and how modern America owed all it was today to the British. Maybe there's some truth in that, but I can't imagine many places in the USA where the claim would go down well, outside the British Embassy in DC and those parts of Manhattan where the Brits cluster (talking loudly in loud British accents, announcing to all "Look how clever I am! British but over here!").

I think I wrote for so long because it is floating my boat to think that people like what I've written. It was Doreen who made the difference. Julian is paid to be there. None of the biddies and codgers have much else going on, and it's an easy shuffle from their rooms to a comfortable chair. Doreen could be home, but she chooses to walk an hour and a half through the dark later, when it's colder and, I daresay, more terrifying, all so she can listen to my tale. It brings a tear to my eye.

Talking of tears, we're going to James Willow in all sorts of bother, and return to the mine.

I rose with the first grey hint of dawn and got busy with the breakfast things. My ma always said you could get three hours work done if you got up one hour early because all the fools who get in your way are still in bed.

I was worried that Silver and Monk had killed Crane in the night, but there was nothing I could do about it if they had, so I reckoned I might as well carry on as normal. That was another thing my mother had taught me, or at least tried to. Don't sit and fret about what might be when you can't do anything about it and there's work to be done.

I collected the chopping board, knife and a side of sowbelly, and laid them out on the outdoor table so I could watch the sky lighten while I worked. Dawn was the most beautiful time of day, especially here in the valley. A jackass rabbit skedaddled from under the table, where it had been looking for scraps I guess, and hid behind a pile of broken lumber. I could still see the tops of its ears.

The bacon was greening, but I'd eaten worse. I liked to think I was an observant girl, but it wasn't until the third or fourth slice that I spotted the man hanging from the aerial tram wire. I left the knife quivering in the meat and walked out from under the dorm veranda to a better vantage.

Yup, I'd thought it was him at first glance. I'd have known that fat form anywhere. Halicore Silver. I shook my head. Here was a fine thing. It looked like Silver had gone and done for himself. Surely not? Surely he wasn't deep-thinking enough to do for himself? Or energetic enough, for that matter.

So, it must have been Crane or Monk who'd hung him. Or bandits? Or the Timbisha Shoshone? No, not bandits, they wouldn't be so stupid as to be out here in the heat. The Timbisha were built differently and didn't seem to mind the hot, so maybe it was them, but I'd never heard of Indians hanging nobody.

So, it was Monk or Crane. But Crane was too decent and Monk was on Silver's side. What had happened? Maybe he had done it himself?

He was twisting slowly one way, then the other. There was no breeze at the dorm shed. Was there wind just a little higher, I wondered, or was it the tension in the cable making him swing like that?

I jumped when footsteps sounded behind the shed. I held my breath as the steps approached. And let it out again when Crane came round the corner.

"Look!" I pointed.

"I saw." Crane stood by me and we regarded the dangling man.

"Is he definitely dead?" I asked after a while.

"I guess so." Crane didn't sound overly concerned.

"Was it you?" I stepped away and looked up at him. I didn't think it was him. If Crane had reason to kill him, he would have just shot the old coot.

He smiled. "Nope. Was it you?"

"Yes, it was me," I grinned at him, "I carried him up there and threw him up onto the wire."

"I was planning to kill him, though," said Crane, as if musing what to have for breakfast.

I looked at him. He wasn't joking.

"He was a bad man, Eleanor."

"He was a nasty man, but he didn't deserve hanging."

"Oh, he did," Crane assured me, "and a lot more."

I narrowed my eyes at him.

"Silver was boss of this mine when it flooded. That's how he knew about The Prize. Think about it. Miners stopped digging at the Fabulous when the flood happened, right?"

"Yes. So?"

"So if nobody's been working the mine, how did The Prize get found?"

"I guess Silver got lucky exploring? Or maybe he was clearing out the dead bodies?"

"Can you imagine Silver exploring? Or clearing bodies for that matter?"

"I guess not."

"Exactly, Eleanor. Silver knew about The Prize before the flood." Crane was looking levelly at the gently spinning body. It was kind of mesmeric.

"But there were fifty men here. If they'd found The Prize before the flood, they could have got it out in a trice"

"If they knew about it."

"You said they did."

"I said Silver did."

I knitted my brow, and he opened his palms at me with a questioning look on his face. He was asking me to work it out myself. My ma used to do the same thing.

So, if Silver knew about The Prize and the other miners didn't … "You reckon Silver knew The Prize was there and he let those miners drown under the ground so he could keep The Prize all for himself!"

"That's it, well done. And I don't think. I know. I also know two of those men were my brothers."

"Your brothers?" *How had he held back from killing Silver sooner?* I pointed at the dangling corpse. "He killed your brothers? We should cut him down, kick him until sundown, and hang him again!"

"Fine idea. I'm your Huckleberry."

"Then we should bring him back to life, make a little slit in his stomach, pull out his guts a dozen yards, and tie them to a tree so he can watch the coyotes eat them!" I'd heard tell that a Paiute had done this to a settler once, and I'd thought about it a lot. How far out could you pull someone's guts before they died? How long did the gutted man watch the coyotes?

Crane gave me a look. "You're a strange little girl."

"I have an imagination is all. But hang on a minute. You reckon he knew where The Prize is at?"

"Yup."

"So why haven't we got it already?"

"I guess he was waiting for more people to die so he'd have to share it with fewer of us, or biding his time for another reason. Whatever it was, we won't find out now."

Suddenly I saw his game. He wasn't all noble revenge. "You were waiting until you got your share of The Prize before killing him!"

Crane smiled back. "Sure was. There's something appealing about so much gold that you'd never need to work again, and I wasn't in a rush for revenge. My brothers are staying dead, whatever I do. And, revenge would have been sweeter once Silver thought he was a rich man."

"Do you have other kin?"

"A sister back East. If she's alive. I wrote her at Christmas, but I haven't heard back."

I wanted to cry for Crane but there were serious things to discuss. "So, who did kill him? Monk?"

"No. It was the same person who did for all the others."

"*You* killed Masterton."

He blew a little laugh out of his nose. "Fine. The person who killed Silver is the one who killed everyone apart from Masterton."

"Well, who killed the rest of them? It wasn't me."

"So that leaves?

"Nobody."

"Nobody?"

"Well, Loretta, but it can't have been her, Mr Smarty-Boots. She can't go underground."

"What if she's been lying about that?"

"I guess, but … but she's a woman."

"Loretta! Monk!" Crane shouted so loudly in the still dawn that I had to take a few paces back. "Come to the dorm shed! Bring no funny business with you and you'll find none here."

Monk arrived a few minutes later, smile stuck on his face, gun strapped to his leg. His smile flickered when he saw Silver hanging from the wire. He pulled his pistol and levelled it first at Crane, then at me.

I put my hands high as I could in the air and said, "I surrender!". Monk was slow as molasses in January, and I didn't want to do anything to confuse him. Crane raised his hands to shoulder height. "No one means you any harm." he said. "We're in this together."

"How the heck d'you get him up there?

"It wasn't me, Monk."

"Then who the heck was it?"

"Loretta."

"Loretta?" Monk spat on the dirt. "Horse crap."

"I don't know the why of it, but the how is easy enough. She's been lying about being afraid of the dark. Once you accept that, you can see she's the only one of us who could have done for them all. Plus I know it wasn't me, little Eleanor's not strong enough, and you're a ten-dollar Stetson on a five-cent head."

"What's that mean?" Monk asked.

Crane winked at me and I giggled.

"Means you're stupid," said Crane.

"I'm stupid? Reckon you're pretty dang stupid insulting a man holding a gun on you."

"I retract the accusation," said Crane.

"What?"

"I'm sorry I called you stupid. And I'm sorry I had to explain the accusation."

I giggled again.

Monk pointed the gun at me, then back at Crane, mouth opening and closing. "You will be sorry, Crane. I still reckon you killed Silver and the rest of them. Convince me you didn't or I will shoot you here and now. I might not be as clever as you, Crane, but clever don't mean nothing out here. Guns is the law in the West, and right now mine's pointed at your gut.

"Guns *are* the law," Crane smiled.

"What? That's what I said." Monk shook his head like a dog annoyed by a wasp, "I know you killed Masterton. Silver told me. So, you did for the rest of them. Has to be you. It wasn't me and there's nobody else."

While they were talking, I sidled to the wall of the dorm shed and grabbed the shovel that had been leaning there since the day I came to the mine. I agreed with Monk. Crane must have killed them all. But I was still going to help him against Monk.

"I killed Masterton because he was attacking Eleanor, fixing to have his way with her."

"Well then he deserved worse than death."

"As do you, Monk."

"*What?* You're dumber than me, the way you talk when I've got a gun. "

I agreed with Monk about that. What was Crane thinking, goading an idiot with a gun? I lifted the shovel and Monk didn't notice. It seemed he'd plum forgotten about me.

"I know who you are. You ain't Monk. You're Rockwell."

It took me a moment to remember who Rockwell was, then I almost dropped the shovel. *Rockwell!* Rockwell was the guy who'd murdered a load of Timbisha and caused the deaths of a bunch more. Monk couldn't be Rockwell, could he? Or maybe there was more than one Rockwell.

I wanted to carry on round behind him with the shovel, but I held back. Dang ground was too crunchy to sneak up on someone who wasn't talking, especially when you've got one leg shorter than the other. There was a long pause. I held my breath and stayed put.

"I'm Monk," said Monk.

"You've forgotten me," Crane said, "but we had dealings before. In Texas. When you were Rockwell."

The two men looked at each other, stony eyed. Crane was shiny with sweat. Monk was sweatier. It dripped from his nose. His gun wobbled in his hand. I was on my toes.

"I was in Texas," said Monk eventually. "I thought you looked familiar. So, I'm Rockwell. What of it?"

I could have run and hit him while he was talking that time, but I wanted to hear more.

"Tell me why you did it."

"Indians wronged me."

I took a step closer.

"You stole a mule from the Timbisha and you killed it. They paid you back fair and square by taking your gear. It was over. Then you killed four of them. Women and children." All the usual humour had gone from Crane. He put me in mind of an avenging angel.

"They stripped me naked and took my clothes, including the hat my pa gave me. I loved that hat."

"And that was fair dues after you took their mule."

"Horse crap. A white man can't wrong an Indian. It's in the Bible."

"Which part of the Bible would that be?"

"I'm done talking, Crane. You know God so well? Go meet him."

He shot.

I charged, swinging the shovel. Another shot rang out.

Monk went down and the shovel swished clean through the air.

I spun round and nearly tripped. When I'd gathered myself, Monk was lying on the ground, looking up and blinking, blood blooming on his shirt. I pulled the shovel back. Monk raised his gun and shot at me. I slammed the blade down with all my strength at his head. It sliced into his skull with the noise of a boot going into deep mud.

I let go of the tool and patted myself. I wasn't shot. Crane, walking towards me, looked unharmed too.

"That man," said Loretta's voice behind me, "could not hit a cow's tits if he was under it."

She was walking up the track from her crib, smoking pistol in hand. She was wearing a belt I hadn't seen before, with a big Bowie knife in a sheaf attached to it.

Crane reached down for Monk's gun.

"Uh-uh," said Loretta, waggling the barrel of her shooter. "Step away from the dead moron. Both of you."

Crane backed away, hands halfway in the air again.

I looked from Loretta to Monk. The shovel was lodged neatly in between Monk's eyes, which were gazing glassily in opposite directions, like a fish's eyes. I'd killed him. He was shot and maybe he'd have died anyway, but everyone dies so that argument was no good. I'd killed him. I was a killer.

"You too," said Loretta, pointing the gun at me. "Go stand next to Crane."

I did as I was told, but I couldn't stop looking at Monk. Was that his *brains* bubbling out around the edge of the shovel?

"On second thoughts," said Loretta, "get in there and have a good look if you like, honey. Death is kind of fascinating, isn't it?"

She sounded different. My mother had always been shy with men, but some of the other dancing woman had been forward, using wit and jokes to persuade men into a dance. Loretta had been more like my mother before, but now she was all confidence and sass like those other women.

Could she really be the killer? Maybe, but it made no sense. Why would she have done it?

I forgot that for the moment, too fascinated by the corpse. I crouched to have a good look at the inside of Monk's head. Funny how that grey mush had controlled his thoughts and actions, and made him the dumb, venomous varmint that had decided to kill four people who didn't deserve it at all.

"Why did you do it Loretta?" Crane asked.

"Do what?"

"What do you think, put beetles in Silver's stew?"

"That was Eleanor."

"Guilty!" I admitted, still marvelling at Monk's split head and the lack of life in him.

"Why did you kill them, Loretta? Happy Days Frida, Indian Moses, Denny, Silver ..."

"It's something I like to do," Loretta confessed, as if she was talking about flower arranging.

I gawped up at her, Monk forgotten. "*What?*" I asked. Had she really said she liked killing people?

"You've killed before, haven't you? Before you came West." Crane lowered his hands. Loretta didn't seem to mind.

"Maybe I have."

"It's why you've fled here, isn't it?"

"Again, I am happy to supply a definite maybe."

"How many people have you killed?" I asked. I didn't hate her for it, or even like her any less. In fact, I was thrilled. *To think, quiet old Loretta was the killer all along! She'd shown those silly men, she sure had.*

"I honestly don't know," she answered.

"You must have a rough idea," said Crane.

"How many breakfasts have you had, Crane?"

"What kind of question is that?"

"Answer it."

"I asked my question first."

"I've got a gun and I'm a killer."

"Fair enough." Crane scratched his nose. "I guess I've had more breakfasts than I can count."

"That's the same with my killing. It's something I do. A lot."

"Wow!" I found myself grinning.

"You going to kill us?" asked Crane.

Loretta looked from me to Crane like she was choosing which shirt to wear that day. I wasn't scared, even though she might shoot me. I don't know why.

"Of course not," she said eventually. "We're friends."

The look in her eyes said different, which thrilled me all the more. "I cannot believe it was you, Loretta! Pretending you couldn't go underground like that. You sure fooled them all, me included!"

"What are you planning to do?" asked Crane

"With your help, I'm planning on getting The Prize, splitting it three ways, and getting out of here."

The idea of teaming up with Crane and Loretta filled me with joy, but there was one big problem. "We don't know where it is." I said.

"I do." Loretta smiled. "I followed Silver. He went into an adit, rubbed off some dirt, and there it was. I don't know why he had to check it was still there. I guess he was kind of gloating. He covered it up again and headed out."

"And you think we should help you, even though you killed the others?" asked Crane.

Loretta looked at him like a ma looking at her kid. Like a normal ma looking at her kid anyway. When I pictured my ma, I just saw someone desperate to know what she should do next.

"Up to you," she smiled. "I'm not going to kill you, Crane, unless you make me. You can go, if you want. Take the girl with you, if she wants. Or you can stay, help me get The Prize out, and walk away richer than anybody you're ever going to meet."

"I'm staying!" I jumped on the spot. I trusted Loretta. So she'd killed loads of people. Nobody's perfect. I'd killed a man myself, and I wasn't a bad person. Once we go the prize out, I could go back to town and my ma would never need to dance again. Picturing her face when I told her made me about as happy as I'd ever been. She'd stop looking worried the whole time and be able to look at me like a normal ma.

Crane nodded. "Alright then, lead the way."

Loretta Cook had lied to the girl. She'd kill them in a heartbeat and lose not a wink of sleep. Sure, she liked them, but it didn't mean a thing. The only reason they hadn't died already was that they hadn't been nearby when the urge was on her. Chances of the urge coming soon were high, and chances of Crane and Eleanor walking out of that canyon were somewhere between slim and none.

ACT THREE, CHAPTER FIVE

Dying in Death Valley

A few of them, Doreen especially, were upset that I didn't mind about Loretta Cook being a mass murderer. I said that attitudes to death were different then, but it didn't help much.

"How can you condone murder?" bleated Mrs Terbangun.

Point is, I liked Loretta an awful lot more after discovering she'd killed a whole bunch of people. I was eleven! Eleven-year-olds are weird. They don't feel the gaze of social expectation so much. As I've explained to the group a couple of times, I'm trying to write from the perspective of myself at that age.

Little Eleanor's views are not the same as old Eleanor's views. I always smile a little when people when people confuse the views of a character with those of the author, as some fools did with that Nabokov fellow. If you think the writer believes what their characters believes, then boy, you are dumber than a bag of wet mice. Admittedly this is a little different because the character is me, but it's eleven-year-old me. If you think that someone as old as me can be responsible for what she thought as a child ... well it's the wet mice thing again, isn't it.

I left them talking about attitudes to death and headed off to write this coming chapter. Mr Hillier-Edwards chased after me (or what goes for "chased" in an old folk's home. He called out my name and came down the corridor bent forward, lifting his elbows higher as if attempting a half jog, but not actually achieving a faster pace than normal).

"I understand," he said. "I have killed seven men that I know of, and

certainly more."

"I guess the War was like the West," I replied, "you had to have a different attitude to death."

"Who said anything about the War?" Mr Hillier-Edwards' eyes twinkled, then he walked away chuckling.

I'm old now, and I've done some weird and incredible things. But young people look at me and think, "worthless old person. Nothing interesting there." I'm not surprised and I don't mind. As I may have mentioned already, I have known for a very long time that all young people are five-cent heads in ten-dollar Stetsons.

What's funny is I'm as guilty as them. Who knows what Mr Hillier-Edwards, Mrs Terbangun, Mrs Hopkins, Mrs Bull, or any of the rest of them, have done? They could have been milliners in Moscow or banana growers in the Bechuanaland Protectorate - or both, for all I know. I must try to find out more about all of them. I'm sure it will be fascinating and surely useful for my writing.

Another Willow chapter now. Chances are I'm going to stay up too late and go on too long. Which, if you've been paying attention and can remember all the way back to the last chapter, is actually a good thing.

Mr James Willow followed Mrs Elizabeth Willow up the curving staircase. When he was a boy, these polished wooden steps had been his ship in a storm, his treehouse in the jungle, his fort on the frontier.

Now they were the stairway to his gallows.

Time was a strange thing. As he'd played here, he'd never imagined that years later he'd be in that exact place, sick with drink and misery, following his wife of just a few hours as she skipped further and further ahead of him, higher and higher out of reach. He looked for ghosts of his child self, hoping to claw some happiness from those days. He could see no ghosts. And who was he trying to fool? He'd been unhappy as a child as well.

He wanted to dance up the stairs like Elizabeth, but he was trudging, drunk as drunk could be. Hugo had told Elizabeth that he was penniless. Her flashing smiles, bright eyes, and whispered promises of congress had become hard stares and poisonous glances of contempt. Willow had drained glasses of wine like a man glugging water after a long ride. He'd toured the room, bumping into people, finished off unattended drinks, aware of the embarrassed muttering of family and guests, burning with shame but unable to stop.

Elizabeth seemed happy now, though, ascending the stairs like a twinkling princess. He didn't know why. She was saying something, but he couldn't make sense of the words. He could only just see her. He felt like he was drowning whilst she skipped along the shore.

Buck up! he told himself.

"Elizabeth, wait!" he managed.

She stopped, surprise in her bright eyes. "It speaks?"

"I want ..." his brain cartwheeled and landed in a pile of its own excrement. What did he want?

"Oh, my mistake. The pathetic drunk only grunts like the pig it is!" she ran on up the stairs and disappeared.

She wasn't in the room that the servants had prepared for their first wedding night. He'd look for her after a quick lie-down. But he was so tired. So heavy. He fell face first onto the bed.

He was woken by screaming.

He knew what it was, knew what he'd find, but still he tumbled off the bed, somehow landing on his feet. He was still wearing his shoes. The joke about shoes in bed came to him. "I have a bad reaction to leather." "How do you know?" "Because every time I wake up with my shoes on, I feel awful."

He giggled until he heard a woman cry out and remembered what had woken him.

He stumbled out as the room whirled around him.

The screaming was louder as he cannoned off the walls towards the noise. He could hear rhythmic, bovine grunting as well now.

The door was open. He recognised Hugo's naked frame, his muscled buttocks pumping in rhythm with the grunting. A dainty hand appeared on his back, then a head around his arm. It was Elizabeth, grinning at James, eyes flashing, like a spoilt girl caught stealing biscuits by a powerless nanny.

James Willow woke. For a moment he thought he was in his cold wedding bed, but no, he was curled up on desert sand and stone. How long had he slept? It was still bright and hot as a furnace, so not long, assuming it was still the same day.

He pushed himself onto all fours, then heaved and bucked and spat, voiding the stringy gobs of bile left behind by his earlier vomiting.

He fell back to sit against a rock. He didn't have the energy to wipe the sweat and spit from his face. He was so very thirsty. He reached for the canteen which he'd spotted mid heave.

It was empty.

Hmmm, he thought. The meaning of the empty canteen grew in his mind like a huge bird coming from a great distance at incredible speed, claws out and squawking.

The sudden horror of the situation cleared his mind.

He had no water at all, and he was already thirsty.

He was going to die.

He was going to die!

No, no. He was an Englishman. Any problem could be overcome by the calm, intelligent competence of an Englishman.

He took stock.

Negatives. He was a day and a half's walk from the town and the nearest water he knew of, other than the poisoned stream. He'd come downhill most of the way, so the uphill return would take longer than a day and a half. The heat was astonishing, he was already very thirsty, and poisoned by whatever foulness had seeped from those dead men. He'd also been shot.

Positives. He had six biscuits, or what the Americans called biscuits. They were actually scones, which seemed more nutritious than biscuits. That was a boon. And the gunshot wasn't so bad. Actually, it was awful, like somebody had gouged a notch in his shoulder with an apple corer, but it could have been worse.

Now weigh the positives against the negatives and …

He giggled. He was going to die!

He could walk back to town. Would he make it? He had drunk so much water on the way here, downhill and in fine fettle. How much more would he need on the way back, uphill, poisoned, and injured? He had none. The heat was like a squeezing fist. His head ached and he would have given his left arm and leg for a drink. And he hadn't set off yet.

Pandora had left with two men and Elizabeth the mule. He could try to catch up to them up and beg for mercy. She had, after all, left him with the canteen, so she didn't want him to die. On the other hand, she'd told Willow to go back to the town. She'd killed Sheriff Marshall for disobeying her.

Also, it was clear she wanted the bounty on Loretta Cook. She'd kill anybody who tried to stop her with that vicious rawhide whip, he was sure of it.

So, back towards town it was then, dying at some point along the way. How far, he wondered, would he get?

He made it ten paces down the broad valley when he stopped. He remembered the look Elizabeth the mule had given him. He remembered the looks Elizabeth his wife had given him. And he remembered the look on the face of the third Elizabeth in his life - Lizzie Salmon. She'd sent her daughter to the mine so she could spend more time with her drug habit. He'd seen her anguish and self-loathing.

He knew self-loathing. Anguish, too.

Pandora was headed for the Fabulous, ready to kill anyone who got in her way. Lizzie Salmon's young daughter Eleanor was at the mine, under the protection of the very woman that Pandora was after, and therefore in terrible danger. How would Lizzie Salmon live if her daughter died? The guilt would finish her.

The side valley of the waterfall and the corpses led westwards down to Death Valley proper, a mile or more below. To get to the mine, Pandora would return to the valley, head south until she reached the building that actually was a stamp mill, then head back east up another tributary valley. Three sides of a square, in other words. Could Willow get there before her by travelling just one side of that square?

The southern side of his valley was high enough that you'd die falling from it, but rough and not steep. Surely he could scale it? If he could, then continue southwards in a line parallel to Death Valley proper, down into any canyons like this one and up the other side, he'd surely come to the Fabulous?

If he reached the mine before Pandora, he could warn the miners and potentially save Lizzie Salmon's daughter. Maybe he could save Loretta Cook? Take her to justice alive and save her from having her neck broken by Pandora's whip?

And if he died of thirst on the way, or succumbed to the corpses' poison, or fell and struck his head, or became a victim of the myriad animals out here that could kill with claw or venom? Well, if he had to die, he'd rather die trying to rescue others than trying to save himself.

Yes. His final act would be saving the life of little Eleanor Salmon, or, more likely, dying in the attempt. Finally, here was something to tell Saint Peter at the pearly gates.

He tied the bag of biscuits - or scones - to his belt, turned south, and strode up the low bank of the dry streambed. His knee gave way at the top of the little slope. He managed not to fall, but he slid back down the scree. He stood, hands on hips, panting roughly through his dry throat. He had failed to climb a slope half a pace high. The valley side was steeper and perhaps forty times the height. And God knew how many valleys lay between him and the mine. Not a good start.

He took the bank at an angle and gained its summit. So, a little thought was needed, that was all. Wit would see him through.

The valley side was higher than he'd judged from a distance and comprised of rock that looked as if it would crumble under the slightest pressure. He stood at the base of the slope, searching hopelessly for a route to the top.

He was on a heroic mission, so bravery should probably a part of that, he thought. Maybe he should start to climb and see what happened? On the other hand, there'd be no heroism in breaking his leg here. He owed it to little Eleanor Salmon to proceed with some caution.

He walked upstream until he found a gap in the rock wall. It was a gully that narrowed to nothing. If he wedged himself at the correct point, he reckoned, he could work his way to the top.

With much effort and luck - he was pretty sure that gravity very decently turned a blind eye at least twice during his ascent - he reached the top.

He stood, heaving and bruised. When he was capable of taking stock, he realised he was in front of a cave on a rock platform so regular and flat that it looked man-made. Jagged stones lying about had a strange regularity. He crouched and picked one up. It was an arrowhead, he was sure of it, more or less the same as the Neolithic arrowheads that he'd found in a badger's diggings near Fenny Compton and brought home to show an utterly indifferent Elizabeth.

And here was surely a stone spear head, and a knife's blade. He looked about, half expecting to see a village of savages nearby. But no, only desolate desert. This had been the tool making place of some ancient people, or possibly modern Indians. If he could go back a number of years - he had no idea whether it was one or ten thousand - there would be people here who could help him.

Time, as his dream of the stairs had reminded him, was strange and cruel.

He looked into the cave; perhaps there'd be a water tank? There was nothing but more worked stone on the floor and scores in the rock where stone had been chipped away.

He tried to eat a scone but managed only half, so gummy was his saliva.

James Willow left the cave and headed on southward across the blindingly bright, baked-hard land. Far too soon, he reached the edge of next canyon running down into Death Valley. He scrambled and half-fell down its side with relative ease then set off across the dry wash, head down and counting steps in an attempt to distract himself from his nausea, exhaustion and pain. The rocks underfoot were larger here, which made the going harder, and there was a plague of spindly but tough bushes with tiny leaves.

Not looking where he was going, he headed down a funnel of vegetation and came to a dead end. There was no way through the tangled bush.

Here was where a real man like Slade - or his brother Hugo - would have whipped out a cutlass, laughed heartily and chopped a path.

Willow turned. He'd have to retrace his steps a good hundred yards. He shook his head and coughed a sob. Tears flowed.

Heroes, he thought, did not cry when their path was obstructed by shrubbery. He wiped his face and headed back the way he'd come, before climbing up onto a rock ledge, picking out a path through the vegetation, then following it.

The roughly stepped side made it much easier to get out of this valley. His nausea was almost gone. He did have a beating headache, his thirst-swollen tongue filled his mouth, his throat felt rubbed raw, his shot shoulder throbbed, and he reckoned that if he lay down, he'd sleep for a hundred years or possibly die, but, apart from all of that, he was beginning to feel actually quite positive about things.

He headed off across the high land between the drainages. He walked for a good long while, picking his way between bushes that looked like holly, and cactuses with spines that looked like the fluffy fur of a baby animal. He touched one. It was not fluffy. Nothing fluffy in the desert, he supposed. Then he wondered what a coyote puppy looked like. Or a baby jackass rabbit.

He was making good progress. Surely the next valley would hold the mine? Almost as soon as he thought that, a new canyon split the land ahead so suddenly that he almost fell into it.

This one was narrow, maybe thirty yards deep and cliff sided. He could see no way of getting down into it, let alone up the other side. *Jump across?* He thought. It was about fifteen paces at the narrowest point he could see. He wouldn't make it halfway.

But he was so tired, and so thirsty, and his shoulder blazed so hot with pain, that he seriously considered trying the jump. He knew he wouldn't make it and he'd definitely be killed falling from that height, but he'd be killed trying to save the people at the mine from Pandora and her men.

It would be a noble death.

Or would it, really? Could it be a noble death if he knew there was no way he'd make the jump? Surely that would be pointless, selfish suicide.

He looked over the edge. His head boggled. It was a long way down to the hard dry ground.

He walked southwards along the gully edge. The valley of the corpses had changed from steep to gentle-sided, so surely this one would too? He went on and on, but it stayed as steep. He pictured Pandora and her men riding easily along the track in Death Valley. He'd never beat them to the Fabulous!

Presently, he came to a declivity which led to a gap in the canyon side. Peering over the gap, he could see that a near vertical chute of smooth rock led around ten paces down to the valley floor. It was a very steep, dry waterfall, worn smooth over millennia by alluvium-filled runoff. If he slid down that ... it would be near enough the same as falling. Two broken legs was the best imaginable outcome.

He walked on along the canyon side. It stayed steep. He could follow the edge of this tributary gully all the way down to the valley, he thought, but that would relinquish the short cut advantage. A sudden cough ripped at his raw throat. Something trickled out of his nose. He wiped it and looked at his hand. Blood!

It was funny, wasn't it? Here he was dying of thirst and his nose decided to leak out what little moisture was left in him. His own nose hated him.

He licked the blood off his hand. It sated him minutely. Odd, he thought. Odd and disgusting.

A rattle startled him. It was a huge serpent, its revolting trunk as thick as the boa he'd seen in London Zoo. It wiggled its nauseatingly fat tail and rattled again, eyeing him with a venomous cruelty that reminded him of his wife.

"I'm not scared of you," he tried to say. It sounded more like a dying dog trying to bark after being squashed by a steam roller. No matter, he thought, chances were the snake didn't speak English.

The snake hissed. That decided him.

He headed back the way he'd come, faster than he'd walked all day. He found the declivity, clambered down it, and sat on the edge of the chute. It was higher than he'd remembered, and as near vertical as made no difference.

God, he thought *if you put this dry fall here for me to slide down, send me a sign.*

He looked around. All was still. There wasn't a cloud in the white sky.

Let us try another way. God, if you didn't *put this chute here for me to slide down, send me a sign.*

He looked around. Absolutely nothing.

It didn't get clearer than that.

Before he could think about it more and stop himself, he pushed himself over the edge.

He felt a joyous rush of abandonment that ended far too quickly. His feet hit dirt. He flew forwards, arms out. A loud snap echoed off the canyon's sheer walls.

He opened his eyes, unsure whether he'd been lying there for just a moment or a thousand hours. He was on his back. One hand was on his chest; one was next to him. Both burned with an extraordinary pain that made him whimper. He banged his head against the sand in agony, then again, then stopped. Movement made the pain worse.

He lays, tears running, wrists on fire. How was he going to get to the Fabulous now? How was he going to stand up?

On the bright side, he'd thought he'd break his legs, so it could have been worse. He tried to laugh and failed again. It was a fitting finale for his tragic life, lying with both wrists broken, on an alien canyon floor where no human had trodden for what - weeks, years, ever?

He closed his eyes. His corpse would be eaten by animals. No, he realised, the cold, sickening hand of terror closing around him. Why would the animals wait until he was a corpse?

He was woken by Elizabeth busying about the room.

"Good morning!" she flicked the curtains open with a bright swish, as if they were any other couple waking on their wedding morning.

For just a moment - perhaps the happiest moment in his life - a fantasy flashed that they'd had the wedding night he'd dreamt of, making love until they fell asleep in each other arms. Then he belched nastily and remembered Hugo's buttocks and her face. His wife's face as his own brother-

He belched again. His stomach heaved. He fell more than climbed from the bed, grabbed the chamber pot, and vomited.

On all fours, he raised his head and regarded Elizabeth with streaming eyes.

"Are you finished?" She was smiling, but it was a tight smile of concentrated hatred.

He nodded.

"Then dress. We are expected at breakfast."

He heard hooves and opened his eyes. Horses were coming down the canyon. *It must be Pandora and her men! But why would she be ...* It didn't matter who it was. People were coming and that meant rescue.

He didn't want to be found lying on the dirt like an idiot. Holding his poor arms to his chest, he wormed his way with shoulder and buttocks backwards to the canyon edge, where he managed to push himself up with his legs, so his back was against the rock, burning wrists resting on his lap. They were still very, very sore, but less painful than before. His left hand was purple and swollen, but his right didn't look so bad. He managed to waggle the fingers on that hand, but the pain made him gasp.

The horses clopped nearer, still obscured by the curve of the canyon. They took longer than he expected. He found himself trying different facial expressions. What was the correct look on the face of a man, he wondered, sitting on his own, miles from anywhere, with two broken wrists, poisoned by decaying corpses, and almost dead from thirst?

Finally, the riders appeared. Indians. Four of them, all men, all riding bareback. All naked.

He tried to shout a greeting, but he could only grunt quietly. *No matter,* he thought, *a noise is all I need.*

The men were muscled and lean. They looked noble, they looked very serious, and they looked straight ahead.

Willow beat his leg against the ground and grunted. The men didn't so much as blink.

"Heeeelp!" he managed, high and pathetic. They rode past as if he were a ghost. Not even a ghost – they would have noticed a ghost. It was as if he wasn't there at all. They rode on and disappeared around the downstream curve of the canyon.

When the last echoes of the hooves faded away, James Willow wondered if he'd seen the naked riders at all. He sat against the rock wall. His wrists throbbed sharply. He didn't mind the pain too much. It was a reminder that he was alive. He wondered how long it would last.

ACT THREE, CHAPTER SIX

The Prize

"Willow must survive," Doreen announced "Or how else would you know what happened? About the Indians and all?"

"She's making up bits too, don't forget," said Mrs Hopkins. "The whole Willow part of the story could be completely fabricated."

"Oh." Doreen deflated.

"That's not entirely accurate," I said. "When I'm writing the parts that I didn't witness myself, the most part comes from what I learnt afterwards."

"But you've given yourself free rein," Julian chipped in, "to fabricate as much as you desire."

"Yes ..." I was wary. Julian's input had rarely proved helpful.

"So, the entire James Willow storyline - the Clemenses, the town, everything - could be concocted. He could die here, and that could be that. Perhaps you found a body in the desert and made up this story around him."

"I suppose I could have done."

"So is James Willow alive or dead?" Doreen was quite fraught.

"You'll find out, I promise," I said.

"Tomorrow?"

"The day after. I promise. I'm writing a 'me at the mine' chapter tonight." Doreen remained far from happy. It pleased me greatly.

Mrs Hopkins approached when Doreen was gone. "You know that the brave thing to do would be to kill Willow, don't you? It will stun the readers and show that no character is safe in your books."

I thanked her for the suggestion, glowing just a little inside because she thought I'd be writing more than one book.

Loretta led us to The Prize. I hung back. Loretta was walking differently now – quicker, and she seemed taller. She and Crane looked quite the couple, striding along ahead of me. I didn't care one bit for the people she'd killed. It was simply marvellous that shy, scared Loretta wasn't shy and scared. But who was she? Was her ignorance of animals and the ways of the West all feigned as well?

The Prize was hidden, to Crane's obvious amazement - and mine too, if I'm honest - along a short passage only a hundred yards into the second lowest adit in Gila Canyon. Loretta scraped the dirt with a trowel and there it was.

It was a seam of white quartz and gold. There was as much gold as there was quartz. If the seam was only a couple of inches deep, there was enough gold there to make anyone rich for life. But the seam was surely deeper than that. Surely there was enough there for all three of us, and our families, to never want again.

Crane wiped the remaining dirt away with a cloth and the gold sparkled all the more.

"Well I'll be a son of a gun."

"Hold your cussing and stand ready with that rag," Loretta commanded. "Eleanor, find another trowel or something else useful and get cleaning."

Loretta and I scraped away more dirt and Crane followed with his cloth, revealing quartz heavier with gold than any of the ore I'd seen brought to the town's mills.

The seam became longer and higher. Then larger still. I helped to scrape some, but most of the time I stood back in wonder. There was already enough gold to buy ... well, anything, and more revealed every moment.

Travelling around with my mother, I'd heard plenty of crazy exaggerations from miners. Lying about what you'd found underground was part of mining. It impressed the ladies in town and it duped investors.

But in all the wildest tales, I'd never heard about a strike like this.

It was a long while before Crane reckoned we'd found the edge of the lode.

"And that's only this part of it," he said, his voice wobbling. "Usually when you find gold-bearing quartz there's similar stuff nearby. Plus, we have no idea how deep this strike runs."

Crane went off to fetch water, food, and the tools we'd need to get the strike to the surface. Loretta and I stayed down there, sitting with our backs against the opposite side of the tunnel, watching The Prize glitter in the candlelight.

I'm not sure why we stayed. I guess it seemed like it needed guarding. Or maybe we'd spent so long fetching and carrying for the men, Loretta thought it was time a man had a go.

"I don't understand why Silver let those fifty men die," I said. "There's enough here to make fortunes for a hundred."

"But think how rich it would make one person," Loretta replied.

"You'd be able to buy a whole country. Who could possibly want that much? It would bring you more trouble than good."

Loretta chuckled warmly. "So, you won't be claiming your third?"

I stared at her. I'd been so excited about the size of the strike and Loretta being a murderer that I hadn't considered my share.

"A third? For me?"

"There are three of us. It goes three ways. I'm sure Crane will agree."

"But what will I do with it all?"

"Travel. Buy things. I'm never going to wear anything second hand again, and I'm going to stay in hotels so smart that they don't look down on coloured people."

"My ma can stop dancing. We'll get a good house in a fancy part of a big town and walk out in fine clothes on a Sunday."

"You do that, and give the rest away. Or keep the rest, in case you ever need to buy a fleet of ships."

I looked from Loretta to the gold, all a-shining and a-twinkling in the candlelight. She wasn't exaggerating. I had no idea how much ships cost, but I reckoned you could buy a whole load of them with that much gold. Maybe all of them. I was euphoric and a little terrified. Would I be killed before I could spend any? Then I pictured Ma's face when I told her that she wouldn't need to dance anymore, and I cheered right up again.

"I have always wanted my own train," Loretta mused. "Maybe a train company, so that they can keep all the other trains out of the way of mine. I'll have a few people to pay off, of course, if I'm going to live so openly, what with all those folk I've killed."

"Won't some of their kin want vengeance?" I asked.

"Everything has a price child, including forgiveness."

We sat quietly for a moment, then I asked what I'd been itching to ask.

"Tell me about killing Happy Days Frida."

There was a pause. I thought I was in trouble, but then Loretta said, "All right. Most times I kill folk because they're in the right place at the right time. Or the wrong place at the wrong time, depending on your perspective. It doesn't matter too much who it is, that's the point. The killing itself is my delight. Just like people who love eating steak don't give too much thought to the character of the cow it came from. Do you see what I mean?"

"I do." I did.

Loretta nodded. She believed me, and that pleased me about as much as anything ever had.

"Every now and then, however," she continued, "I get fixed on somebody. I'll come across someone hateful, simply begging to be killed, and I am smitten. Waking, sleeping, walking, washing, I cannot focus on anything but bringing that person's life to an end. However, when you choose a specific victim like that, it's a whole lot trickier than a little bit of arbitrary slaying."

"Like trying to catch a particular fish, not just any fish in the river."

"That is exactly it. They've got to be far enough from others so nobody will see or hear, then you've got to get away without being seen, then you've got to make it look like you were somewhere else … And that's just for starters. Kill someone you hate, and the first thing everyone is going to ask is 'who hated this person?' and eyes will turn to you. Choosing a target is a fool's game."

I thought about how horrid Happy Days Frida had been. "But sometimes you have to."

"I'm glad you understand. It's nice to talk about this. I never have before. It's so hard not to rush because every fibre in you is pulling at your skirt tail, begging you to rush. Happy Days Frida presented a problem because, boy, that woman would not stop asking to be killed. First time she deigned speak to me I'd just put Silver's supper bowl in front of him. I was new to the mine, hoping for a little sisterly solidarity from the only other woman. *No Loretta,* Frida said in that bossy voice. *Serve the lady first, not the men.*

"Where I come from, we serve the boss first," I told her. Frida didn't even hear my reply. She'd already gone back to talking with Monk. That was how it went. Frida never replied to anything I said. I wasn't important enough for her to waste her breath.

"Now, I'm used to being looked down on. It's useful. I've killed more people than I can count because people don't even begin to think that it could have been meagre me. Usually, I don't mind it when people look down on me. I tell myself it's how they've been brought up, and I know I'm good as anybody. But there is a line. Frida crossed the line straight away and kept right on going."

"So how did you decide to use the lion's claw?"

"I'm getting to that. So Happy Days Frida kept on begging to be murdered. One evening as we cleared the table after dinner, she said that dark-skinned people were no better than animals. I was standing right there."

"I remember! Crane told her off for it."

"He did. I guess that might be why he's still alive."

I shivered, half with fear and half with excitement. I was sitting in the dark with someone who killed people for the fun of it! I wasn't too scared though. I knew she wasn't going to kill me.

"I looked for an opportunity. But she always had Monk nearby. She had him like a whipped hound. It was frustrating. It was like she knew someone was after her and she'd hired a guard. She had him hooked by promising herself, but never giving. She even told Monk she was scared of savages and got him to loiter nearby when she was in the outhouse.

"I found the dying lion that very night, in the tunnels above the camp where nobody goes no more. I like it up there. No drowned miners."

"Are you scared of ghosts?"

"No. I don't like the stink of rotting people."

"Hmm. I don't mind it."

"I like you, Eleanor. So, I put some candles out to watch the lion die. She wasn't that happy to have me there. She couldn't move, but she kept sticking her claws out and pulling them back in. That gave me the idea."

"The lion claw!"

"You got it. When she died, I chopped off her claws and bound them to a hatchet handle. It was a lucky find. God was smiling on me the next day, too. Frida pretended it was her monthly time, but I knew she'd had her time the week before, because I do the laundry."

"I remember!" I said, "You were sick too that day, and had to go ... you weren't sick either!"

"You got it. I went to my crib, picked up the lion claw club, then went straight out back into the tunnels and up the hill. There's a good, shady spot up there where you can watch the whole mine without being seen.

"After a while the men went down into Gila Canyon, then you headed off looking for lizards or whatever."

"Tarantulas that morning, I think."

"Tarantulas, then. It's funny, when you bunk off like that and watch the world going about its normal business, everything seems muffled and distant, like you're watching through a veil from a different world. That's how things looked that morning. I wasn't far off giving up when Happy Days finally emerged, backpack on. She went about gathering supplies, all bent-kneed and palms splayed, like a sneaking child that knows she's being naughty.

"Keeping high above her, I followed her as she climbed the side of the canyon, crossed the high ridge, and headed down into the next canyon. I knew where she was going from my exploring. There's a way into the Fabulous tunnels from that next door canyon. I knew I could get there quicker underground, so that's what I did. I waited for her in the door of the adit.

"I heard her coming after a while. She sat on a rock in the dry bed below and went through her backpack. I'd been planning to wait for her to come into the tunnel, and mayhap I should have done, but the lust was on me. I snuck out, far from silent, but Frida was like a man. She was busy in her bag, and once she was focussed on a task she ignored the rest of the world.

"I hit her in the side of the head, hard. She fell, then turned and looked at me. That's my favourite bit. The confusion. The realisation. The fear. Best of all, the hope. *Surely it was all a prank?* I watched her go through all these, then I swung the claw and ripped her smug face apart from ear to mouth. A couple more whacks to her neck, then I sat back to watch her die, while she watched me watching her die."

I was going to ask some questions - had Happy Days Frida said anything? Why didn't she try to fight back? - but Crane returned with the tools and supplies in a barrow. He spoke quickly and set to work like an excited schoolboy.

I watched Loretta watching him. She had a funny look on her face, like a horse lover watching a foal at play. Might they get hitched? Crane didn't seem that much more upset than me that Loretta had killed all those people. She was clever and beautiful. I reckoned any man could love her, if he could overlook her hobby.

I guessed that was a pretty big if.

We worked all day and then some, carting barrel loads of that super-rich ore out of the adit and hiding it where we all agreed was clever. It would have to be processed to get the gold out, but we had a plan for that, too.

It was past dark when we gave up for the day and sat at the table under the eaves of the big dorm, munching quietly on hastily heated beef and beans. I thought we were too exhausted to talk, but Crane proved me wrong.

"Something happened to you, Loretta, to make you how you are. But I reckon you only kill people that deserve it."

Loretta raised an eyebrow but carried on chewing.

"But you need to stop killing people," Crane continued, "unless the situation arises when you have to."

"Like if someone was trying to kill her?" I asked.

"That would be a good example," Crane nodded. "So how about you pledge not to kill any more folk?"

"I will try," said Loretta.

"Okay," said Crane, sounding unconvinced. "So, I guess Denny, Indian Moses, and Happy Days Frida all did things that I don't know about to make them deserve death?"

Loretta fixed him with those fine eyes, icy-blue even in the candlelight. When she'd finished chewing, she put down her fork. "If they did, I don't know what it was."

"Then why did you kill them?" He asked

Loretta smiled. "Because they were there."

I squirmed. Loretta Cook was a stone-cold killer!

Crane laughed. "You're a mad murderer!"

Loretta laughed back. "I guess I am."

"So you really might kill us in our sleep!"

"I never killed anyone in their - oh, tell a lie, yes I did. A couple of folk, in fact. I won't kill *you* in your sleep. Not tonight. I need your help with the gold."

"You'll hold yourself back from killing us because you need our help?"

"That's about the size of it." Loretta took a big sip from the cup of whiskey, then levelled her eyes at Crane. "You reckon you're a good man. I reckon you're probably thinking by now that you should hand me in to a lawman, to stop me ending the lives of any other good folk."

Craned nodded. "I would do that if there was a lawman worth spit this side of the Rockies. There isn't though, so I guess what I'm really thinking is that I'm going to have to dispense justice myself."

"You're going to kill me?"

"When we're done here, and Eleanor's clear and safe, I guess I am. It's simple math. I kill you, and a murderer goes to hell. I don't kill you and a bucket load more innocent people have their lives cut short. I have to do it, unless you can convince me you're not going to kill any more."

"Don't *tell* her if you're going to kill her!" I could not believe the idiocy. "And don't kill her!"

"Everybody dies, Crane," said Loretta, as if I wasn't there. "Everyone I killed was dead already. We're all dead already."

"I'm not dead already, and I'm glad I'm not," Crane countered. "Life's the only thing we've got, when it comes to the rub. That's why stealing it is the greatest crime of all."

I thought Crane made a reasonable point, but Loretta seemed amused. "What are you eating?" she asked.

Crane looked down at his bowl, then upwards. I followed his gaze to the stars. There were about a million tonight, twinkling in the black like the gold in The Prize. "You're going to tell me that a cow's life is worth the same as a human's, aren't you?" he said.

"A cow's life is worth something, isn't it?"

"Sure."

"So how many cows' lives equal one human's?"

"I don't think there are enough cows."

"Then make some up. How many?"

I left them arguing about cows, did the dishes, and headed for bed. As I walked, I looked up and saw Silver still swinging from the tramway wire, looking like he was made of silver in the starlight. In all the excitement, I'd plum forgotten about him. I guess we'd have to chop him down soon. If someone happened along, he'd take some explaining.

We carried on the next morning. My job was mostly fetching water and food as the other two worked. We still had no idea how deep the seam went into the rock.

"Reckon we should go to town and get some help?" Crane asked during one of their rare rests.

"Because that worked out so well for Silver?" Loretta replied.

"Yeah. We could get unlucky and hire a mass murderer."

"That's certainly a hazard."

"Who could easily stop killing people."

"That's like saying a fat person could stop being fat."

"They could!"

"Sure, but very few do when they try because they don't really want to, and food is delicious."

I headed out again to get water. We already had plenty but we'd use whatever I got, and I thought I'd best leave them to their lovey-dovey play fighting.

The thick heat of the day hit me a few paces from the entrance, and I slowed my pace accordingly. The light at the tunnel mouth was so bright it almost knocked me back. I stood, blinking, waiting until my eyes could bear it.

When I did finally get my vision, I was surprised to see a chubby man with a pointed beard looking straight at me. He was holding a revolver in one hand.

My heart fell into my stomach. I knew the gold was too good to be true. Here was a bandit for sure, come to take it all.

"Hello?" I said.

He chuckled. He had red cheeks and a kind face. Maybe he wasn't a bandit. "You made me jump like a racoon surprised by a snake, coming out of that adit all of a sudden like that!"

"I didn't mean to startle you. Sorry. How can I help you, mister?"

"Who else is down there?" he asked.

"There's a small army and a whole tribe of Comanches." I replied.

He chuckled. "Got a bunch of redcoats in there, too?"

I nodded.

"You sit on that there rock and stay quiet." Beardie pointed his pistol at a rock, then waggled it at me.

"Can I sit in the shade?" I asked.

He looked confused for a second, then apologetic. "Sure, sorry, should have thought of that. How about under that ledge yonder?"

"That'll be just fine, thank you."

I sat on one side of the canyon and Beardie stood on the other, where he could cover the adit mouth and me with his gun.

He kept looking along Gila Canyon, as if looking for someone. "What's your name?" he said after a while.

"Eleanor Salmon. What's yours?"

"Craster Bellamy."

"Craster?"

"It's a place in England where my parents came from. I was born in America. I've never been to England. I mean to go one day and head for Craster."

"Why?"

He chewed his lips, and his beard rotated like a skunk's tail. "I never thought about the why of it. Maybe just to see the look on people's faces in Craster when I say I'm called Craster."

"Seems a long way to go just to see English people confused for a moment."

"I guess it does. You're a clever girl, ain't' ya?"

I was about to agree, but I heard footsteps crunching along the gravel bed of the canyon. It was a man and a woman. She was tall and confident, rawhide whip at her waist. She had a white shirt tucked into blue men's trousers at her narrow waist.

The man was taller and nasty looking, with a chin like an ore stamp and a big pistol on his hip.

"Howdy, Pandora," said Craster whose ma and pa were from Craster, standing up straight like a kid in a schoolhouse. "This is-"

"Eleanor Salmon," said Pandora.

I blinked. *How did she know my name?*

"Howdy, Eleanor." She was pretty but she had mean eyes. "I'm Pandora Jones. They call me Pandora Catastrophe Jones. I'm sure Craster's told you his name by now, he's a friendly sort, and this here is Gerald Potts." She hoiked a thumb at stamp-chin. "He ain't so friendly." There was an edge to her voice. Coupled with her killer eyes it made me shiver despite the heat, and I didn't like the look of Gerald Potts one itty bit.

What's the situation?" she asked Craster.

"This one came out of there." He pointed at the adit.

"How many men in there?

"I dunno!" Craster Bellamy admitted cheerily. "She said there's an army, some Comanches, and a company of redcoats. I suspect she was exaggerating."

Pandora turned to me. I did not like the look in her eye.

"How many people are in the mine, Eleanor?" She asked.

"Like I told your friend, there's a small army and-"

"Your mother is Lizzie Salmon. She's a whore in the town." Pandora's face was deadpan, but I could feel the threat.

My head got hot. I was not far off attacking her, pointless as that would be. I fixed her eye with mine.

"My mother. Is. A. Dancer," I said.

Pandora shrugged. "Whatever you've got to tell yourself. Point is, I know who she is and where she is on any given day. And what she's doing every night."

Treacherous tears of rage made me blink.

"So," Pandora continued, "tell us the truth or, when we're done here, we'll pay a visit to your ma. Are you old enough to understand what that means?"

The big henchman, Gerald Potts, smiled at me like a boy who likes killing birds might smile at an injured bird found in the woods well away from anyone. I was more scared of him than I was of Pandora. He was huge and looked about as kindly as a scorpion, but he had a crafty glint to his eye too.

Craster Bellamy widened his eyes and smiled in an 'I'm-sorry-but-this-is-happening-anyway' expression. I'd seen the look on some of the men who'd come to dance with my mother. I hated those men more than the ones who scowled at me.

"I'm old enough to understand," I said, "but I still don't want to tell you."

"Is that what you'd like me to tell your mother? I know what Silver found here. I want it. I've killed people for an awful lot less. You would not be the first child I've done for."

"You proud of killing children?" I asked.

For the first time, her expression flickered away from super-cool, in-charge beauty. She sighed, looking down, then up at the sky, then back into my eye.

"I don't suppose I am," she admitted. "But that doesn't change anything."

I felt sick. What could I do? Crane was most likely to come out first, pushing a barrel of ore, since it was his turn to take a load of gold to the hiding place. But what if they worried why I hadn't come back with the water? Crane was the better miner, so he'd probably stay working while Loretta came looking for me …

"There's only one person down there," I tried.

"Where are all the others?"

"Dead."

"Dead?" asked Craster. "But you can't be here on your-"

"Shush, Bellamy," said Pandora. She'd come from up the hill, so I guessed she'd seen Monk and Silver's bodies. We had, I had to admit, left the camp in a state that might trouble the casual observer. "Take the girl up to the mine buildings. Do not let her out of your sight."

I was up and walking before Pandora could ask for more details about the one person I'd said was down there. Now it didn't matter who came out first. Pandora would capture him or her, but the other one could rescue the rest of us. I hoped Loretta stayed behind, because Crane might hesitate before he killed Pandora and her men.

Loretta hefted another chunk of ore into the barrow. It was hard work, but she'd done harder.

"Don't reckon this one will hold any more," she told Crane. "Your turn for a run."

"Sure." He downed tools, grabbed the handles, and headed off.

Loretta bent to pick up a chisel but was interrupted by Crane hollering over his shoulder, "Eleanor's been gone an awful long while."

Now Loretta thought about it, she had. Much longer than normal. She stood back up. "I'll come with you."

She followed Crane out of the tunnel, closing her eyes at the glare.

"Hold it right there," said a woman's voice.

Loretta stepped back, hand on her revolver, and opened her eyes. Light blinded her. A whoosh of air, then a fearsome grip snapped onto her wrist. She wrenched at it.

"Don't tug darling, or you'll get shot," said a confident, female voice.

She blinked until her vision returned and saw a big man with a huge revolver trained on her and Crane. The woman was holding the rawhide whip that wound painfully about her wrist.

"I'm going to give you enough wiggle room to toss that gun on the dirt," said the woman, "but try to point it at anyone and you'll lose your head."

The whip loosened and Loretta did was she was told. The lunk came over to pick up her gun, all the while keeping his own gun trained on Crane. When he was back covering the both of them with his pistol, the woman flicked her whip. It snapped off Loretta's wrist like a well-trained snake. The woman began to coil it

"What the heck is that?" shouted Crane, pointing up the slope.

Loretta ran for the adit mouth. A shot rang. Stone chipped and pain flashed across her face but she carried on, sprinting into the dark. She was around a corner and deep in the darkness before the next shot rang out. She stopped running and felt her way to a broad support beam that she could hide behind.

Loretta took her Bowie knife from its sheaf and waited, hoping they'd come along the adit after her.

Willow Cannot Weep

Julian has looked up the word "Okay" in an encyclopaedia and announced that its first use was later than the period I'm describing.

"What do you mean, its first use?" I asked.

"The first time it was used was when it was written-" he began.

"Jinglewangers," I interrupted.

"What?" he replied.

"Tonight, I'm going to write the word 'jinglewangers'. Would you say that's the first ever use of the word?"

"No ... "

"No, because I just said it."

"So?"

"So, first time something's written doesn't mean that's the first time it was used, does it?"

Julian gulped at me.

"You have to admit she's got you there, old man!" said Mr Hillier-Edwards, rocking back and forth on his feet, as he does when he's amused.

James Willow followed Elizabeth to breakfast on the first morning of his life as a married man. His hangover was like a diseased cat clinging to his skull, toxic claws piercing bone and brain.

The corridor to the dining room was a gauntlet to run - or stagger. Light poured through the windows like liquid poison, and he knew what it was to be a vampire.

His new wife hadn't waited for him. He hadn't seen her since she'd skipped away down the stairs like a selfish lamb. He could hear her now though, laughter chiming like happy funeral bells, overlapped by Hugo's deep guffaws.

"You're late, James!' Hugo bellowed when he appeared. "Didn't you hear the breakfast *horn?*"

Elizabeth laughed. His father and mother joined, looking confused. The only other genuine laugh was a surprised titter from a serving girl. So, the staff knew already. Of course they did. Hugo had been making a joke about a cuckold's horns. Married less than twenty-four hours and already a cuckold. If the staff knew now, the village would know by the end of the day, the county by the end of the week.

He sat, hoping coffee might help his dreadful physical and mental predicament.

What could he do?

In the end, over days, weeks, months, and then years, he did what men like him have been doing for centuries, millennia, maybe longer. He did nothing.

James Willow didn't know how often his brother Hugo visited their cottage on the estate, because he came when James was out. Sometimes he met him leaving.

Elizabeth was cold, snubbing him at every turn. She laughed at his earnest but cack-handed attempts to consummate the marriage. Soon she gave birth to a daughter.

A little over a year later, his wife had a son, then another daughter. The wedding remained unconsummated. Hugo brought the children presents of wooden animals - a goat, a deer, a highland cow. Always an animal with horns.

Willow played with the children, read books, walked in the countryside, became involved in village affairs, and generally behaved like a gentleman. He didn't know what else to do. Nobody seemed to mind what he did.

By the time they were one, three and five years old, he loved the children with a passion that surprised him. One day, walking in a February drizzle, he wondered which one he loved most. He concluded that he probably did love them to different degrees, but it was like looking into three boxes, each containing a different strength of blinding light. The lights might be different strengths but they all blinded him, so their relative brightness was irrelevant. Such was his love for his children.

It was returning from that very walk that he found his eldest, Rosie, embroidering with her nanny.

"Oh, it's you," said the child. "I expected Uncle Hugo."

"Would you have preferred Uncle Hugo?" he asked.

"Oh, yes."

"Why?"

She'd looked at him appraisingly for a long while, then said "He's better than you in every way. And you're worse in every way." She'd returned to her embroidery, utterly unaware of the devastation wreaked by innocent honesty. Or was it innocent? Even as young as she was, was she goading him? Half of her came from Elizabeth, after all, and half from Hugo, who was hardly a delightful character.

"Oh, I'm so sorry," cried the aghast nanny. "She don't mean it, they repeat what they've heard at this age ..."

"You're not my real daddy anyway," chimed in little Rosie. "Uncle Hugo is."

The nanny turned beetroot red and hung her head.

Willow walked back out and kept going walking for hours. Walking calmed him. When he was sufficiently calm, he knew what to do. He had to leave. It was that or suicide, and he was too scared to kill himself.

The final humiliation was asking Hugo to fund his passage to America.

"Now the children are old enough to see what you are, it's probably for the best," Hugo said.

James wondered if Hugo had told Rosie. But he didn't ask. He needed to leave, and he needed the family money that Hugo controlled.

Staging a suicide had been Hugo's idea. *Better for everyone* he'd insisted.

Better for Hugo, James Willow had thought. It left the path clear to Elizabeth, and it paved that path with honour. *Hugo's a good chap,* they'd say. *Stepped in to look after that poor woman and her lovely children after that cowardly cad took his own life.*

But he'd gone ahead with it.

Willow had taken passage to America with enough money for food and meagre board for a few weeks. Hugo had made him beg even for this, and given it only on the assurance that he would never return to England.

Hugo left a pile of Willow's clothes on the beach in Norfolk and arranged for them to be found. Even in this last act Hugo had sought to humiliate him, by choosing the very safest, least dramatic coastline in Britain for James' final, desperate act. Anybody visiting the site - his children, for example – would not be inspired by the poetry of Willow's despair as they might on, say, a craggy Cornish cliff. They'd simply think what a sad fool he'd been, if indeed they could be bothered to ever make the pilgrimage to such a dreary spot.

I must never be pushed around like that again, Willow resolved. *I will have my vengeance on Pandora. I will recapture the mule, Elizabeth, I will give her a new name that reflects my new life - Liberty, perhaps - and I will begin again.*

This is the dawn of the James Willow that should have been!

He opened his eyes, a little surprised to find he was still alive. While he'd been making his fine pledges, one part of his brain had suspected that he was in purgatory and that he'd have to live his new life in heaven, if God accepted victims of their own weakness.

He was sitting against the canyon wall. It looked hot but he felt cold. That probably wasn't a good sign.

His wrists throbbed, the left more than the right. He could lift the right without too much agony. He pressed his palm against the dirt, and it was bearable. He tried the same with his left and cried out.

He sat back. The agony in his arm subsided, though his whole body ached.

But he was alive.

And he was not going to be cowed again. Not by Pandora, nor by this desert.

Pressing his feet into the dirt and wriggling his back up the rock, he managed to stand. He walked a few steps, but the movement hurt his left wrist too much. He tried to lift his left hand using the fingers of the right, but that was too painful for both arms. Finally, he managed to use the back of what he laughably thought of as his good hand to lift and tuck his left hand into his shirt.

He trudged down the canyon, nauseous, dizzy and buffeted by waves of pain from his damaged arms. Slowly, he adapted to his miserable condition and began to walk faster and more firmly. His mouth was gummed with a saliva that tasted like excrement. His head felt like an anvil whacked by a blacksmith in a blindingly lit furnace. He couldn't even consider climbing the canyon walls, so he'd have to go the long way round. But he was up, and he was headed for the Fabulous. He couldn't hope to overtake Pandora, but he still might save little Eleanor Salmon.

He was going to get to the Fabulous if it killed him.

He made it forty yards along the even surface of the canyon floor before the world whirled and he staggered and fell, crashing down on his left wrist and crying out.

He blinked and waited for the pain to subside just a little before pushing himself to his feet again, using his right hand and cradling his poor left to his stomach.

He stood. He had to face it; he was not well. The light was burning agony. He squeezed his eyes tight and realized that they were dried out. He had no tears. He wasn't sweating either. *That's not good,* he thought.

He looked up. Through blurred vision he could discern a bend in the canyon a hundred paces ahead. He'd make it that far before he died, he decided.

How many more paces to the Fabulous? Ten thousand? More? He knew he could make it. He'd failed his own children. He'd failed himself. No more. He was going to get to the Fabulous and he was going to save that dear, defenceless child.

ACT THREE, CHAPTER EIGHT

The Art of Torture

"Willow is going to live," Julian told Doreen. "Eleanor wouldn't have been able to make up such a complex story. He must have told it to her afterwards."

Is that true?" Doreen asked me. Her concern for Willow's welfare is touching. I suppose when your husband lets you walk miles in the dark and the rain while he drinks in the pub, you look for a hero where you can.

"I can't tell you, Doreen," I said. "It will spoil the story."

"He is going to live," insisted Julian. "Leaving a chapter hanging like that, with us thinking he must be about to die, is called a cliffhanger. It's a very basic, beginners' writing technique. If I was Eleanor's editor, I'd suggest she used it less, if at all."

Mr Hillier-Edwards appeared, an uncharacteristic no-nonsense look on his face. "Julian, has Mrs Salmon given you permission to use her first name?"

"Well, not as such."

"Then please do not. Moreover, why do you think she couldn't have made up Willow's story? Do you think she's not capable?"

"Or too old?" asked Mrs Terbangun from her chair.

"Or is it because she's a woman?" asked Mrs Hopkins, storming across the room. She's speedy when she wants to be, that one.

"It is all three of those things," said Julian, rather bravely I thought.

In the silence that followed, I swear you could hear the eyebrows raising around the room.

The secret of being a good general is knowing when to retreat, said somebody once - Napoleon or Wellington, I think. Or was it Lee? Maybe it was all of them.

Julian was not a good general.

"She's not capable because she's never written fiction before. One cannot just become a writer by wanting to be one. And yes, she is too old, in the sense that her prose is outdated. She has learned nothing from modern writers because she hasn't read modern literary fiction, and one can simply not be a good writer without being a contemporary writer." His tone was reasonable and persuasive, as if he truly believed the crap he was spouting and expected the others to understand and change their minds. "And yes, sorry, but being a woman does not help. There are some capable female writers, but they are few. Mrs Salmon is not one of them."

He looked about, smiling condescendingly, as if he'd cleverly convinced a group of idiots to replace their daily bourbon biscuits with plain ones.

The group stared back at him.

I left. I may not have written much, but I do know that hearing someone say you can't write does not help, and I had a lot to get down that evening.

I was surprised by Julian's attack, but I have taken over his writing group and denied him editorship, so I can understand his rancour. Don't misunderstand me, I don't forgive him, but I do understand him. He is young.

He's also stupid, patronising and disrespectful as hell. What was he thinking, attacking old people about being old? Did her really think we'd all go "golly, you're so right, you're a thirty-year-old genius and we're all a bunch of fools who've learnt nothing in our shared thousand years or so on the planet."

What a cretin.

Anyway, he deserves no more thought. Time to get back to the Fabulous and write about what was happening with me.

Craster Bellamy followed me up the canyon towards the mine office. When we got there, I spun round and punched him in the groin.

"*Oof!*" he cried, gripping his nethers.

I ran. I tried to run like I'd seen others run, headlong and fast, but I couldn't of course. It was like being in a dream. It seemed ridiculous that I couldn't go any faster. The invaders' three horses, tied to the rail at the end of the big dorm, watched me with pitiful eyes. I didn't want their pity.

I wanted to run!

"Stop or I'll shoot!" shouted Bellamy.

I kept going.

There was a bang and a p-tang! as a bullet bounced off a rock.

"Next one hits you! I'm a better shot than I look!"

I stopped and turned.

Craster Bellamy was standing by the dorm shed, pistol pointing at me. He held the gun steady, despite the recent blow to the balls. The gentle man was harder than he looked.

"I'm sorry, my sweet," he said. "I'd love to let you go. But Pandora will kill me if I do. She nearly killed me when I lost the mule."

"How do you lose a mule?" I couldn't help but be interested.

"It was my watch last night when the Indians took it."

"Did you go to sleep?"

"I'm pretty sure I did not. They're sneaky varmints."

"And you're sure Pandora will kill you if you let me go?" I tried.

"For sure."

"She looks so nice."

"Oh, she's a fine-looking woman, but she's about as nice as a shaken sack of rats. Better people look, the meaner they think they can be, in my reckoning. Pandora Catastrophe Jones is the finest looking person I ever saw, and the meanest too. Proves the point, you see?"

It didn't prove his point though. She was just one example and that wasn't enough to prove a point. My ma had explained that to me. But I wasn't going to quibble. "I won't cause any trouble if you let me go. I'm just a girl."

"The mule was just a mule, and it wasn't even ours by rights, and she nearly killed me over that. If she knew they took my rifle, too, I reckon she would have killed me. So, sorry, but I ain't going to let you go."

"They took your rifle?" yelled Pandora Catastrophe Jones, striding up the slope from Gila Canyon. Crane walked after her, followed by Gerald Potts. Potts had his gun held out front, pointed at Crane.

Bellamy looked at her, mouth opening and closing. If I could have run faster than a crippled tortoise, I'd have high-tailed it there and then.

"Craster," said Pandora, once she was near enough not to need to raise her voice again, "it's not the loss of the mule or your rifle that concerned me. It was you letting Indians so near our camp when we were asleep. They could have taken a lot more. You lost ten percent of your share of the gold for that. Now I know there are thieving Indians running round armed with a very nice Henry, you've lost twenty."

He looked at his feet. "Sure thing, Pandora. Sorry."

"Apology accepted. Don't do it again. Now tie Crane to that chair." She pointed to the stout chair that Silver had always favoured. "Potts, cover him."

I thought about slipping away while they were tying Crane to the chair - they took a while over it - but Pandora fixed me with a smile. She looked up at Silver, who was still hanging from the tramway.

"Love what you've done with the place," she said.

"We would have taken him down." I was embarrassed. "We've been busy."

"Sure. Hauling out gold to make you rich is more important than a dead man's dignity."

"We didn't know how!" I blurted. "He's a big man, and-"

"I'm joking," she interrupted. "I knew Silver. He doesn't deserve cutting down. But how did he get there? He didn't seem like your suicide type."

"That's what I thought, so I was very confused when he did kill himself." I smiled at her. I wasn't going to let this lady browbeat me too much, no matter how lovely and nasty she was.

"Well you're a sassy one, aren't you?" she said. Then she went over to Crane. "Give me your knife, Potts."

Potts took a long blade from his belt sheaf and handed it to her.

With no ado at all, she thrust the knife into Crane's shoulder.

I gasped. Craster Bellamy grabbed my shoulders. "Best not interfere, child,' he said.

Crane didn't make a sound, but his eyes were screwed shut. Then he opened them, and I hated the tears that spilled. They were real tears of pain that he couldn't have done anything about, but I felt bad for him because I thought he'd think that Pandora might think he was scared or upset or something. His next words changed that, though.

"Thanks," he said, rolling his shoulder. "The muscle was a bit tight in there after hefting all that gold. What's next?"

"Maybe an eye?" Pandora put a finger to her mouth as if pondering which cake to choose. "Possibly an ear. We'll see. I don't want to make you a woman just yet, but that's very much on the table should it be required. Or you could tell me where the gold is now and save us some pain. Well save you some pain, anyway."

Crane laughed. "You haven't tortured much, have you?"

Pandora shrugged. "Not a great deal. You?"

Craned nodded. "I've seen a bit. It's a long way from as simple as it seems."

"Really? Surely I simply hurt you a lot and you tell me things."

Crane shook his head. "Oh no, no. There's much more to it than that."

"Enlighten me, please."

I looked from Pandora to Crane. This was a very strange conversation for torturer and tortured to be having. Crane was positively flirting. Sure, she was lovely, but she'd just stabbed him! Men are strange, I decided. Women too, for that matter.

"Torture works through fear," he continued. "You hurt me. I'm scared of what you'll do next, so I'll tell you where the gold is before you can hurt me more."

"Yeah. That is exactly what I am doing." She sounded a little impatient and I understood why. Nobody likes it when people explain the obvious. "So, are you going to tell me where the gold's hidden before I injure you permanently or not?"

"Two things. First, I know you're going to kill us whatever happens, so a permanent injury isn't a problem."

Pandora tilted her hat and gave a little nod. *They were going to kill us whatever happened!* I looked over my shoulder at Bellamy. He gave me those sorry-but-not-sorry eyes again. Potts grinned and winked. I don't know which one I hated most. Actually, I did.

"What's the second thing?" Pandora asked.

"Say I tell you where the gold is now. Say I say it's at the top of the mountain, in a combination safe. The combination is one, nine, zero, eight."

"Shall I go?" Potts asked, looking up the mountain uncertainly. "Might take me a couple of hours."

"It's not there." said Pandora. 'What Crane here is saying is that he'll lie to me to stop the pain, and I'll send one of you on a wild goose chase. You'll get back with the news he was lying. I'll torture him some more and he'll lie again. That, he's trying to tell me, is the problem with torture. People lie. Especially when they're going to die anyway."

"You got it!" said Crane. "You are a smart one. This could go on for days. So how about you don't torture me, and we share The Prize? There's enough to make us all rich for life."

"The Prize?" asked Bellamy.

Crane smiled at him. "It's what we've been calling the biggest gold strike you ever did see. We've already got millions of dollars out. There's a lot more. Working together-"

"Potts," interrupted Pandora, "shoot his knee."

"Hang on," said Crane, "you haven't understood a thing."

She smiled sweetly. "Oh, I have understood. When there's a problem, men like to tell women there's only one course to follow. Inevitably, that course benefits the man to the detriment of the woman. Inevitably, he's talking bullcrap and there's more than one course. Shoot, Potts."

It was a powerful pistol. Crane's knee and the chair leg exploded. He fell face forwards and screamed. It was the second worst noise I ever heard. Then he sucked in a breath and panted and tried not to cry out again; that was the worst noise I ever heard.

Pandora walked over and grabbed him by the belt and hair and heaved him around, so he was looking at me. His face was a mess of snot, tears and agony. My heart was fit to burst. I tried to wrench free and go to him, but Bellamy had me tight.

"Right now, child, you two will make a good pair," said Pandora, "because he'll always walk peg legged. It'll be the work of moments to shoot both his legs clean off. Potts?"

Potts raised his gun.

"No!" I cried.

"Oh," said Pandora, "would you rather tell me where the gold is?" She sounded nice, concerned even, like she was asking whether I wanted to carry on with a Sunday stroll or rest on a bench awhile.

I looked at Crane. I'd have given all the gold in the world to stop him being hurt more, but I reckoned if I straight out told her she'd kill us both anyway.

"Will you promise to let me and Crane go without any more hurt if I tell you?"

She nodded.

I'd have believed a rattlesnake quicker. How could I make sure she wasn't lying? I thought of what was most dear to me. "Swear on your mother's life that you won't hurt us no more and I'll tell you."

"Okay, I swear-"

She was interrupted by a loud, metallic clang.

There was a judder and a whirr as the aerial tramway started up. Silver jerked and headed off down-canyon. An ore cart swung out of the tram house to follow. The wire sagged so much under the weight of the loaded cart, I thought it would break, but it didn't. The cart bobbed off down the slope, following Silver, who danced a macabre jig on the swinging wire.

"Who else is here?" Pandora asked, unclipping her rawhide whip.

I looked at her, thinking I'd better tell her because I didn't want her hurting Crane.

The whip lashed and stung my shoulder.

I touched the wound then looked at my bloody fingers.

I stared at Pandora through my tears, enraged. She was coiling her whip.

"I am eleven years old!" I shouted at her.

"I'd had a lot worse than that by the time I was eleven. Now tell me who else is here or you'll get a lot worse too."

"I was about to tell you!" I sobbed a little, stalling for time.

"Quit stalling or I'll kill your friend."

"It was Loretta. There are just three of us left. I swear."

"Loretta Cook," said Pandora. It wasn't a question. How *was* she so well informed?

"Potts, run and stop the tramway. But be careful. Loretta Cook is a killer."

"*She* is a killer that I should be worried about?" scoffed Potts. "A woman is going to get the better of me?" His voice dripped with mocking disbelief.

Pandora looked at him.

"Sorry," he said.

"Go and get her."

We watched him head up the hill. He disappeared behind a shed. A horrible scream ripped through the hot, hazy air, then there was silence.

"Potts!" shouted Pandora Catastrophe Jones.

No answer.

"Come out, Loretta, or I'll shoot the girl!"

No answer.

Pandora strode over to me, grabbed me by the shoulder and pulled me away from Craster Bellamy.

"Shoot her in the leg, Bellamy."

"Which one?" he asked, taking his pistol from its holster.

"You choose," she said.

"Threaten me instead," said Crane. "We got a thing, me and Loretta. She's more likely to come out if you threaten me."

Pandora let go of me and loped over to where Crane was propped up on his elbows. She kicked him hard in the face and he slumped.

"Last chance Loretta! Come out or the girl gets it!"

We listened. All was silent. A zebra-tailed lizard had climbed onto the table and was pumping up and down on its forelegs, watching us.

"Do it," she said.

Bellamy took aim.

ACT THREE, CHAPTER NINE

Elizabeth Rescues Willow

I delayed the start of last night's reading, waiting for Julian.

"He's not coming," said Doreen.

"We told him to sling his hook," said Mrs Bull.

"Editorial decision by the editorial team," said Mr Hillier-Edwards. "We couldn't have someone being rude to our creative type and jeopardizing the writing process."

All the biddies and duffers, plus Doreen, were smiling and nodding.

"He didn't upset me," I insisted.

"But it is better without him here, isn't it?" said Mrs Hopkins.

I wanted to say it wasn't. I wanted to say that I wanted everyone to hear my story, even its detractors. Also, I'd never have started writing if it wasn't for him. But the fact was, I was happy to see the back of the jumped-up toerag.

"Perhaps we can manage without him," I said.

And now, For Doreen's sake, let us see what Mr Willow is up to.

James Willow reached the bend in the canyon. He was pretty sure he did, anyway. The light was a piercing pain, and he could see only blurred shapes anyway, so he kept his eyes closed most of the time, only opening them to check for direction and major obstacles. Minor obstacles he stumbled over. His thirst was extraordinary. He would have given his arms and legs for half a cup of water.

He tripped over boulders - he assumed they were boulders - they could have been lumps of cheese or holidaying dolphins for all he knew - but he made it to the curve in the canyon and stumbled on. Every fibre in his body begged him to throw himself down and die.

No! He said out loud. He was not going to give up again.

Elizabeth the mule brayed in agreement.

Yes, that's right, you good mule, he thought. *You never gave up on me. You never-*

He opened his eyes.

There was something mule-shaped in his way.

"Elizabeth, is that you?"

He found the last moisture in his body and blinked it into his eyes. It was Elizabeth, hung with bulging sacks that looked a lot like waterskins, and other bags.

Shortly afterwards, he was feeling a lot better. The mysteriously reappearing mule carried easily enough food and water to get him to town, and a loaded Henry rifle.

He was at the mouth of the side canyon at the edge of the main valley. He could head north, back to town. Or he could follow Pandora and her men south to the Fabulous and see if he wasn't too late to save little Eleanor Salmon, and collect the bounty on Loretta Cook.

With a good amount of painful heaving, he mounted Elizabeth. She didn't seem to mind. Without any instruction, she walked off downslope, sure footed on the alluvium. When they reached to the valley, she headed south, towards the Fabulous. Willow clung onto her back. It was not comfortable, but it was around a million times better than walking.

It wasn't long before he saw the stamp mill and the base station of the aerial tramway, but it took a while to get there.

"*That's what a stamp mill looks like!*" he said out loud.

From the distance Willow had thought it was a little shed, but the building housing the base of the tramway turned out to be a huge wooden hall. Elizabeth stopped outside it. Willow slipped off. His right hand was more or less working, although still painful. His left was still pulsing pain and useless. It took him quite a while to work the rifle free of its strapping, but finally he managed.

He climbed the steps into the tramway building, figuring if he could get it started then here would be an easy way up the mountain. Just days before, the idea of riding in a bucket suspended high about the ground would have terrified him. Now, in the crushing heat, weary as a man could be, it seemed a pretty marvellous conveyance.

There were cogs and drums and levers and empty tins and wrappers. There was a cart in the station and more dangling up the hill, but no obvious way to get them going.

He was contemplating a set of leaves and gears, willing them to start, when there was a crack and a groan and suddenly the wire and the cart began to move.

Marvelling at the power of the mind, he mounted steps up to a little platform and half jumped, half fell into the cart as it passed.

Moments later he was looking out of the aerial ore truck as it headed up the canyon. Elizabeth, ever smaller, watched him go.

ACT THREE, CHAPTER TEN

Pandora on Top

For the first time, the codgers and Doreen thought the chapter was too short.

"At least you won't have to walk too late," I said to Doreen.

"Oh, I don't walk anymore," she told me. "Your Pandora's inspired me. I told Gary he could go to the pub after he'd picked me up from the bus stop and dropped me home. It works well. I prefer having him out of the house while I do the housework and cook our tea."

Small steps, I thought.

I told them I had to head upstairs to write the final chapter.

"Maybe the last chapter of this book," said Mr Hillier-Edwards. "We're all looking forward to the next story already!"

So here I sit, at my vulture's perch, in what I call my turret atop the castle, to write the end of this story. Back we go to the Fabulous. It was so many years ago, but when I close my eyes, I am right back there, an eleven-year-old girl having the adventure of her life in the rocky heart of that insanely hot valley.

Pandora had me by the shoulders. Craster Bellamy's gun was pointed right at me.

Bellamy looked at me with those eyes again. *I'm so sorry I've got to do this, but I've got to do this.* I didn't want my last sight to be those hateful eyes. I was a kid, but I understood what it was to know you were doing wrong and to do it anyway. Maybe kids understand that better than grown-ups do. Maybe kids aren't so good at lying to themselves.

His finger squeezed on the trigger. He raised the barrel to point at Pandora.

"I ain't going to kill a child for you, Pandora."

He really should have just shot her without the preamble. As he fired, she flung me one way and dived the other. I never did find out where she kept her concealed pistol, but it was somewhere pretty handy because she fired before she hit the ground.

The bullet hit Craster Bellamy's chest. Blood sprayed like a geyser. There was so much. I had to jump out of the way to avoid getting soaked. The man himself looked down, face a picture of despair, then staggered back, arms waving. He fell onto the blade of the circular saw, which lodged in his back and kept him standing there, gushing his life out as if there was a hose pointing out of his chest. It was a sight to see.

"Well, I'll be," said Pandora, lying on the dirt, the little, smoking gun in her hand.

Bellamy jerked as the gush subsided. Finally, he was still, drenched in his own blood and surrounded by a pond of it. I'd never known a man, even one as fat as Craster Bellamy, could have so much blood in him.

I was still staring when Pandora Jones grabbed me by the shoulder.

"If Loretta won't come to us, we'll have to go and get her."

She turned me round to leave, but I shouted, "Wait!"

"What do you want?"

"I want to check on Crane."

She let go of my shoulder. I ran to him. He was out cold but breathing. His shoulder wasn't bleeding at all anymore. His knee was still oozing out a little bright, fresh blood, but not gushing.

"That's not much bleeding," said Pandora. "He'll be fine. Well, at least he would be if I had any plan to leave him alive."

She pointed her little gun at his head and pulled the trigger.

"No!" I shouted, running at Pandora.

She held me at arms length as I tried to hit her. I was trying with all my might, but she just held me there with one arm.

I gave up and looked at Crane. He looked the same. No brain splatter. I looked back at Pandora, mouth open like a dimwit.

"Damn gun didn't fire," she shrugged. "I'm a little surprised that the lack of a gunshot noise didn't alert you to that fact."

I stood back, feeling foolish yet again.

"I'll kill him later. He ain't going anywhere."

She went over to Bellamy, took his gun, and said "come on!"

Pandora headed up the hill. She was cautious, half crouching, checking every hiding place from every angle.

I tagged along behind, feeling sick with misery. My shoulder throbbed where Pandora had whipped me, but I was pretty much okay physically. My mind was whipped though. After all I'd thought about Bellamy, he'd died trying to save me and it was all my fault, so it was like I'd killed him. And Crane was going to die as soon as Pandora found and killed Loretta. And I couldn't do a thing! I was completely useless! Pandora wasn't even bothering to point the gun at me as she searched for Loretta because she knew I wasn't a threat. I was following her because I didn't know what else to do. I should have gone and found another gun – there were plenty about the place – or run away or done *something* but I'd failed and failed again, and I couldn't think of anything to do apart from follow Pandora like some idiot sheep. Actually I take that back. Sheep in those parts were pretty clever.

Meanwhile the aerial tramway trundled on, carts coming up the canyon, disappearing into the tram shed for a few moments, then heading back down. Loretta had been cunning to send what we'd dug of The Prize down the mountain, I guess. The weight of it would make it stop at the bottom.

We came across Gerald Potts' body. There were two chisels stuck in his stomach - presumably the cause of his scream - and his throat was slit. Where his neck was sliced open, you could see his trachea and the end of what I guessed was a sliced vein.

"Eleanor!, Eleanor!" I heard. I recognised the same frustrated tone that my mother used when I'd been distracted by something and she'd been calling for a while. "What's wrong with you?" Pandora said. "I've never seen anyone stare so hard at a corpse."

"Just interested, is all."

We reached the tram shed. There was an adit cut into the mountainside ten paces away. Pandora seemed very interested in that, with good reason I reckoned. That's where I'd be hiding if I were Loretta.

Loretta had Potts' gun now so it would be an easy thing to fire from the darkness of the tunnel at anyone in the bright light. Pandora had worked this out too, by the way she was keeping to the side of the entry.

"Do you know how to stop this thing?" she nodded at the tramway.

"Yup."

"Then get up there and do it, please." She looked back to the adit.

"Why do you want to stop it?" I asked.

"I know I said please," she was still peering at the adit, "but it wasn't a request."

"It won't help."

"I know the gold is in the cart she sent downhill."

"And you want to bring it back up, right?"

"Yes." she sounded exasperated. I recognised that tone from my ma. Funny thing was, I liked Pandora, even after all she'd done and planned to do. I thought she was clever and ruthless and daring, and beating the men at their own games in the manly world of the West. I wanted to be like her. Even though she didn't know squat about how aerial trams worked.

"You can't bring it back up," I explained. "It works by gravity. To bring a full cart back up, you'd have to put a heavier load into carts at the top. We pretty much filled the cart with quartz and gold - which is about the heaviest thing in the world - plus there's Silver's weight. Since you can only load one cart at time, it's impossible to bring the gold back up."

"That's a stupid system."

"It works if you're loading carts up here and emptying them in the valley, which is what it's meant for."

She wrinkled her big nose.

"What happened to your leg?" she asked.

"One's shorter than the other. It's how I was born."

"I'm sorry about that."

"Not your fault."

She nodded and looked about. She seemed nervous and undecided, with good reason. Loretta was lurking nearby. I could feel it. If she headed down to the valley now, Loretta could follow her and kill her whenever it took her fancy.

She looked at me and chewed her lower lip.

"You deciding whether to kill me?" I asked.

She nodded.

"Because you don't want to kill a kid, but if you leave me alive I might come for vengeance when I'm older?"

"Yup."

"You don't need to kill me. I'm not like other people."

"I'm beginning to realise that."

"Everyone going for The Prize was worse than you, except me and Crane. Take The Prize, leave us alive, and I promise we'll never come after you."

"I don't like people telling me what to do. Plus, I like life, and you may believe you won't come after me now, but gold does funny things to people. So, I'm sorry, sweetie. Hold still and it'll be quick." She lifted Craster Bellamy's big pistol and pointed it at me.

James Willow knelt up in the cart as it coasted uphill, gently bobbing. A couple of bighorn sheep peered at him from a ridge. Downslope, the view of the valley widened and widened.

Had he not felt so awful, he managed to realise, he might have appreciated this new method of mountain climbing.

His head pulsed and ached like it had been crushed between two locomotives and he felt about as strong as a butterfly. But he was finally, genuinely hopeful that he might make it to the Fabulous. He wasn't sure how he was going to get out of the cart at the other end, but presumably if they put ore in the things at the top, then it couldn't be so hard for the buckets' contents to go the other way.

Looking ahead for the mine, or anything that wasn't rocks or sheep really, he saw something odd coming towards him on the downward wire. It was a hanging man, he realised; a big, fat, dead fellow. The poor chap's face was horribly swollen and his tongue stuck out, as if in one final, incongruously petty insult. The hanging corpse sailed by, rude and macabre, turning slowly as it descended towards Death Valley proper.

What was happening up there?

He went over a rise and saw the large shed which must be the end of his ride. He wished the journey was a lot longer.

There were two blurred figures standing near the shed. One was small. A girl, he realised. It must be Eleanor Salmon. The other was a woman. Pandora.

He was seventy paces away when Pandora raised a pistol and pointed it at Eleanor. Willow flipped the rifle up, rested it on the edge of the cart and looked along the sights. He blinked and blinked again.

Everything was really quite blurry still, but he didn't need perfect vision. His left arm was still useless but, resting the rifle on the edge of the cart, he needed only his right.

He'd been in his school rifle team. It was the only sport he was any good at, if you could call it a sport.

He fired.

Pandora hesitated.

"Don't kill me," I said. "I can be your sidekick."

She sighed.

"Unpaid."

She looked up to the heavens then down at me.

I don't think she was going to shoot me, but her gun was still pointed at my head when there was a sharp pain in my calf and the boom of a rifle rang out.

"Sorry!" shouted a man. "It's the sights, they must have been knocked!" He had a strange accent.

I looked it my calf. It was bleeding, but not too much. The bullet had skimmed it. There was a man's head poking up out of an ore cart, coming closer along the wire every moment.

Pandora aimed at the man and fired. He ducked and the bullet pinged off the metal cart.

"Follow me!" she said, grabbing my wrist.

She'd made it only a pace when two more shots rang out, this time from above us.

"What the heck!" Pandora ducked into the adit. I stayed out in the open. Two men and a woman were coming down canyon towards us.

Pandora looked round the wooden doorpost of the adit entrance and took a shot. The men crouched, rifles pointed, but the woman carried on skipping and sliding down the scree.

"Eleanor!" she shouted.

It was my mother!

"Ma! Don't come any closer. It's too dangerous!"

It was a silly thing to say because it only sped her up. Pandora took aim.

I looked back just in time to see the man with the rifle in the ore cart disappear into the tram shed. Then the wire stopped – I guessed the cart full of gold ore must have reached the bottom.

I limped towards Pandora.

She fired at my mother again. She missed, but Ma kept coming, running now, darting between bushes and discarded mining equipment.

"Miss Salmon, please slow down!" shouted one of the men who'd come with her. Even though it was a desperate shout, I could tell he had a refined east coast accent. Where had she found him, I wondered?

"Please, don't shoot!" I shouted at Pandora. She pointed the gun at my ma.

My ma was nearly on us, running straight. There was no way Pandora could miss.

There was an almighty boom.

"Eleanor!" Someone was shaking my shoulders and calling in a voice that echoed about inside my head. "Eleanor!"

I opened my eyes. I was lying on my back. There was someone above me. It was my ma!

I reached up and hugged her.

I wanted to hug her forever, but I also wanted to know what the heck was going on.

Up the slope, the two men who'd come with my ma were emerging from the tram shed with the man who'd come up in the cart and shot me.

By the way they were chatting excitedly, they knew each other.

I looked at the adit where Pandora had been. It was collapsed.

I stood up and headed towards it.

"No, Eleanor," said my mother, "you do not want to see that."

Funny how your parents don't know you very well.

Pandora was half buried by rubble. Her open eyes were bulging and bloodshot, staring at me. Her lips opened and closed like a fish's. She was alive, but she wouldn't be for long and she knew it. I could see the disbelief in her eyes. She was a golden goddess, skipping across the world of men doing as she pleased. She was going to live forever. She looked straight at me. I could feel her pleading to stay alive as she died.

I knew it was awful. Her light had seemed too bright to be snuffed out like this. I knew I ought to cry. But all I was was interested.

There was a cough.

Ma and the three men were looking at me. Two of the men were very well dressed and looked so alike that they must be brothers. The other looked like he'd been dragged backwards by a galloping horse through a hedge and then through a war. His arm was tucked into his shirt, and his skin was blotchy, part sickness-pale, part burnt by the sun.

"I'm so sorry for shooting you. Are you alright?" asked the scruffy one. He had the very strangest accent - feminine, clipped, and elegant.

"I'm fine," I said, looking down. "I'm just nicked."

"Oh good. It was the sights, you see. I really am a very good shot, and I had your best interests-"

"It's okay. But save the rest, please. We've got to get to Crane."

Pausing only to take Pandora's rawhide whip from her hip - I decided she'd want me to have it - I headed off down the slope fast as I could with the others following. They soon overtook. I fell in with the broken fellow. He really did look like he'd been dragged over mountains, beaten up by a team of strong men, then dragged back again. So he was going about my speed.

"Who are you, then?" I asked.

"James Willow."

"Where are you from?"

"England."

"Across the ocean England?"

"Yes."

"That explains the voice."

"I daresay it does."

"What are you doing here?"

"I came to rescue you."

"Me?"

"You. Your mother told me you were here."

"I see. But instead, you shot me."

"Yes. Sorry about that."

"That's okay."

"Things have a habit of going wrong for me."

"That must be annoying."

"You get used to it."

"But you did save my life."

"Did I?" The Englishman jolted and brightened about a hundredfold. "Are you sure?"

"Sure. Pandora was about to shoot me and you distracted her. Then the others turned up. If you hadn't shot, she would have killed me before they got to me. You saved my life James Willow."

"Well I never!" Despite his injuries and general near-deadness, Willow grinned like a loon.

I don't think Pandora was going to kill me, and I'm not sure what made me bend the truth like that, but it sure seemed to cheer the fellow up, and that made me happier.

We walked around the dorm shed.

Crane was sitting now, and he'd managed to tie something around his shot knee, but he looked awful. Not as bad as Craster Bellamy though, still held up by the circular saw, pale because all his blood was sprayed all around the rocks, the shed, the table where we ate our meals, the chairs, the tins, the mining kit … you get the idea.

"I look awful, don't I?" said Crane. I nodded. "Don't worry. My knee - or what used to be my knee - has numbed a bit. All this blood belongs to that poor fellow." He nodded towards Bellamy. "What happened? It looks like he exploded."

I was about to say he was shot when Crane noticed my mother and the other three.

"Miss Salmon! What a delight to see you! And I take it you fellows are friendlies?

"That we are, sir," said the younger of the well-dressed men. "Friendly as they come, and here to help. I'm Samuel Clemens and this fine-looking man," he gestured towards the other, "is my brother Orion. What can we best do for you?"

"And I'm James Willow," said James Willow, easing himself onto a chair, despite the blood all over it.

"Pleased to make your acquaintances," said Crane. "Are Pandora and her men accounted for?"

"They are." I said. "Loretta's disappeared."

"Where is she?"

"I don't know. She went into the mine. She could be anywhere."

"Could that be her?" asked Orion Clemens, pointing down canyon.

There she was, on horseback, heading down towards Death Valley.

"That's Delores!" said Willow

"Uh, no," I said, "it's Loretta."

"Not the woman, the horse." He stood up with difficulty.

"Please, lend me whichever of your rifles is better," he asked the Clemens. "I left mine in the hanging cart."

"She's too far."

"I can hit her from here."

The Clemens looked uncertain.

"She's a murderer," said Willow. "She definitely killed her husband, her husband's parents, and three other innocents from her town. They reckon she killed many more."

"He's not lying," said Crane. "She kills for fun. Give him the gun. If he can shoot her, it'll save a lot of lives."

"It's too far."

"I can hit her."

"You shot me when you were trying to hit Pandora at half this distance," I muttered.

"Yes, and I explained. That was the sights. That's why I need one of your guns." He looked down the canyon. Loretta would be out of sight soon. "Please."

Samuel Clemens held his rifle out, butt first.

"Shoulder rest?" asked Orion.

"Please."

With the younger Clemens' help, Willow rested the gun on the older Clemens's shoulder, took aim and squeezed the trigger.

A puff of smoke exploded from a rock a good five yards from Loretta. Woman and horse rode out of sight round a corner.

EPILOGUE

The next weeks were very happy ones.

I guess I hadn't really noticed how awful it is to be surrounded by awful people, but being with decent folk was a huge relief. It was like somebody had been blaring a trumpet in my ear all the time and I kind of got used to it, but when it stopped it was the best feeling in the world. Being with my ma was best of all, not only because I was with her, but because she was free for the first time in a long time. She was funny for a little while, getting used to life without opium, but it was still great to be with her.

The Timbisha Shoshone who'd delivered Delores to Willow and saved his life had followed him to the Fabulous. I wondered what their motives were at the time, but found out later that they were simply interested. They liked to watch the white man's antics in the same way some people like to watch plays. Anyway, they appeared and insisting on taking Willow and Crane. We were pretty sure that their intentions were good and, sure enough, Crane and Willow returned about a week later, all patched up and chipper.

Crane was mobile enough to hobble around giving instructions. Willow helped out at the cookhouse a bit, and wasn't that useful really, but it was him who persuaded three Timbisha men to stay and help with the mining. He'd picked up enough of their language in a week to do that. It was the first sign that, pointed in the right direction, James Willow might make a go of the West after all.

The Clemens also stayed to help. For two well dressed pilgrims, they certainly knew a lot about mining. I guess they were both really clever about pretty much everything. While Crane organised the getting it out the ground and processing bit, the brothers did the smart stuff. They worked out how to get the gold from the inside of a Californian mountain to the inside of a bank.

Everyone agreed that Crane and me should have forty-five percent each. Willow, the Clemens brother and my ma took two and half percent each. Sounds an unfair split, and I always thought it was, but it was the Clemenses and Willow's idea, and they insisted. Two and a half percent was still an awful lot.

The only payment the Timbisha would accept was the dozen finest horses in town.

I'd like to say that I put my money into good causes and became a veterinarian like I'd planned, or a teacher or something useful like that. I'd like to say that, but it's not what happened. I was far too selfish, far too rich, and the world was far too exciting.

EPILOGUE PART TWO

The biddies and the crones clapped, which was nice, and Mr Hillier-Edwards produced a couple of bottles of champagne.

Mrs Bull was in particularly high spirits after a glass or two. We were talking about how we might go about editing the book.

"Let's club together and rent a riverboat!" she said. "We can moor it at the end of the garden and go up and down the Thames discussing your book and anything else that comes to mind!"

"Well, that's a marvellous idea," said Mr Hillier-Edwards. "I've piloted a few boats in my time, and would be very happy to take the helm ... assuming nobody else wants to, of course?"

"Here's another idea," I said. "How about we get a big yacht - I'm talking ship size - hire a crew and a medical team, and spend a few months cruising on the Mediterranean? You can helm as much as you'd like, I'm sure, Mr Hillier-Edwards."

"What a lovely idea!" laughed Mrs Bull.

"We could really do it," I said.

"But how would we pay for a boat like that?" asked Mr Hillier-Edwards.

"Did you not listen to my story?" I asked, placing a hand on his arm.

EPILOGUE PART THREE

(from Eleanor's great-grandson, Angus Watson)

And that, dear reader, is my great-grandmother's story. Maybe I liked it more because she was my great gran, but if you enjoyed it half as much as I did, you'll be wondering if there's more. Eleanor said towards the end that she had other tales to tell. But did she write any of them?

I've asked around. Well, I texted my American cousin who's more interested in family history than the rest of us combined. It turns out that there is a mysterious, heavy trunk that once belonged to Eleanor Salmon in the attic of my aunt, in Pennsylvania, USA.

Perhaps there are more books in there? Or maybe it's full of gold? You may be wondering where all the money went. I certainly am, because it didn't make it down the family tree as far as me. I guess she carried out her threat to make her children earn their own money... Bit rich from someone who got rich from being in the right place at the right time, but there you go. I'm not bitter ...

My aunt has never opened the trunk, and – her words not mine – has become too much of an old fatty to fetch it out of the attic. I go to America whenever I have the excuse – I love the place – so in a couple of months I'm going to head for the Pocono Mountains, near Scranton, Pennsylvania, and rummage in my aunt's attic.

There could well be more writing in there, so keep an eye out for another book. Of course, the trunk could be full of gold, in which case keep an eye out for a portly Englishman walking around London town next to a lady in a golden hat.